J. D. WILLIAMS

Born by Song

First edition

ISBN: 9798218318956

This book was professionally typeset on Reedsy.
Find out more at reedsy.com

Contents

About Born by Song

Following her recent success and newfound fame after competing on *Next Real Star*, Julia and Raine must confront the ultimate pain that comes from an unspeakable loss. Julia and Raine fight their demons as they struggle to hang on to one another, while trying to maintain their sanity in a world spinning out of control.

Born by Song is a dual POV, female rock star, soul mates, sweet with spice, open door contemporary romance novel.

Julia Tate Song Series

Bound by Song leads book two, *Born by Song*, and the final book, *Blessed by Song*, through the popular music industry as Julia Tate becomes a beloved singer-songwriter against all the odds, inspiring millions of fans. Julia strikes a powerful chord as she encourages women to follow their own dreams of career, motherhood, and love. The background world of music is positively intertwined throughout the books, adding to the allure of celebrity, while giving real insight into the challenging world of a popular recording artist.

Series: Bound by Song and Born by Song, available now; Blessed by Song, coming early 2026.

For more information, go to www.jdwilliamsbooks.com

Cover Design: Original *Bound by Song* design by Logan Bartels. *Born by Song* cover design and *Bound by Song* revised cover by Britt Wilson with Author Services Australia. Website by Artillery Media.

First edition January 2024

Acknowledgments

Thank you to my family, friends, and followers for your support. There are too many to thank here, but every like, comment, and share are greatly appreciated. Thank you to two wonderful editors (K. and B.) who helped with their guidance and expertise. To every person who has streamed a song, read pages, downloaded a digital book, ordered a paperback, given a rating and/or a review, thank you isn't enough. The book and music markets are tough—thank you for giving this work a chance.

There are two people I should have thanked in the first book. Jim Koudelka, a music instructor who helped me for years—thank you for being so generous with your time, talents, and arrangements, especially with someone who was so "green." And thank you to Ellen Britton, guitar instructor extraordinaire—thank you for giving me a musical voice, I am forever grateful.

Special thanks to Jill, Gary, Sydney, Levi, Sharon, Carol, Don, Ron, Louie, Julie, Kim, Roxann, Pamela, and many others for liking so many posts ... I see you. Thanks to my dad for being the kind wonderful person you are, and thanks to Chris for everything, you are my rock.

There are resources listed at the end of this book. "The Four Tasks of Mourning" found in the book by J. William Worden, PhD ABPP, "Grief Counseling and Grief Therapy, Fifth Edition: A Handbook for the Mental Health Practitioner – Grief Counseling Handbook on Treatment of Grief, Loss Bereavement," are noted in several resources and mentioned in this book.

Dedication

I dedicate this to anyone who has suffered an unspeakable loss. I may not have captured this perfectly, but I try to show the utter heartbreak and sorrow that comes after the loss of a life that carried so much hope, while also portraying how many people learn to live with their grief. This book is for you.

This book is dedicated to my mom, and also to my dear friend Bryan, two people I miss.

Chapter One – Raine and Julia

I'm careening through the streets of Nashville at record speed. I've already called the hospital, and as I glance down at my beautiful wife, her face contorted in pain, it nearly destroys me. It's too soon. The baby is coming too soon.

"It's okay, love," I manage to get out, my constricted voice betraying the fear consuming my body. "Just hold on. We'll be there in a few minutes."

Julia groans, her head thrown back against the top of the car seat. Her eyes are shut from the pain.

I gun the engine even harder as we take the on ramp and my tires scream toward the hospital. Why did we move to the country? I should have life-flighted her to the hospital. My mind is racing and I'm silently pleading with God to get us there on time. She's barely six months pregnant with our child. It's just too soon.

I'm trying to keep it together, but the cramping in my abdomen is unlike anything I've ever experienced. Waves of pain sear through me, but I can't let Raine know how bad it is. I'm losing our baby with every second, and my heart constricts so hard I think it will explode from my chest.

I look up at Raine, purposefully avoiding the blanket wrapped around my waist. It's warm and wet, and I can't bear to look down. Raine's brow is deeply furrowed as he tries to maneuver down the street. I've never seen him look this stressed or frightened.

"Hon … don't worry. It'll be okay," I say as I drop my limp hand on his leg.

1

Without looking away from the road, Raine puts his hand on top of mine. It's so warm and comforting. I'm trying to stay focused, but all I want to do is sleep, so I close my eyes.

"Julia ... Julia!" Raine yells at me and my eyes flash open. I blink quickly trying to stay awake.

He yells, "Stay with me!"

I manage to croak out, "I'm here. I promise. I'm here."

But I'm already feeling the loss. I've lost our baby.

When I finally pull up to the emergency room entrance, several staff members are waiting outside for us. After I had called the hospital, I called Julia's best friend, Tracy, and she's standing there as well.

Our car screeches to a stop as several people run to us. I had told them to look for a black Jaguar.

When I touched Julia's hand, it was ice cold. I'm doing my best to keep my fear in check.

As the staff starts to help Julia out of her car door, I jump out and run to her side. She passes out. As they pull her limp frame onto a gurney, I look down at the blanket lying on the car seat. I've never seen so much blood in my life.

"Raine ... Raine! I've got the car," Tracy yells at me as she grabs the keys from my frozen hands and pushes me toward the building. My heavy legs struggle to follow as they rush Julia inside.

Nurses wheel Julia through double doors into a room as I stagger behind. The emergency team quickly puts an IV in her arm and yells to get a fetal heart monitor. The hospital has called our obstetrician, and Dr. Henley is on her way. I watch helplessly as they plug Julia into machines and listen to the monitor on her stomach, trying to find a heartbeat. My eyes glass over. There's no sound coming from the machine. How my heart aches to hear the tiny heartbeat I've heard so many times, but there's nothing.

Our doctor finally arrives and catches my eyes as I stand in the doorway. She grimaces. We're in good hands with Dr. Henley. She's one of the best.

I look at Julia lying there. She's so still and slightly blue, which shocks the hell out of me. But her monitor is beeping out her heartbeat. At least Julia has a heartbeat.

Chapter Two – Julia

When I finally come to, bright lights hurt my aching, swollen eyes. I squint up toward the windows and see Raine standing with his strong arms stretched wide against the windowsill, looking out like he's seriously studying the leaves on a tree. Before he notices I'm awake, I cautiously peer down at my midsection, but I already know what I'll find. The roundness I've seen for the past several months is noticeably smaller. The baby's gone.

I look back at Raine as his head swivels toward me. The rims of his usually dazzling green eyes are red. I've never in my life seen him cry, and the ache in my heart drops to my stomach. I've caused this. Raine collapses into a chair by my side and takes my cold hand in his. I notice how his hand seems to engulf mine, but at least now my hand isn't blue.

"Hey," I manage to croak.

Raine tries to muster a smile, but more tears form on his lashes. His head drops to our hands.

"It's okay," I say picking up my other leaden arm and placing it on his head. "I know. He didn't make it."

Raine pulls his head back up bringing his moist eyes to mine as he softly strokes my hand. "I'm so sorry, love," he whispers and my heart shatters. For some odd reason, he's apologizing to me, when this is clearly my fault.

"Why are you sorry?" I squeak out through my own stifled sobs. "It's my fault. I shouldn't have toured. I knew it, and you knew it. You even told me to slow down, and I didn't." As the former winner of the music reality show *Next Big Star*, I'd toured with the other contestants up until just a few weeks ago. Obviously, it'd been too much, especially at my age of forty-one.

"What? What do you mean it's your fault?" His eyes search mine questioningly. "It's no one's fault."

I'm silent as I look at him but then I look away at the wall, which has some awful picture of a tree in a barren field. I try to focus on the picture. Raine's look of sorrow is so intense, it's all I can do not to lose it. My throat constricts as I struggle to hold back sobs. Raine stands and places his body next to mine on the slim bed, engulfing me in his arms as I turn into him, burying my face against his chest. My sobs start; I can't help it. As we cry together, Raine somehow manages to hold me tighter until we both finally fall asleep, exhausted.

The next few days are a blur. Tracy, who is not only my best friend but also my personal assistant, has been making most of the funeral arrangements. Raine and I will bury our young son at a cemetery a few miles down from our new home.

We bought our home shortly after I'd won *Next Real Star,* and I moved from Nebraska back to Nashville after our hasty marriage in Napa. At that time, I was already pregnant. Everything back then was such a whirlwind.

For days now, our family has been arriving from around the country. Raine and Tracy have been swamped with all the details, and I haven't been much help. I was in the hospital for three days and now I'm at home, but all I'm doing is lying in bed. Raine has been coming into our room and trying to get me to eat, but I don't want anything. I can't feel a thing, and I don't want to. I'm numb and I want to stay that way. I want to stay in my bed cocoon and hide away from the world.

Chapter Three – Raine and Julia

"Did you try to get her to eat something this morning?" Tracy asks as she walks into our kitchen swirling her long blonde hair with her hands on her hips, glaring at me with that usual all-knowing look.

I've just picked up a tray of hot tea and some soup. "Good lord, woman, every damned hour I've been trying to get her to eat," I exclaim. "Who do you think you're dealing with? I love her!"

It's then that Tracy must notice my complete and utter exhaustion. A look of sympathy crosses her face. We both have been running so hard trying to take care of Julia and the funeral arrangements, neither of us are taking care of ourselves, and it's showing on our faces and in our tempers.

"I know … I'm sorry," Tracy replies. "Let me take that tray to her," she says, taking the tray from my hands. "Maybe I can work my magic. You both have a tough day tomorrow, and Julia needs to get some nourishment, or she'll never make it through the day."

Tracy must sense my relief. Ever since Julia came home, I've tried to get the love of my life to react in any way. But she's jailed herself up in our bedroom with the blinds tightly closed and sleeps as though she hasn't slept in years.

##

There is no way on God's green earth I would have missed Tracy's loud steps and heavy sigh. Elephants are quieter. I hear her place the tray on the nightstand next to me, and then she walks over to the blinds.

"This room is dark enough, we need some light in here," Tracy says as she

6

bangs open the blinds. Bright sunlight streams into every crevice. There's no place for me to hide.

I peer up from under my covers and then bury my head back into the pillows, hiding so only a tiny bit of my face is showing.

I hear Tracy stomp toward my bed. "You need to eat something, my friend. I'm not "Mr. Nice Guy, Raine" walking around on eggshells. You're going to eat."

I pull back the covers a smidge to look at my friend, but I don't really see her. I'm squinting through the bright light as my head throbs from too many tears and frantic tossing and turning all night long. I absentmindedly run my hands over my stomach as my face is swallowed up in silent pain. I still can't believe he's gone. My baby boy is gone.

Tracy walks over and sits on the edge of my bed. "Please, Jules, you've got to try and eat something. I don't know what I'm going to do with Raine if you don't try."

At the mention of Raine's name, I lift my head up and blink at my friend, giving her a slight nod. Almost worse than losing my beloved baby boy is the thought that I'm hurting Raine in any way. I've already destroyed him. I lost our baby. *Me.*

I try to rise up on my pillows, but my arms fail me, and I fall back. Tracy leans over and props a few pillows behind my back. After I settle back against the pillows, I lean toward the tray and pick up the cup full of tea, but my hands are shaking, and I struggle to get the tiny cup to my lips.

"Any honey in this?" I ask. "You know it won't help me hit the high notes without honey," I manage to squeak out.

"Of course," Tracy responds. "You've got me trained well."

I take a slight sip, and I have to admit it feels good against my raw throat. "You mentioned Raine ... where is he?"

"He's here. He was headed in here to make a food attempt, but I thought I'd take a stab. He's a pansy-ass when it comes to this sort of thing." Tracy says it with a smirk, but there's a dark tone to her voice, and I can sense her worry.

At that description of Raine, I smile slightly. Raine is never weak, so to hear Tracy refer to him in this way is funny.

"Now, how about some of this soup?" Tracy reaches over and picks up the bowl looking down inside and raising her eyebrows. "It looks like some sort of vegetable concoction, but if "Mr. Producer" fixed it, there could be some sort of mystery meat in here, too."

I give my dear friend a half-hearted grin as she scoops up a spoonful, and I lean toward her to try it. I have to admit, I'm more than famished. Whatever Raine has made has never tasted so good.

Tracy looks down at me and relief washes over her. They both have been worried about me, and I'll admit I've been worried too. And I still am. I don't know if I'll make it through this.

I'm silently watching Julia with Tracy as tears stream down my face. Tracy got Julia to eat. Thank God. Losing the baby has been more than a devastating blow to me and it's about killed Julia. The thought of losing Julia forever is something I can't even fathom, and I've been consumed with worry. As I lean against the door frame, the heaviness of the past few days hits me like a two-by-four. Tomorrow we'll place our tiny baby boy into the ground. I have no idea how I'll get through it, and I can't even comprehend how we'll get Julia through the day.

I walk back down the hall to my den, shut the door, and sit in a chair by my desk. The weight of the past few days is more than I can bear.

At the hospital, I tried bargaining with God, but it was no use. They couldn't save our son, and now I'm angry. Angrier than I've ever been in my life. Not only angry at God, but mostly angry with myself for letting my wife continue to tour as long as she did, when I knew it was getting too hard on her. I knew it, but I let everyone around me, even Julia, talk me into letting her continue. I could see she was exhausted, but I did nothing to stop it.

I'd watched how tired Julia was getting, trying to make it through shows, interviews, and meet and greets with fans. While she tried to stay off her feet as much as she could, it probably was too much. I don't know if I can ever forgive myself for not making her take more time to rest, but she loved being out on stage performing for her fans. I don't blame her for that, not at all, but maybe she should have stopped sooner. Who knows? At least Julia is still alive. Dr. Henley was able to stop Julia's bleeding during the miscarriage. It was touch and go and we weren't sure she was going to make it. Now I don't know if Julia will make it mentally. I know she blames herself. But I don't blame her; it just happened.

Later that day after Tracy has gone home, I quietly open our bedroom door and walk toward the bed. Julia's eyes are open, and she's staring out at the pastureland behind our house. I moved the new bassinet, which used to be in this room, into the nursery so she wouldn't have to see that constant reminder.

Julia speaks softly before I'm at her side, "We won't need that porch swing now either. You need to take it down."

I stop short. "I can do that if you want. How about we wait a few days though?" I take the final few steps and sit by her side, looking down at her pale face and sorrow-filled beautiful blue eyes, which have deep dark circles surrounding them. Julia has never looked this tired or sad in all the years I've known her, and I've put her through hell more than once.

"Whatever." She rolls to her other side away from the windows. Since we came home from the hospital, we've barely touched.

I take the plunge, reach out, and put my hand on her shoulder.

"Honey, you're not alone in this."

"I know," she whispers, emotionless.

I take it further, cause I'm always one to push, and I lie down next to her with my stomach against her back, pulling her body to mine. She remains stiff against me, but after a few minutes, her body softens, and I can hear the slight sound of her crying into her pillow.

"You're not alone," I whisper into the back of her long, dark hair.

After a few moments, Julia croaks out, "I know I haven't been very strong these past few days. I'm sorry if I've let you down."

"You haven't let me down. You never have."

"You know what, Raine?"

"What, honey?"

There is a long pause before she speaks. "We have to give him a name," and at the end of her sentence, Julia's voice cracks, and her words make me catch my breath. A couple of moments later she continues, "We didn't decide on a name, and we have to give him a name."

I clutch her body against me even tighter and after several minutes, I respond, "How about we name him after our fathers, Jonah Christian Wagner. He'll be our angel waiting for us in heaven."

Julia takes a sharp breath at the mention of heaven and her shoulders start to shake with sobs. Without saying anything, Julia gives me her hollow, blue eyes and tear-streaked face and nods as I lean down and kiss her lightly on the lips. She nestles close against me. I hold her like this for several minutes, stroking her hair until she drifts off. It's a restless sleep, but I can hear her light snores.

I quietly pull myself up from the bed and walk over to the back window. Although it's close to dusk, I still have enough light as I stare at the porch swing, and an overwhelming sense of anger overtakes me. Grabbing my work boots, I storm out the back toward a wood pile. I grab an axe sticking out of a piece of wood. I want to hit something, and destroying wood seems like the best option right now.

Chapter Four – Julia

The day of the funeral is nothing more than a sickening blur. I dress up and ride in a car to the small church near our home. We're surrounded by friends and family, but I don't see anyone. My baby boy, Jonah, is in a tiny black casket, and all I can do is aimlessly stare at it.

Raine clutches my arm and leads me where we need to go. People talk to me, but I don't hear what they're saying. Most of the press are staying away as Raine requested, but a few paparazzi bother us at the church and at the cemetery. Raine scowls at them. He's always my protector.

The cemetery is the hardest part. I can't fathom that they'll lower my baby boy into the cold, dark ground. I didn't want him to be cold.

"Julia, you've got to get in the car now," Tracy says, approaching me as I sit staring at the tiny coffin. Most people have walked away, leaving me alone. They can tell I don't want to be bothered. I vaguely hear Raine's voice nearby thanking some people, but everything seems out of body, like I'm in a hollow tube with muffled movement and sound around me. Our families are here, and Raine has to make sure everyone is taken care of and has a ride back to our house.

Finally, I whisper, "I can't leave him. I don't want him in the ground."

I feel Tracy standing right next to me. "I can't imagine what this is like, Julia. But he's with God now. God has him in his arms and is holding him safe until you see him again."

I can't fathom a God that would do this. Tracy reaches out and takes my hand, gently pulling me up. Raine is watching from a few feet away. When I meet his eyes, it's a gut punch. The pain staring back at me is overwhelming.

My beloved husband, the father of our tiny baby boy, has tears streaming down his face. I quietly walk to him, and his strong arms engulf me. He smells and feels like home and despite where we are, right now, I'm safe. Raine gently steers me away from the scene toward our waiting car. A few lingering guests watch with tears in their eyes.

After we settle into our car and start the procession back to our house, Raine speaks. "I thought they did a good job … the service was nice."

I nod and then look out the car window. I don't remember a thing about the service. The only image that is permanently seared into my brain is of Jonah's small casket. Raine reaches over and grabs my hand as we ride back in silence, both caught up in our own personal misery.

We're such a long way from where we were just a few months ago. Thinking back to how Raine and I reconnected less than a year ago when I won the music reality show he judged, how I became a hit singer and songwriter, our whirlwind Napa wedding, followed by the announcement of our pregnancy. And now this has happened and destroyed our safe little world. I'd been right when I told Tracy on our wedding night that no one gets everything. No one ever really does, at least not in my mind. They never do.

After lunch back at our home, once the guests and caterers have left, I'm sitting on the back porch with Raine and Tracy. Raine has already poured a large glass of bourbon. Tracy made me a warm brandy concoction, and it's soothing my mind and helping take the edge off, but I'm not sure it will really help. Luckily, our families are staying in a hotel to give us some space. I don't want Tracy to leave just yet. Raine and I don't have much to say to one another right now. We're there for each other, but everything seems off. And after the day we just had, I'm not ready to be alone with him.

"I see you cut up enough firewood to last for a few years," I say to Raine with a crooked grin.

Raine nods, looking toward the wood pile as a slight smirk crosses his face. I see a few pieces of the now missing porch swing in the pile as well, and a gut-wrenching pang hits me. I don't cry though. I don't have any tears left in me.

Raine takes a long sip of his drink, then takes his now empty glass and heads through the French doors toward the kitchen. Tracy's eyes dart to mine, but we don't say a word. We both know he'll drink heavily tonight.

"Maybe I should go, Jules ... I think you both need some time alone."

"Don't you dare leave. I have no idea what to say to him right now. He's in the mood to drink tonight. I need you here a little bit longer."

"Okay. I'll stay for a bit, but you two need to talk."

"Talk about what? I caused this, Trace. I know that and Raine knows it too, even though he won't admit it."

"Bullshit ... it's not your fault and you know it," Tracy says as she slides closer to me, resting her hand on my back. "These things just happen." After several minutes, Tracy adds softly, "You guys can try again one day."

With that mention, I sob out loud. I can't help it. I want Jonah. I want my baby boy. I had so much hope for him. I can't even think about trying again.

I sit outside with Tracy until we get cold, and then I walk her out to her car and give my good friend a bear hug. I reluctantly head back into the house to try and talk to my husband.

I walk down the hall to Raine's studio, and I hear him playing his guitar. I peer in the doorway. His back is to me, and he's looking out the window. He's playing a melody I heard him play a few weeks before I lost our baby. I spin away, pressing my back against the hallway wall.

I walk back down to the kitchen and grab my own bottle of brandy, and then I head toward our bedroom for a hot bath. I can't face him right now.

Chapter Five – Julia

The next few days pass the same way. I basically ignore Raine until we meet up each night in bed. By the time Raine enters the bedroom, I'm asleep, a bottle of pills lying next to me on the nightstand. I phoned my doctor about not getting any sleep, and pills were the answer. I'm taking pills while Raine has his bourbon. Other than the moment at Jonah's funeral, we haven't touched each other. For some reason, it feels awkward.

Late one morning, I'm waiting for Raine in our breakfast nook. Raine's frame fills the doorway as he enters the kitchen. His normally perfectly coiffed hair is ruffled up, and he looks like he hasn't shaved in a week. Although he looks rough, my heart flutters at the sight of him.

"Morning," I say searching his face.

He grunts as, clearly hungover, he heads straight to the coffee maker.

"Dr. Henley called yesterday and wants to see us in her office later this afternoon. Can you make it?"

Raine's facing the cupboard and hesitates for a moment. Then he reaches for a cup and proceeds to pour a cup of strong black coffee.

"Of course, wouldn't miss it," he says, sarcasm pouring from his lips.

I don't respond. It's obvious how much he blames me. And then he walks right out without saying another word. I look out the back window and sigh, staring at the huge pile of wood, which still contains our porch swing. I'm glad that it's gone.

Later that day, we drive in silence toward downtown Nashville. I think Raine purposefully puts the car stereo on loud, so he won't have to talk to me. I can't tell if he's pissed at me or at the world. He's really good at being pissed off at the world.

As we pull into the doctor's office, I reach out and place my hand on top of his. I see his raised shoulders go down as he softens for a moment. He looks at me, love clearly showing in his eyes. He must see the dark, puffy circles surrounding my seemingly permanently sad blue eyes. Raine reaches out and gently touches my face as he gives me a slight smile. I lean my head against his hand.

"Did Dr. Henley say *why* she wants to see us?" Raine finally asks.

"She has some information she wants to tell us. Said it was important."

Raine finally pulls his hand away and we get out of his car. He reaches out and takes my hand, leading me toward my doctor's office.

"Not really what you had expected to hear, was it?" Tracy is on the other line, listening to every word I'm relaying about our recent doctor's visit.

"No ... I think I'm still in shock. It's one thing to think Jonah's death was because I toured too late into my pregnancy, but quite another to find out it really was my fault."

"How can you say that? Dr. Henley told you it wasn't your fault!" Tracy practically screams at me through the phone.

"But it was ... my body failed me," I say, with surprising calm, as I'm even more resolved in the fact that I failed Jonah ... and Raine. The doctor told us that the placenta had actually detached from my uterine wall. It's called a placental abruption and is a bit more common with women experiencing pregnancy at an older age. "How will Raine ever forgive me for having a weak body? And what if I can't ever have another baby." I'm starting to tear up and I'm sure Tracy hears it as my voice quavers. "What in the world do we do now?"

"Dr. Henley didn't say you could never have another baby. You can try again, and there are other options. Adoption ... surrogacy ... there is another way."

But I'm not listening to my friend. I'm too caught up in the failure of my body. "Raine will never forgive me, and, frankly, I don't think I can forgive myself."

Tracy responds with anger, "That's just foolishness."

But I'm not listening to her. My mind is made up. Even though Dr. Henley said it was something medical, I pushed myself too hard and toured too long while pregnant, and at my age. I knew better and should have made different choices. I lost Jonah and broke both our hearts.

Chapter Six – Raine

I'm sitting at the bar when Bret, my good friend and famous country artist I produce, walks in to join me. Bret's tall and everyone says extremely good looking—like Matthew McConaughey. He's known to attract attention, especially from his female fans. I see him as the same smart-ass singer-songwriter I've known since before he was famous, who's not only my golfing buddy, but my one true confidant in a town where it's not easy to find true friends. We're meeting at a golf course where the staff know us and people generally leave us alone. I start the conversation before he can even order his drink.

"The doctor said the placenta pulled away from Julia's uterus. Literally her insides failed her. It's why we lost him the way we did."

"Oh man, I am so sorry," Bret mumbles out.

"This is killing her," I reply. "I can see it, Bret. Julia already thought the miscarriage was her fault, and now she thinks her body failed her. I don't blame her at all … this just happened."

"Does Julia know that?"

"I've tried to tell her, but she won't listen." I pause, looking down into my drink, and I give it a good swirl before continuing. "I may lose her over this, Bret. We may not recover. Julia can't stand to be in the same room with me."

"Just talk to her. Don't stop trying to talk to her."

"I don't know what to say to her! I'm so fucking pissed. Pissed that this happened to her … to us. She didn't deserve this. Maybe I did because I'm such an asshole, but she didn't. She didn't deserve to get hurt in this way." And then my voice catches as I continue, "It never crossed my mind that we'd lose him, even while she was touring. I tried to talk her into slowing down a couple of times, but I never thought we'd actually lose him."

Bret places his hand on my shoulder as I stare down into my drink. I think my honesty about this has shocked us both. It's not often that we talk about anything too serious, but I'm glad that I have someone I can vent to … at least just a little. But I still feel lost.

"Raine … don't let this come between you two. Not after everything it took to get her back. I know how much you love her, and that's enough."

I nod in agreement and I take another drink, but it's much easier said than done. There's an impenetrable wall neither of us can seem to break.

When I pull up the driveway, Julia's Jeep is out in front of the house, not in the garage.

"Julia?" I yell loudly as I stand in a very quiet front foyer.

Julia's tiny voice responds from up above. "Up here."

When I enter our bedroom, she's standing over a giant suitcase that lies open on our bed. I stop cold in the doorway. "What's this?" My hands defensively go to my hips.

Julia pauses with a blouse in her hands, "I've called my sister, Jody, and I'm going to go stay with her for a while. I think it would be good to get away—get some fresh air up in Montana."

I'm stunned as I walk toward her, but she gives me a look that stops me in my tracks. I've seen stubborn Julia before. One hand runs over my unshaven face and through my hair. I take a step toward her, and then I just stop. My fears are coming true. Julia wants to leave me.

"I don't think leaving right now will help anything, babe." I move closer and step behind her, putting my arms around her. She instantly tenses up.

"Raine … I need to go. I did this. I caused us to lose him, and I need a break. I need to clear my head for a while."

"Julia, no, please don't do this. And what about your songwriting? You need to keep working on your songs." I pause and continue in a whisper, "I don't want you to leave. Please don't leave me, Julia."

"I was the one who continued to tour, even when you asked me to stop. I think about that practically every minute … no, every second of every day since we lost him." And the level of her voice rises a little as she pulls away from my arms and sits on the bed, staring up at me. Her head falls down and she looks away from me. "I should have listened to you," she continues, and the tears start to roll from her eyes. "But I was selfish … all I could think about was me and how it felt being out on stage, and how much I loved being out with the fans. Look at what it cost us? And right now, I can't see straight. I don't feel anything." She manages to look up at me and my heart breaks a little bit more. "I love you, Raine, but I don't love me right now. I failed us, and I don't know if I can ever live with that. Every time I look at you, all I see is sadness. It tears me in two. I did this to us."

I manage to pull her back up and she lets me take her into my arms. My lips are pressed against her hair. "Jules, it just happened. That's what Dr. Henley said. I know you loved it out on stage, I get that, and it didn't cause any of this. You didn't fail us." I squeeze my arms tight around her and she starts to soften, but then she quickly pulls away.

"You can't change my mind, Raine. I'm going. Just for a little while."

I stare at her for a long time, but I recognize the look on her face. Her mind is set, and there is no way to talk her out of it. A trait I used to love, but right now despise.

"Fine," I growl as I storm out of the room. I head toward the kitchen and the safety of a bottle of bourbon. But a deep sense of doom overcomes my mind and my heart. She's leaving me.

Chapter Seven – Julia and Raine

As my plane taxis toward the gate in Helena, I start to panic. Why am I here? I already desperately miss Raine, and during the flight, all I could think about was our baby boy, Jonah. I cried the entire way from Nashville to Montana, and my arms ache. They ache to hold my tiny baby boy.

I make my way toward baggage claim, and as I step off the escalator, I see Jody waiting for me. She walks up and enfolds me in a huge, sisterly hug.

"Jay and the kids with you?"

"They're waiting in the car. I thought it'd be easier to meet you by myself."

"Yeah. I bet no one has any idea what to say to me. I don't even remember talking to you at the funeral," and my voice breaks on the word "funeral." I look away, trying to compose myself.

"Once everyone gets over the awkwardness, it'll be okay. They all just feel bad for you and Raine."

At the mention of Raine's name, I grimace, and slight tears start to form. I look away, trying to hide it.

"Was Raine okay with you coming here?"

"No. Not at all. I tried to explain that I just need some time away, but he doesn't get it. It's all been too much for me ... for us."

Jody nods as we pluck my suitcase from the spinning carousel, and then head out to the waiting car.

##

I'm on the phone with Bret. "She left. Julia went to see her sister for a few days."

"Maybe that's a good thing?" Bret responds. "It gives you two some space and time to feel better. Maybe you'll miss each other."

"I don't want space," I say, my anger rising with each syllable. "I need to be the one taking care of her, and we need to be together. This is a fucking mess."

"Give it a few days, and then head out there and join her. Have a mini vacation?"

"Maybe. Do you wanna write tonight?"

"Would love to, but I've got a party to go to. You should come along? Be good for you to get around some other people."

"I'm not good company right now."

"If you change your mind, give me a buzz, and I'll come pick you up."

I hang up and walk around my too empty, silent house. I climb the stairs and slowly open the doors to the nursery. We'd decorated it in a light blue with darker blue trim. It has a simple contemporary sailor design. I walk over to one wall with wallpaper trim that has tiny sailboats, and I start to pick at it. Maybe I'll have the room redecorated? If I change the room before Julia gets back, it'd be one less reminder for her. I start to tear at the wallpaper, and I keep at it until I've peeled most of it off the walls. Then I move the furniture, carrying the smaller pieces down to a storage room on the first floor. This keeps me busy and thankfully away from the liquor cabinet, because right now, that's all I can think about. One big, fat glass of bourbon.

My phone buzzes and I see a message from Julia.

'Arrived safely at Jody's. Call you tomorrow.'

I send a text back, 'Okay, good. Tell everyone hi.'

It's like we're strangers. Gone are our "I love yous" and tender words of caring. They've been replaced with empty phrases. I can't tear down this nursery fast enough.

##

After tossing and turning all night, I walk out of Jody's guest bedroom at ten the next morning. It's Saturday, and Jody and her husband, Jay, are

21

seated around the kitchen table finishing up a late breakfast.

"Hey, Jules. Coffee's still warm."

I nod and grab an oversized cup, filling it to the top. Many times, during the night, I'd woken up startled, reaching out for Raine. The heaviness in my heart is overwhelming and my senses are in overdrive. I miss him, but when I think about going back home, to that house, waves of nausea crash over me. I've lost people I've cared about in my life, and pets too, but this grief is unlike anything I've ever experienced before.

"I'm thinking about doing some shopping today in town, and then maybe dinner and a movie tonight," Jody says. "You game?"

"Sure, sounds like fun." There is no fun emanating from my voice or eyes. But getting out will keep me occupied and get my mind off of how much I miss Raine, and our baby Jonah.

From the corner of my eye, I catch Jody and her husband Jay exchanging glances. I'm making them uncomfortable, and they don't really know what to say to me. I wish to God I was back in a time when my presence didn't make people uneasy, but here we are, in my new fucked-up reality.

Later that day as we stroll through an outside mall area, I'm surrounded by mothers and their babies. They're everywhere. Each stroller is like lightning striking my heart, and in one short hour, I'm sure I'm having a panic attack. I steer my sister toward a nearby restaurant, one I'm sure will serve us alcohol. The weight of hopelessness is overpowering, and I can't seem to catch my breath. I order a Bloody Mary. My sister doesn't say a word, and in fact joins me.

"Started to panic," I say as I pick up my glass, taking a long drink. "Too many reminders."

"I'm not sure where to take you or what to do," Jody replies. "Seems like everywhere we go, there's a reminder."

I give her an uncomfortable nod and then look down at my now almost empty glass. The drink doesn't erase the all-consuming emptiness, but it temporarily eases some of my anxiety, so I don't feel like I'm losing my marbles at the mall.

"Have you talked to Raine today?" Jody asks. "Your phone's buzzed a few times." Concern ebbs from Jody's voice.

"Not yet. It's so weird ... I don't know what to say to him right now. It's just awkward. On the plane I was reading about couples and grief, and the article said many couples don't survive a loss like this, which is terrifying."

"You'll make it. Just takes some time, but eventually you'll need to try and talk about it."

I nod and pause for a few seconds before replying, "You know what would be nice ... before our wedding, I got Raine a ring from a local store in Napa. I've always wanted to pick out something special for him. I'd like to find the perfect ring for him. Maybe we can look for something here?"

"That's a great idea. I'm sure he'd love that."

At least now we have a mission to keep me busy, which may help ease my troubled mind and heart.

Chapter Eight – Raine

By the next morning, I've completely torn down the nursery, and now an interior designer is standing next to me taking notes.

"I want it simple and very elegant. A perfectly organized closet with lots of room for her shoes and boots. I've never met a woman with more boots."

"How about a dressing table inside the room?" the designer asks.

"Yes, that'd be perfect. I want everything accessible, and I want a full wall mirror on one end."

The house was initially built with the nursery attached to the master bedroom. The nursery overlooks one of the prettiest parts of our land, which includes a small lake. I'm going to completely redesign the room into a special closet Julia will love. Hopefully it will help ease the ache of what the room was built to hold. With the thought of little Jonah, I let out the heavy sigh I've been holding, and run my fingers through my too long dark hair. I've been trying to keep my mind occupied with this room, and when it drifts to Jonah and what we've lost, the hollowness in my heart overpowers me. Somehow, I get my mind back on track.

"How soon can you start?" I ask.

"We'll start immediately. What's your deadline?"

I pause. That's a good question. I have no idea what the deadline is. I don't know when my beloved wife will come back, or if she ever will. A deep fear strikes me to my core that I've lost her forever. "Not sure. Let's say no longer than a month."

I hope some time will help Julia heal, but at the same time, I want to bring her home. I want Julia with me where she belongs.

Last night, I missed not having her body next to mine—it didn't feel right. All I want is to feel her arms and legs entwined with mine. What tortures me the most is the smell of her perfume. It's everywhere. Last night, I got out of bed and grabbed one of her shirts from the closet to hold it against me as I slept. I wanted to be close to her in some way.

I scan my phone as I walk out of what will soon be the closet of every woman's dreams. There are no calls and no texts from Julia. It'll be close to dinner time in Montana. Suddenly the air around me is stifling. Never in my life have I felt this out of control. I want to run out of this house and go straight to a nearby bar, but with my own fully stocked liquor cabinet, that doesn't make much sense. So I rationalize. A little drink with dinner never hurt anyone. But if I don't hear from her soon, I'm going to call. I'm not going to lose her.

Chapter Nine – Julia

I stagger into the guestroom. We walked and walked for hours to different jewelry stores until we'd found the perfect ring. It's platinum and it has several large black and white diamonds around the band. Although it's not as garish as my similar wedding ring, it will suit Raine and his large frame well. I relax against the pillows and I'm holding the ring up to the light just as my phone rings. It's him.

"Hey hon, was just thinking about you," I say softly. I hear Raine exhale on the other end of the line.

"Well, I wanted to give you some space, but I broke down. Miss your voice."

I smile as I reply, "I miss yours, too." A long pause. "Are you keeping yourself busy and out of trouble?"

"Trouble … yes. But not really busy. I've got a few new projects I'm taking a look at. There's a new female country-pop artist they want me to produce."

I pause as a familiar pang of jealousy hits me. Raine has a prior history of questionable infidelity, and then there was Bethany, his former background singer who tried "outing" our relationship during *Next Real Star* and caused us so much trouble. I can't help but pause. "I see," is all I say.

Raine senses my hesitation. "Don't know if I'll take it though. Bret and I need to finish up his latest project, and it has several new tracks. I might be too busy." A slight pause before he continues. "When do you think you'll come back home?" I can hear the slight desperation in his voice.

"Not sure, hon. I can't seem to keep my shit together right now. I had an anxiety attack today at the mall. I don't really want to say much more about it. I don't think I can be in that house right now."

"Darlin', it's hard for me to be in this house too, especially when you're not here, but it's our home. I want you here with me. It's not your fault, Julia."

I'm quiet. I don't know what to say as the tears start, and my hand goes over my mouth to try and stop the sobs.

"Are you there?" Raine asks.

I whisper back, my voice filled with the emotion I'm trying to keep in check, "Yes. I'm here … I need to go now. We're headed out to dinner."

"Okay. I'll talk to you tomorrow."

"Sure, hon. Tomorrow."

As I hang up, I can't stop the tears. Does Raine really forgive me, or is he just saying that to get me to come home? How could he forgive me? If only God had saved our son. When he didn't, I figured it was karma getting back at me. In some way, I probably deserve what happened, and God wants me to suffer for something. I'm just not sure what that something is, and I sure as hell don't forgive myself.

I put my cell phone in my purse and then walk into the guest bathroom. I've looked rough before, but never like this. The reflection staring back at me through the mirror is someone I've never seen before. "Sad" doesn't describe it with my shrunken eyes, sallow skin, and hair that needs more than a good washing. I've never looked this tired before in my life. "Defeated" comes to mind and that word has never, ever, entered my vocabulary. I shake my head, run some cold water, and then splash it over my face. It helps a bit as I look back up, staring at my reflection once again.

A few of my fans noticed me today while we were shopping. The news of my miscarriage has been fodder for the tabloids. Thankfully, most people avoid me, or they give me sympathetic glances, which only makes me feel worse.

I pull my makeup bag and hair brush out, trying to fix my spider web hair. Then it's time for my face, but it's almost impossible to put mascara on lashes that are constantly moist with tears, and my dark circles are no use. They can't be covered up.

I miss Raine more than I can stand, but what do we do now? When I'm around him, I only feel guilty. The weight of the loss is unlike anything I've ever experienced. One minute I'm functioning and the next I'm drowning in a sea of torment and tears. I walk out of the bathroom and pull out the ring I bought for Raine. Will this ring mean anything to us after this?

Later that night after tossing and turning for hours, I wake up and sit straight up, gasping for air. "He seems so real!" I say out loud to the ceiling. "God, he seems so real!" I sob. I dreamt I was holding my tiny dark-haired baby, Jonah, and he looked up at me and smiled. While the dream itself was comforting and soft, a harsh reality greets me.

"God! I will never hold him! Why … why!" I exclaim out loud, glaring up at the heavens. My anger toward God erupts from every pore. "What did I do?" My head drops to my hands, and I cry like I haven't ever cried before.

Chapter Ten – Raine

I hang up with Julia and stare at my cell phone. It might be good for me to get out and not think about anything tonight. I don't know how to deal with the ever-growing distance between me and the woman I need more than air. I text Bret.

'Is there a party or something going on tonight? I need to get out of here.'

I pace around the room waiting for Bret's response. I'm about to jump out of my skin, waiting for him to text back.

Finally, I get a response, 'Will pick you up in an hour.'

When I hop in Bret's car, I have no idea where we're going and, frankly, I don't care. I had to get out of that damn house. I can't stay cooped up in a house where every room reminds me of Julia, and what we've lost. It's too much. Bret senses my mood.

"You just want to grab a bite to eat? We don't have to go to this party."

"No. I want to be around small talk. Nothing real."

"O-kay. We're going to Sean Nicholsen's house. You met him once, remember? He's that young writer with seven songwriting hits who just signed a major deal. I mentioned him the other day." I shake my head as he continues. "Anyway. Will be a lot of young people … not our typical crowd."

"Young is good."

I catch Bret's eye. He can't miss my permanent frown and my hands that keep clenching and unclenching. I'm in a mood and wound tight, that's obvious. My gut is screaming that heading to this party isn't a good idea, but I'm determined to go somewhere, anywhere but staying in my claustrophobic house.

I enter the party and notice an energy I haven't felt in a while. People are alive; it's palpable and despite my mood, it's refreshing. It's definitely not dark and dreary, but there's agitation in the air, which fits my mood. Bret's brow is furrowed with worry, and inside, I'm a little worried too. I'm coming out of my skin, and it shows.

We walk up to the bar area in the front room. Bret seems to know many people in the room, but I only recognize a few faces. It doesn't take long before a couple of younger women approach us, because when I'm with Bret, it always happens. Women are not afraid of coming on to him.

"Bret, darling, haven't seen you in a while, I've missed you," one of the girl's purrs. Bret looks down at the pretty brunette with striking almond brown eyes and basically shrugs off the innuendo. I watch in amusement until it's my turn. The young, petite blonde with her offers me a drink.

"Thanks, honey, but I can get my own drink," I brusquely reply. I can't help it. I'm so used to having Julia close by. People know who she is, so women rarely approach me anymore. I'm clearly out of my element.

I lean toward a bartender and ask for a bourbon, neat. I look over at Bret, who nods at me, so I order another for my friend. When I have my drink in hand, I survey the room. The new, young Nashville crowd is everywhere. And right away a pang hits my heart. I miss old Nashville, and the way things used to be. And *damn it*, I miss Julia.

Bret grabs me and we walk around the mansion, finally settling in a near-empty pool room. We set up the table to play. The two young women who'd approached us earlier follow, but I give them a look that clearly relays we aren't interested. Eventually, they leave. Coming to this party was likely a bad idea, but staying in that house all alone was a no-go.

We play a round of pool, and Bret easily wins. I'm basically just going through the motions. I stopped playing several times to bring us more drinks. I need to keep them flowing and not think about anything. Bret's arranged a driver, so we don't have to worry about driving. We're getting a really good buzz on. As we start round number three, a couple of young guys walk in, challenging us to a game for money. I give Bret a sideways grin and brief nod. Why not?

We start the game, and I can hear these young guys banter about several of the women at the party and how they're going to score. When I was younger, I might have been one of these guys, but right now, I'm disgusted. My mind goes to Julia and how I miss not only her maturity, but how she keeps me away from all this bullshit.

Of course these young guys know who Bret is and maybe they know who I am, but I'm not sure how they fit into the Nashville music scene. I roll my eyes at Bret. He shrugs his shoulders at me, trying to laugh it off.

After three glasses of bourbon, my edginess is taking hold, and these young guys are feeding it. One of them speaks to me after he misses a shot.

"Okay, grandpa ... your turn."

I must have noticeably bristled because Bret's eyes get huge. *Grandpa?* Seriously? This guy must be an idiot. "Didn't anyone ever teach you to respect your elders," I sneer back.

The guy gives his friend a hearty laugh. They're cocky and immature, and it's all I can do to keep my cool.

Bret tries easing the slow-burning tension in the room. "Kids ... I'd be careful about waking up the bear," he laughs while looking at me, but I'm not amused as I stand there with my arms crossed, staring at this young tool. These punks aren't getting the hint.

I walk up to the pool table and take my next shot, and then I continue to run the table until Bret and I have won. One of the kids is reluctant to pay and at first, I'm ready to let it go. I don't care about the money, but the bourbon starts to win.

"So, you cocky little shits challenge us to a game and can't pay up?" My voice booms. I stand tall, my chest out as I take a step toward them. I must look fierce, because Bret quickly walks over, putting a hand on my chest, stopping me.

"We're cool, we're cool," Bret says as he swings around, placing himself in front of me and the young guys. They look scared. Good.

One of them speaks, clearly the least intelligent of the two, "You think you're such a hot shot producer, but you don't have any idea who I am, do you? You can't talk to me like that," he says, with as much emphasis as his tiny little body can relay.

I'm oblivious to who this kid is, and I don't care. I side-step around Bret until I'm standing face to face with this guy. I'm a good six inches taller as I tower over him. Sweat starts to form on the kid's brow. Bret runs and gets back in between us just as a small crowd gathers in the doorway, clearly hearing the argument. This won't reflect well on me, a mature, well-respected producer, to be picking on some kid, even if the kid is a dumbass. Albeit the fact that he may be a successful person in our industry doesn't matter in the slightest to me.

I tightly grip a pool cue, pull it up in front of me and easily snap it in two, startling everyone around us. Bret, who, luckily, stands almost as tall as me, grabs me by my shoulders, steering me out of the room, and out of the house to our waiting car as many onlookers silently watch. I'm loudly cussing the entire way as the bourbon has taken over my vocabulary. I don't think I've ever dropped the "F" bomb more in a two-minute span. People gawk at us the entire way.

As our driver pulls away, I run my hands through my hair, bellowing at my good friend. "Why did you do that? Why did you get me out of there? That little shit should know better than to mess with me!"

"That little shit is one of the hottest pop writers right now, and you need to act like an adult. I knew this was a bad idea," Bret says, letting out a heavy sigh. He grabs his phone and tries to ignore me, his inebriated friend.

"I don't care who he is," I skulk, slouching down in the back seat of the SUV, folding my arms tightly across my chest. "He's an idiot."

Bret scowls at me. "True. He's an idiot, but that idiot is running the show on the pop charts right now."

I'm silent during our ride home. I don't give a shit. I'm angry. Angrier than I've ever been in my life. I know it isn't about the kid, it's about Julia … and it's about Jonah. I've got a burning hole in my heart, and I need to fill it up. I'm pissed off, lonely, and trying to take it out on someone or something else. I have all this anger and no way to let it out.

Chapter Eleven – Julia

I stumble out of bed. I had another dream of cradling my young son, healthy and alive, and it's haunting me. I wander out to Jody's living room and sit in an alcove by the front window that overlooks their property. It's a clear night in Montana, and the stars fill the luminous night sky. And I can't miss the moon. Its bold light illuminates everything, making the snowy ground sparkle and glow. It comforts me a little to know that somewhere, my baby Jonah is up there.

I wake up in the same spot as the sun starts to rise over the tree line. I rub my cramped neck while I roll to my side and stretch. I hear a noise and look over to see Jody making coffee in the kitchen. She obviously didn't care that I was sleeping in the alcove. I catch her eye.

"The bed was too soft," I say sarcastically as I continue to rub my tight neck.

"Yeah, other guests have complained that bed is too darn comfortable. They want a rock-hard wooden bench, too," Jody says, smirking back at me.

"Well, rock-hard nails it," I say, continuing to stretch my stiff back and neck.

"Seriously … are you okay?"

"Yeah … just a bad dream." After a few moments, I say, "Tell me, do you believe in heaven? Do you think there is more after this, an afterlife?"

"I sure as heck hope so. Why?"

"I had a dream about him … about Jonah. It was so real."

"What was it like?"

"I was holding him … as a baby. He had a full head of really dark, thick hair just like Raine's, which is not surprising," I say, looking down with an embarrassed laugh, realizing how odd it seems to laugh as I haven't laughed for some time. Thinking back on my dream, I continue, "His hair even stuck up a bit on top." And then I'm lost in the image of Jonah running through my mind.

Jody chimes in, "I believe dreams can be real in a way. Maybe what we want to happen or even images of what might have been. Who knows? Jules, have you thought about talking to someone about what happened? A counselor or something? It might be good for you to talk to someone about this?"

"I hadn't thought about it. Probably would be a good idea, though," I say, my voice trailing off at the end. I really don't want to talk to anyone about Jonah or Raine, but hearing Jody mention it makes me realize it might help.

Jody walks over and hands me a hot cup of coffee, and I let it warm my frigid hands. Lately, the cold seems to penetrate down to my bones. I take a sip, relishing the liquid as it warms my throat. Odd, I haven't really noticed little things like this for days, and it's strange that a simple cup of coffee makes me realize this.

"I'll think about going to see someone, but you know what I really want is a nice massage," I say as I roll my tight neck. "I need to work some of these kinks out."

"I know just the person. She's a miracle-worker."

Jody picks up her phone and quickly dials a number before I can object. I look back out at the snow-covered, mountainous scenery and let the breath I'm always holding out. In a small way, I'm rejoining the land of the living, but I still feel empty. Frankly, I don't think I deserve to feel anything.

My mind drifts to Raine and suddenly I desperately need to talk to him. I head to the guest bedroom, pick up my phone, and call. It rings and rings until eventually going to his voicemail. I look down at my phone, but I don't leave him a message. It's several hours later there and he's probably still sleeping, but something in my gut makes me pause. What if Raine isn't alone and he didn't want to pick up? Although I don't really think he's cheating, an image of him with another woman crosses my mind. Raine is probably as lonely as I am, and I'm instantly anxious. He wouldn't, would he?

Chapter Twelve – Raine

I didn't hear my phone ringing. A bulldozer could have taken the entire house down around me and I would have slept on and on. Bret dropped me off after my repulsive party behavior. I was half drunk and finished the deed on my own, stumbling around the house, walking from room to room with a bottle of bourbon in my hand, trying to ease the ache in my chest that never leaves.

At some point, I poured myself into bed, and that was the last thing I remember. The sun blasts through the windows as I roll toward the nightstand, squinting hard at my phone, and this is when I notice the missed call from Julia. *Son of a!* I bolt upright but instantly sway, holding my head. I'm still drunk. I fall back against the pillows, with my phone above my eyes trying to read the time. It's after ten a.m. Shit. Julia's going to really wonder why I haven't called her back. I again try to rise but my stomach flip flops, and I run to the bathroom before my liquid dinner ends up all over the place. Drinking a bottle of bourbon on an empty stomach was not my best idea.

I get my shit together and decide texting Julia is a better option.

'Hi, sweetie. Just noticed you called. Sorry I missed you, was sleeping in a bit.' I hit send and wait for a few minutes, but silence greets me in return.

I stumble to the kitchen to get something for my aching head. My phone buzzes and I quickly grab it. It's a message from Tracy.

'You have a story on TMZ's website, big fella.' Tracy scolds. 'Better tell Julia before she reads about your little adventure.'

"Damn it!" I exclaim out loud. I do a frantic search and it's not hard to find. The story depicts me as a big, egotistical bully picking on a tiny, hot-shot

36

songwriter. They've posted a video, pictures, and even some quotes from people at the party. I've screwed up and I've got to tell Julia, and fast. This is the last thing we need. The story makes me look terrible.

I dial Julia's number, and she picks up after a couple of rings.

"Hi, Raine." Her voice is cold, and instantly I wonder if she already knows.

"Hey, honey," I say sweetly. Every syllable ringing in my skull.

"I noticed you sent me a text," is her frosty reply.

I'm even more worried. "Yeah." There's an awkward pause, before I finally take the plunge, "I need to tell you something."

"Yes?" I hear the worry in her voice with one word.

"I went out with Bret last night and … it didn't go well," I say with trepidation. There's silence, so I jump back in. "There's a story on TMZ … it's really not as bad as it looks." I'm rambling now, and the words are pouring out. "I didn't beat anyone up, nothing really happened. Just some words exchanged with some cocky little shit head."

I hear Julia exhale loudly on the other end, and I can envision how pissed she is at me right now.

"Start at the beginning and tell me what happened."

I relay my version, omitting the many glasses of bourbon, and any girls hitting on us.

"Doesn't sound so bad," Julia says with a slight laugh. "Sounds like that kid is clueless. I can literally picture you towering over him. I'm sure you scared the crap out of him."

"Yeah, he wasn't the sharpest, but it wasn't a shining moment for me. And, of course, someone took pictures and got everything on video. I look like an angry asshole."

"Well, honey, I hate to break it to you, but you can be an angry asshole," Julia says with an outright laugh this time, and it makes me laugh with her. "I'll check it out, but I'm more concerned about you." She asks softly, "How are you?"

I lie. "I'm okay. Trying to stay busy." I pause for a few seconds before continuing, "I had the bright idea that going to a party with Bret would help … but clearly, not a good move."

"I don't think you should beat yourself up over it. Like I said, that kid seems like a punk, and I know your patience with punks," she teases.

I like hearing her mood lighten up a bit. "You sound like you're doing better. Are *you* okay?"

There's silence. Too much silence before I hear her tiny voice, "Yeah. I'm okay. Some bad dreams, which I'm sure is to be expected. And the panic attack I mentioned at the mall the other day, but other than that, I'm hanging on."

My stomach drops with her words. I know she's not okay, and I don't know why I asked or why I'd expect to hear anything different. I don't dare touch the topic of her bad dreams; I can only imagine.

Julia continues, "Jody thinks I should see a counselor or something. Might not be a bad idea."

"Hmm ... well, maybe, that is a good idea." I pause. "I miss you, Jules. I want you to come home." The toll of last night and how much I miss her is emphasized with every syllable. I hope she hears it.

"I miss you, too, hon, more than you know."

"Then why not come home?"

"I've told you. I can't walk into that house right now. And I hurt you ... I hurt us."

"Julia, you didn't do anything ..."

She cuts me off. "I can't talk about this right now."

"Then I'm coming up there to see you."

"I don't think that's a good idea right now. It would break my heart to see you."

My hand clenches at my side. I need to think clearly before I say anything else. I sigh, "Then what am I supposed to do?" My tone is fierce and I'm sure she can tell. Right now, it surprises me how quickly I get angry at even the slightest thing. I don't want to take my anger and stress out on her, but sometimes it just comes out.

She responds calmly and firmly, "Be patient with me. This can't last forever. I just need some time."

"Fine." My head is pounding like a jackhammer is pressed against my forehead, and all I want to do is get off of this phone. "I've got to go." And then I slam my phone on the counter, shattering the plastic cover, which is supposed to be unbreakable. I shrug it off, grab a bottle of Tylenol and another bottle of bourbon, and head straight for my studio. What's the use? Why stop now?

Chapter Thirteen – Julia

When I walk back into Jody's living room, my sister and niece, Sarah, are crowded around a phone. The guilty looks on their faces give them both away.

"Don't worry, Raine just told me. Is it that bad?"

Jody looks directly at me and shrugs her shoulders with a look on her face that lets me know he's had thousands, if not millions, of streams.

"Jeez … it must be bad," I say with a laugh. For some reason, it strikes me as funny that Raine almost caused a brawl and I continue to laugh, which eventually makes Jody and my niece laugh with me. "Okay … let me see it."

After watching Raine's video clip, I miss him even more. Raine looks absolutely terrible, like he hasn't eaten or slept in days. He's thin, too thin. For a moment I consider hopping on the next plane to take care of him, but I'm pissed, not only that he hung up on me, but I'm pissed at myself, the moon, the stars, everything.

I change the subject. "So, Jod, any luck with the masseuse?"

"You have an appointment right after lunch."

"Yes! After that, we all need to go shopping." I've decided I want to treat my sister and niece to a shopping spree. The fresh Montana air, change of scenery, and now some new clothes are bound to help me.

After a much needed, relaxing massage, we go to the largest mall in town. It feels forced, but I'm doing my best to have fun and not think about anything. We hit several stores, and I treat the girls to new outfits, manicures, and pedicures. We're about to leave the mall when an overzealous fan approaches me.

"Julia!! Julia! ... Can I have your autograph?" The young girl's voice carries across the marble stone, attracting the attention of several shoppers. I usually carry a Sharpie with me just in case, and I smile as I'm digging one out of my purse.

I give her a broad smile, "Sure, what's your name?"

"Charli ... oh my gosh, you don't look so good," Charli says, the brutal honesty spilling out of her mouth as she steps closer to me. Charli's mother stares at me in shocked horror.

I laugh it off, "Yeah ... well, I just came from a massage, and I don't have any makeup on."

"No. It's not that, you're still heavy," Charli continues without any filter. "I thought you'd be much skinnier now."

My face must have fallen. I haven't thought much about the baby weight I'm still carrying, or paid attention to how much my stomach still protrudes, but obviously this young girl noticed.

"Charli!" her mother scolds. "You don't say something like that!"

I look at them both and muster a smile, "It's okay. It's the truth. Maybe I needed someone to remind me," I joke as I uncap my pen.

I sign the autograph and pose for a picture with the girl. Self-consciously, I try to suck my stomach in, but it's no use. It's a reminder, and I need to lose this reminder as fast as possible, especially before I see Raine again.

Jody grabs my hand as we quietly walk away. "Some people are clueless, Jules. Don't pay any attention to her."

I nod, but my mind is racing. Here I am, fat and depressed, and my marriage is hanging on by a thread. It's hard not to feel devastated.

When we get back to Jody's house, I insist on going to the gym. After working out for a good hour, I call Tracy and tell her about my dreams and the young girl's comment. Tracy's supportive as usual, but it doesn't take the edge off my fragile nerves. I'm anxious and unsettled, as if I'm becoming unglued. I've got to call a counselor tomorrow. It's the only thing that may help battle my demons head on. And I have to talk to Raine. After our conversation earlier today, I don't want a rift between us. With everything else going on in my head, I don't need that too. I need to take control and try to save my life, and my marriage.

Chapter Fourteen – Raine

I'm sitting in my studio, fuming. I'm pissed at myself, not Julia. Our call sucked, that's clear, and I've got to get a better grasp on my raging emotions.

I send Tracy a text, letting her know Julia's all caught up about the TMZ fiasco. Then I send a text to Bret apologizing for my idiotic behavior.

Bret sends a message back. 'Dude, you look like shit in the video, but I look pretty damn good. LOL.'

My first inclination is to tell him off, but Bret's right, I do look terrible. I text back, 'You're a dork.' Then I shut off my phone. I don't want to talk to Bret, or anyone else, for the rest of the day.

Even though I still want to drink, I put the bottle of bourbon away and figure I need to take my frustrations out in a different way. I put on gym clothes and head to the workout room in our house. Julia insisted on having a workout room with everything she'd need to lose her baby weight. We have an elliptical machine, spin bike, treadmill, and weights. I'm going to sweat the liquor out and take control. Julia said she didn't want to see me right now, but screw that. I'm going up to Montana and I'll bring her home as soon as I can. And when I get there, I want to look good.

After an hour and half workout, I grab my computer to check on several projects. It's Sunday, and I've got a busy week coming up, which is good. It's the only thing keeping me sane right now.

I walk into my studio, pick up my guitar, and start messing with the melody I've been writing about my son. Maybe it's cliché to write a song about becoming a father, but years ago I heard a song, a beautiful lullaby, that another artist wrote about her son, and it stayed with me. Maybe I can turn my anger and emptiness into something meaningful.

I work on my song idea for hours, never noticing the sun going down. Finally, late into the night, I walk straight toward the liquor cabinet in my studio. It's too easy, and right now, I need it. After what I've just written and without Julia nearby, I want to erase everything for a while. As I pour a glass, my phone buzzes. I grab it hoping it's Julia, but it's Tracy.

I pick it up without any real enthusiasm. "Yes?"

"Hey, Muhammad Ali," Tracy says with obvious sarcasm. "Get in any more fights today?"

"Not funny," I say, but it makes me chuckle. "What's up, Trace? I checked my schedule for the week, and it looks good. Thanks for keeping me busy."

"Yeah, I am, but that's not why I called."

"What is it?" Instantly my stomach falls to the floor. This has to be about Julia.

"When was the last time you talked to Julia?"

"This morning … didn't go well."

"Well, I just got off the phone with her. I think she's worse. She's having nightmares about … him." Tracy can't say Jonah's name.

I sigh, and Tracy continues. "Julia mentioned she's going to start therapy, which is good, but she also talked a lot about her weight. I guess a fan told her she was fat."

"That's ridiculous," I say, my voice rising. "She was *pregnant*," and my voice drifts off at the end.

"I know … but this could be really bad. She had a major eating disorder once, Raine. Really major. With everything going on, I think this may trigger a relapse."

I absentmindedly run my hand through my hair. Great, it's not like I have enough to worry about with her thousands of miles away, and now she's not eating. *Damn it! Why didn't she, or even you, tell me this before?* I crab at Julia's dear friend, who has become one of mine. I can't help it.

"Julia didn't want you to know. She was in treatment for years and had it beat," she says, but I can hear the worry in her voice. She continues, "Julia has a tendency to hardly eat, and exercise too much."

"I'm glad *someone* finally told me, but what can I do?"

"Remind her to take care of herself, make a conscious effort … and tell her that she looks good. Talk to her on Skype or something so you can see her."

"I always tell her she looks good. I'm glad you told me, Trace. This was something I should have known."

After I hang up with Tracy, I pick up my glass of bourbon and down it. I can only imagine how Julia's expanded stomach is making her feel. It's a constant reminder that we lost Jonah. I'm helpless and I don't do well with helpless. I grab the bottle of bourbon and head back to the studio. It's going to be a long fucking night.

Chapter Fifteen – Julia

After dinner, I return to my room and send Raine a text. I have to talk to him. He texts back that he'll Face Time me in just a few minutes. Well, that's odd. We hardly ever use that app. Skype sometimes, but only every once in a while. I immediately accept his face-to-face call.

"There you are. I had to see your face," Raine says, but it seems forced, like he's trying to be upbeat.

"Wish I would have known you wanted a visual, I would have at least put on some makeup," I say, trying to cover my face as I run a hand through my hair. Hot mess is an understatement.

"I've seen you many times without makeup and you're more beautiful without it."

I look away from the phone. I don't look good and his attempt at flattery makes me uncomfortable.

Raine continues, "First, sorry about earlier and the hang-up. I shouldn't have done that. What can I say, I'm a dumbass."

I smile at his comments, "You're not a dumbass, and you know it. It's okay. We're both frustrated."

"Yes, I am frustrated," Raine says, suddenly serious. "I want you here. It would make you blush if you knew what I'd do to you right now."

I laugh out loud, and again it strikes me as odd. Hearing my own laughter feels off. "I'll bet. You know, the doctor said I couldn't have sex for a month after ..." and I just stop.

Raine quickly jumps in. "Time's almost up, and I could be there in a day," he teases. But he's serious, waiting for my reaction. I pause and he continues,

46

"I did have Tracy clear my schedule in two weeks. I want to see you."

I turn away from the screen, hesitating, but I quickly look back at my beautiful husband before I relent. I can't help it. I miss him. "Okay, in two weeks. We'll make it work." I smile at him and then tease, "We'll have to get a hotel room though … you have no idea how much I want to be alone with you right now.

Raine gives me a big, toothy grin. "Good. I'll have Tracy book the ticket."

"And Raine?"

"Yes, sweetheart?"

"Try not to notice how much I've gained, okay. I still haven't lost any weight."

"Honey, I told you once you could weigh three hundred pounds, I don't care. You're beautiful. It's one of the reasons why I wanted a visual tonight. I need to see your face. It tears me up when you're away."

I smile at the green eyes staring back at me, and there's a sweet smile on his lips. I try to capture this image until I'll get to see him.

"You know one thing we haven't tried?" Raine asks with a mischievous grin.

"I have no idea, but you are going to tell me," I respond dryly. With Raine you never know where he's going to go.

"Face Time sex."

And my head goes back with laughter. "True, but not tonight. There's too much of an audience in the next room."

Raine nods, a subtle smirk playing on his lips. "Well, I had to at least mention it."

"But seriously, hon, how are you feeling?" I utter the words most men hate, and Raine is no exception.

"I've started working out and I'm staying as busy as possible."

"Yeah, me too, I guess. I'm calling a counselor tomorrow. I need it. Maybe we could both see someone when you're here?"

"Maybe. Well, hon, I'm gonna try and get some sleep tonight after last night's escapade."

"Yeah, I watched it. It was funny," I say as a huge smile breaks across my face.

Raine grimaces. "It was rather absurd. I'm now known not only for being an arrogant asshole, but a big bully, too. Just what I need."

"It will pass. Things like that always do. Get some rest and I'll talk to you tomorrow."

After I put my phone down, I walk to the full-length mirror and give myself a good look up and down. I frown at my image. I look heavy. I don't want Raine to see my stomach like this, so I have two weeks to lose weight. I instantly drop to the floor and do sit-ups until the burn in my midsection makes me stop. I stare up at the ceiling as a lone tear runs down the side of my face. It hits out of nowhere and I can't control it. Will I ever feel good about anything ever again?

Chapter Sixteen – Julia

I open the door and walk down the hallway with trepidation. Jody got a reference for a doctor in town, and I'm here for my first appointment. Right now, as I stand outside the door, I'm not ready. Talking about Jonah with a stranger has made my old friend stomach acid churn.

This morning, I went for a long run in the cold Montana air, and it felt good to sweat. I now have a two-week goal to meet, and I don't have a minute to waste. I know I'll have to tell the counselor about my bouts with anorexia, and I dread going through the story, but it's a part of me. Tracy mentioned my illness on the phone the other day. She knows I can easily fall back into old habits, especially when I'm riding this emotional roller coaster. Anorexia can take a hold of me, and I can get obsessed with food and exercise. My two addictions. I've never mentioned it to Raine because it happened so long ago, but with the turmoil I'm now under, I realize it's a battle I'll have to fight. Some people turn to drugs or alcohol; I have a problem with excessive exercising.

I finally get the nerve to knock, and a deep voice responds to come in. Andrew Montgomery, Ph.D., is the name on the door. "Ready or not," I whisper under my breath.

An hour later, I'm sitting in my rental car, spent, and my emotions are raw. I peer into the rear-view mirror and wipe away the black mascara stains from under my eyes. I can ruin perfectly good makeup in a record-setting amount of time. I need to compose myself before I head back to Jody's. I drive to a nearby coffee shop called Scenic Drive, and after fixing my face the best I can, I head in.

As I approach the counter, the server gasps loudly. *Damn!* I still forget that people sometimes recognize me.

"Hi … um … Ms. Tate," the young girl says. Her big, brown eyes are wide, and she slightly stutters. I give her a sympathetic smile before she finally sputters out, "What … can … I get you?"

"Just a small cappuccino, non-fat please," I say, giving her a big smile of encouragement.

She walks to a back counter to make my drink as I glance down at my phone, noticing several texts from Raine. I'm sure he's wondering how it went with my new counselor. I'll get back to him in a few minutes. I've got to get my shit together first, but first I need to get some perspective on my hour-long session where it seemed like I bared my soul out to some doctor I'd just met.

During my session, I'd rattled off the key details: pregnancy, miscarriage because I was touring too late into my pregnancy, followed by a nervous breakdown and my marriage hanging by a thread. Dr. Montgomery listened quietly, acknowledged my comments, but fought me on the "miscarriage was my fault" point. Everyone fights me on it, but my head and my heart tell me it's all me. *Me.* Why can't someone see it from my point of view?

The young girl finishes making my drink. "I'm in the same grade as your niece, Sarah. She said you were her aunt. Wow. She's lucky."

"Yes, Sarah's my niece, but I don't know if that makes her lucky," I say with a wink, trying to make a joke. It must not have worked, because the young girl looks at me like I'm off my rocker. I add, "Would you like a picture?"

"Oh my gosh … I'd *love* one," she practically squeals, which makes me laugh.

She quickly steps from behind the counter as a few other people watch her pull her phone out, and then I lean in for a selfie. The other bystanders soon go back to their own business. Luckily, most people leave me alone when I visit my sister. When I'm in this town, it's like being anonymous, and I'm grateful for that, especially now. When I've visited a few times with Raine, we've enjoyed the anonymity.

I grab my drink and sit by the huge fireplace in the center of the room to enjoy a quiet moment to myself. I'd brought a journal with me, and I open it up to write about my session. My goal is to not only get out of bed, but also out of my head. Seriously, right now, that's all I want. Every day is a struggle, and it's only getting worse, not better. Dr. Montgomery explained that this is a normal part of the grieving process, and that I'd go through the tasks of mourning, which he says we'll go over in our next session. I know what he's telling me is true, but nothing feels normal to me. No one should feel this low. And it's likely that my fucked-up determination is keeping me from actually feeling what I need to feel. I despise being lazy, but right now all I want to do is sleep all day. My body is heavy and sluggish, and my brain can't process this, not to mention all the unhinged thoughts swirling around my head. I've never felt such despair—there is no way in hell this is "normal."

I try not to think as I start to write, putting all my feelings down on paper. Dr. Montgomery thought this would help me sort out my pain, but my mind keeps drifting to Raine. Dr. Montgomery reminded me that Raine's reactions and anger are likely normal for him. We're processing our pain and grief in different ways. Raine's pissed. That's obvious, but he's trying to hide it from me.

My phone buzzes again. Raine's clearly worried, so I send him a quick message.

'Hi, darling. Session went okay. I'm destroyed as you can imagine. But I think this may help me.'

Raine responds back immediately, 'Okay. Been worried. Can you talk later?'

'Of course, I'm getting coffee right now, but I'll call in an hour or so?'
'Perfect.'

I shake my head and go back to my journal, trying to write down more thoughts, but it's difficult as random tears fall on the pages. It's a challenge, but I'm able to write about how much I miss Jonah, and how much my arms ache, which I've read is common. It's a physical reaction from not having him to actually hold.

When I've finished, my pages look like a semi-wet, garbled mess, but it's a start. I put my coffee down, wipe away a few remaining tears, and stare into the fire for a good few minutes. I don't know how this will ever get any easier. My heart is absolutely broken into tiny fragments, and there is no hope of fixing it. Not ever.

Chapter Seventeen – Raine

I think I'm having a panic attack or maybe it's a heart attack, I'm not exactly sure. My heart is pounding, so hard I can feel it pulsating in my ears. I had a few glasses of bourbon last night, but nothing crazy, so this shouldn't be alcohol related.

I stumble out of bed and manage to make it to the bathroom, where I splash cold water on my face. With my arms stretched wide on the counter, I study my reflection in the mirror. God. I look tired. This morning is one of the first times I woke up and remembered my dream. It was a doozy.

I was lost on some street and every time I went around a corner, I was back where I started. I stare at the empty space around Julia's sink. Her things are gone from this room, and from many places in the house. It's one more reminder that tears me in two.

I stagger back to bed, sit down, and pick up my phone. I have a writing appointment in a little over an hour, and there's no way I can chill out enough to go.

I'm talking the instant Tracy picks up. "Can you reschedule my appointment this morning?"

Tracy gives me a dry reply, "Good morning to you, too. Sure. Why?"

I trust Tracy implicitly, but I don't want her to know I may be having a panic attack. "Some people are coming to the house today to work on that surprise closet for Julia."

"Okay. Consider it done. I'll try to reschedule it to later this week."

I hang up and flop back on the bed. I'm literally exhausted, but at least my heart rate has slowed. The overpowering sense of sadness that comes over me is new. I've never felt tortured in my life, except for when I almost lost Julia during *Next Real Star*. I think back to that time, which seems like an eternity ago. It's amazing how that reality show brought us together, but almost tore us apart at the same time. Now, we're faced with a real-life tragedy. Instead of experiencing an amazing time in our relationship like we expected, we are now facing something that may destroy us.

I make it to the kitchen, thinking a good breakfast will help, but as I stare into the fridge, nothing looks good. I've never been in a funk like this in my life. This house is like a tomb, and I just want out.

I call Bret. "Let's hit the golf course. I need to get out of here."

Although it's only sixty degrees outside, Bret doesn't question me, and agrees to meet me at one of our favorite courses.

As we're riding along in a golf cart, I'm unusually quiet. Bret finally breaks the silence.

"Okay, what's up?"

I look away at the slowly passing scenery before us. "I think I'm depressed. I have never been this down in my life and I literally ... I don't know what to do."

"Understandable. When are you going to see Julia?"

"Two weeks."

"Why don't you go a little earlier and surprise her. I bet she'd like that."

But I'm not so sure. Julia's been adamant about having some alone time. I'd have to fly out without Tracy knowing. I'll think about it.

Bret continues, "Although I haven't been there, with what happened, I think you're allowed to be angry and depressed. Why don't you get out of here? Go clear your head like Julia, and Montana might be just the place."

"If I go, I might never come back," I joke. But I'm sort of serious. Every fiber of my being wants out of Nashville. I thought Julia was running away, but now I get it. I want to run away, too. This crushing sense of loss is more than I can bear.

That night, I book my ticket. I'll leave five days earlier than I'd planned. I've got some appointments and writing sessions that I can't cancel, so this is the earliest I can go. Next, I send Tracy an email telling her to hold off booking any more appointments, claiming I'm having more work done on the house. I hope it'll sway her from peppering me with questions. Tracy is intuitive, but it's a chance I'm willing to take. I've got to see my girl and bring her home.

Chapter Eighteen – Julia

I'm arguing with Dr. Montgomery.

"Julia, I need you to talk about your hopes and dreams for Jonah, it will help you process the pain of your grief."

"I've already told you about my dream. Those were my hopes and dreams ... that I'd have a son, who would have a life with us. What more do you want from me?"

"Then I want you to explain exactly how you feel about losing Jonah and losing him the way that you did. How does it make you feel? Not just the facts and what you think you want me to hear."

And this is how it went, back and forth for the entire hour. Now that I'm leaving my second session with Dr. Montgomery, I don't feel any better, and actually, I thought the conversation would kill me. I could barely breathe during the session, and now the way my head feels makes a migraine seem like a cake walk. Dr. Montgomery continued to explain that I'm going through the usual stages of grief, and he gave me a book to read on the four tasks of mourning. The first task is to accept my reality and what we've lost, and the second task is to process the pain and my grief. He's pushing me on the pain and grief part, and it's too much, too soon. I can't even think about the two remaining tasks ... they seem too far away and out of reach.

I head to the gym before going back to Jody's. Each day my new routine begins with running in the cold air around Jody's property, followed by a very healthy breakfast of egg whites and oatmeal, and then I drive to Dr. Montgomery's, where I fall apart. Finally, I hit the gym again to clear my head. I can't worry about my heart right now. The ache is unbearable.

As I drive away from the gym, I call Raine and get his voicemail and leave him a message. It's nearly noon in Nashville and he must be in a session.

I walk into my new favorite coffee shop, get my drink, and pull out my journal. I read through some of my entries and then start writing. In some ways, I'm working on my anger with God. I still think we lost Jonah because of something I did, but I'm becoming a little less angry with God. Only a little.

It's easy to be pissed off at God, and for the past few days as I look up toward the heavens, I can't understand why we were hurt in this way. We didn't deserve it. We deserved a healthy baby. Jonah's due date would've been the twenty-first of February. My stomach churns as I think about how I'll get through that day. My arms still ache to hold him, and I wonder if that will ever leave me. If only I could have held him ... just once.

Chapter Nineteen – Raine

I'm still convinced I'm having a heart attack. Last night, I polished off another half bottle of bourbon because, like a fool, I thought it'd help me sleep. Same process equals the same results. And I had the same nightmare I've had for days, where I'm lost on the street and I keep coming back to the same place. What the hell does it mean?

I call Tracy and again ask her to reschedule a meeting with one of the labels in town with some lame excuse.

Tracy's not buying it. "Raine, I can't keep making these appointments if you're going to cancel." Her frustration is apparent. "Of course everyone understands what you are going through, but your reputation is on the line."

"Tracy, just do it. Please." And I basically hang up on her. I don't have the patience for her or anyone else right now.

I throw on workout clothes thinking a good, sweaty run on the treadmill will help me get a hold on this anxiety. I've got to try something. I can't keep waking up every morning like this. The only bright spot that's keeping me going is knowing I'll see Julia in a few days. That hopefully will take some of the edge off.

As I'm running, my mind goes back to the fateful night when I drove Julia to the hospital. As the nightmarish event replays in my head, my heart speeds up. That must be it. My nightmare is reminiscent of that drive to the hospital when I was helpless, watching the life seep out of my wife and unborn son, and I couldn't do anything to stop it.

I jump off the treadmill, look down at my phone, and see I've missed a call from Julia. I instantly call her back.

58

She picks up right away, "Good timing." She sounds good today.

I smile to myself and instantly notice how my body relaxes when I hear her voice. It soothes me. I'm reluctant to ask about her sessions but I take the leap, "How'd it go today?" I hold my breath hoping for a good report.

"Honestly? Brutal."

"Right, well, understandable." I want to casually mention my own turmoil, but I don't want to alarm her. Still, I take the plunge. "I'm not sleeping well myself." I pause wondering if talking about my own pain is selfish in light of hers.

Julia asks softly and with genuine concern, "Are you okay?"

"Nothing I can't handle."

"Raine, you could talk to someone in Nashville about what happened. It might help?"

"I've got Bret. He's been good about getting me out."

"Okay ... I get it." But I hear the frustration in her voice. She changes the subject. "What do you have planned for the rest of the day?"

I lie. "Some appointments." I have nothing planned for the rest of the day, and my heart starts to race at that thought.

"Well, I'm headed to a late lunch with Jody, and then I'll be back later. No one will be at their house later. Phone sex?" she teases, but I think she may be serious.

"You have no idea how good that sounds," I reply.

"A date then?"

"You got it."

I put the phone down and sigh, running my hands through my too long hair. I'm starting to look like I'm stranded in a mountain cabin without a mirror and no grooming utensils. I need a haircut, but that would mean going out in the real world and right now, I don't want to go anywhere. I'm becoming a recluse, which suits me just fine.

I walk to the studio, pick up my favorite guitar, and continue working on the song, my tribute to Jonah. I'm engrossed with finishing a demo of the song. And with a bottle of bourbon at my side, I completely miss Julia's call later that day. She tries me three different times, and I miss every single call.

Chapter Twenty – Julia

I try not to put too much stock into Raine's little white lie. I'd already talked to Tracy, and I knew he didn't have any appointments. Raine, ever my strong husband, is hurting far worse than he's letting me know. And now I'm worried, more than ever. Maybe running away to Montana wasn't my best idea. Now that I'm here, there's nothing I can do to help him back in Nashville. It was selfish of me to have left, but I couldn't see straight and still can't. Raine will drink to avoid his pain, and he's good at it. I hope deep in my heart that it won't get out of control. Raine's been more open with me since we reconnected during *Next Real Star*, but he's not one to delve deeply into his emotions. He needs to reveal what he wants at his own pace, but this loss is killing him as much as it's killing me.

I wonder what it'd be like to feel whole again. I'd give anything to be back before the miscarriage happened and have a chance to make different choices. I'd give anything to have a chance to undo my mistakes and remove this guilt, this feeling that I've destroyed our lives. If only I could have one day to not feel this never-ending sense of loss.

Later that night, I try to call Raine again, and again. After the third try, I call Bret. "I need you to check on him. I promised to call him later today and he didn't pick up. He's missing appointments, Bret. Tracy told me."

"He's not going to like me interfering, Julia, you know him. I'm going to piss him off, and I don't want to witness the Raine I got the other night—that was a shit-show." Bret's trying to joke, but he's serious. I get it. He doesn't want to poke the bear.

Even though I'm physically sick with worry, I smile at the image of a pissed-off Raine berating some poor young punk. The video was actually quite impressive.

But I get back to my purpose. "Bret, I need you to do this. Please go over and check on him."

"All right, I'll do this 'cause I love ya, Jules," he says, but he's clearly not thrilled.

Chapter Twenty-One – Bret

When I pull up to Raine's house, it's dark. I go to the front door, ring the bell, and nothing. I knock and wait but no one comes, so I try the door and it's unlocked. Not a good sign. I take a peek into the kitchen, and it's a mess. Empty food containers and bottles litter the counters. Great. I'm fearing I'm going to find a half-crazed man peeing into milk bottles. I walk down the hallway off of the foyer and see the light to Raine's studio is on.

As I walk toward the studio, I hear a guitar and Raine cussing. "Dude, you down there?" I call out, not wanting to startle him.

The guitar stops. "Bret?" Raine asks, his gruff voice responding with surprise.

"Yep."

"Come on in," Raine slurs, and it's exactly what I suspected. I walk into the room, glance at Raine, and wonder if he's bothered to bathe. He definitely hasn't used a razor in days, and I can see a half-empty bottle of bourbon on the floor next to him.

"Come listen to this," Raine says as he gives me a sideways, half-drunk glance. Raine sets his guitar down and gestures for me to take a seat. I sit on the couch across from the mixing board as Raine hits a button in front of him, and a guitar part starts. It's pretty, but sloppy. The vocals are in tune but slightly out of sync. I can make out the lyrics and I nod toward Raine. It's clear what the song is about, and it's also clear Raine didn't have his shit together when he recorded it. This isn't like Raine. Whenever he's in the studio, he's a consummate professional. He's never like this. No matter what is going on in his life, he takes his studio work very seriously.

"Raine, I need to get you out of here. Let's get some dinner?"

"Not hungry. I need to finish this song."

"It sounds almost finished, and it's really pretty. I bet Julia will like it."

At the mention of her name, Raine grabs his phone and sees the three missed calls. "*Son-of-a*! I missed her calls. I've got to call her back."

"Let's get something to eat first."

"I told you, I'M NOT HUNGRY!"

I decide to use the one weapon I have: Julia. "I talked to Julia today, Raine. She knows you're missing business appointments, and she called me, worried. You've got to get your shit straight for her."

At the mention of her name, Raine collapses against the back of his chair, and he looks straight at me. "But she's not here, Bret ...she's not here," he croaks out, almost with a sob.

Raine looks like a lost little kid. I've never seen my friend in such a state. "She'll come back, but right now, we're headed out for a meal and some coffee."

After several moments, Raine reluctantly lifts his eyes up to mine and nods. He stands up from the mixing board and staggers out the door as I follow right behind him, my arms outstretched in case he falls. At least I've gotten him up, and now, I hope, I can sober him up. The jig is up. Raine's hurting more than anyone could have known.

After we have some coffee and food, I bring Raine back home and decide to stay in a guest room. Raine agrees to go to bed, but only because I promise to call Julia and let her know he's okay.

I call Julia as promised and the fear in her voice is evident, "You got him in bed?"

"Yeah. I didn't realize how hard he's taking this ... and how much he misses you. I don't think he knows how to function anymore when you're not here."

I hear Julia sigh heavily on the other end. "We're going to see each other soon. I'm hopeful it will help."

"He's drinking a lot. More than he has in a long time. From now on, I'll check on him every day. He knows you called several times and that he missed them. It was all he talked about all night. He's so afraid of losing you."

"Tell him it won't happen. I will never love another."

Chapter Twenty-Two – Raine and Julia

It's the day of my flight to Montana and I'm having second thoughts. Bret's the only one who knows I'm leaving a few days early. He's been supportive, but I have no idea what kind of reaction I'll get from Julia. The past few days have been some of the most difficult of my life. I've talked to Julia every day after her counseling sessions, and then again at night, but it's been all I can do to keep my shit together.

I usually stay cooped up in the house working in the studio. My studio is the one place where I can really release it all; my fears that I'll end up completely alone and the hollowness that consumes me night and day. And although not everything I'm writing is good, it's keeping me sane. Bret's been in touch with me every day and is trying to keep me sober, but it's been a battle. A deep ache fills my heart. I don't think I can get past it. Bourbon seems to be the only thing that keeps me from going over the edge.

On the plane, I want to order a drink, but I have to be coherent when I arrive. Julia will never forgive me if I step off of the plane drunk. As I board the second plane in Denver, I send Julia a text letting her know I'm on the way. Let the chips fall where they may. I need to see my wife.

##

I jump when I see Raine's text. He's surprised me, but instantly I'm filled with exhilaration that he'll be with me in a few short hours. I don't know if I'll still feel guilty when I see him, but I can't wait to feel his arms around me. After Bret told me what's been going on with him, I've been scared to death about his drinking. Maybe our time together will help ease some of the ache about Jonah, and with the thought of my baby, my chest heaves with sobs that I somehow stifle. I've gotten good at keeping myself from coming apart at the drop of a hat.

The past few sessions with Dr. Montgomery have been especially brutal. Although I appreciate his technique of making me work through my grief, each session is a boxing match, and I'm getting pummeled. He won't let me off the hook about my eating disorder, but so far, I think I'm keeping my weight obsession under control.

I walk out of my temporary bedroom and see Jody sitting in the kitchen. "Raine's on his way," I casually mention.

"Here? He's on the way now?" Jody says, as her eyebrows raise with surprise.

I give her a silent nod.

"Well good, I think? Is this a good thing?" Jody asks. She gives me her big sister questioning look I've come to expect and appreciate.

"Yeah ... I think so. I need to see him. I'm going to run to town and find us a hotel room, pick him up, and we'll talk in the morning."

I rush back to the guest bedroom and quickly pack a bag. With the thought of seeing him in a few hours, I have more energy than I've had in many days. Raine does that. He always lifts my spirits.

##

As the plane touches down, I say a silent prayer thanking God for getting me on the ground sober. It was one of the longest plane rides of my life. I'm a bundle of nerves when I walk off the plane and sweat starts pouring out everywhere. What will I say to Julia when I see her? Will this be awkward?

The airport is very small, and it isn't hard to find her. The moment my eyes find hers, I'm struck by an inner peace I haven't felt in weeks. She always calms me down, and damn, she looks good. Thin, but good.

Julia smiles as I walk toward her. It's almost like we're in slow motion, and if people stop and notice us, I don't see them at all. When I reach her, I swoop her up in my arms and everything disappears. I kiss her hard on the mouth, and my one free hand that's not holding a bag, grabs her by the waist and pulls her in tight. She responds by kissing me back and her arms encircle my neck. God, I missed feeling her against me. We finish and she looks up at me and smiles. We don't say a word as we walk out to her car, hand in hand, just happy to be together.

"It's colder here than I remember," I say, rubbing my bare hands together as she starts up the car.

"We usually visit in the summer, not the dead of winter," Julia teases with a sideways glance. "But for the next few hours, I'll keep you busy and hopefully warm," she says giving me one of her gorgeous smiles. "I've rented a room at a nearby hotel. Thought that would be better than Jody's."

I grab her free hand, bringing it to my lips. The smell of her perfume, one of my favorites, instantly fills me with longing. "How far away is the hotel?"

"Not far," she says with a knowing smile. "It won't take us long."

"Well, I personally hope it takes you all damn night."

Julia laughs, and it sounds like music. It seems like years since I've heard her beautiful voice in person.

Once we get to the hotel and settle inside, we don't waste time. I throw my luggage to the floor and gather Julia's tiny frame in my arms. I can feel her ribs through her clothing, which is concerning, but I don't say anything. After what Tracy told me, I figured she hasn't been eating much and has lost some weight, but she's lost more than I would have thought, and her baby bump is almost completely gone.

I pick Julia up and practically throw her on the king-sized bed with a laugh coming from deep in my chest. Although her bright blue eyes still look sad and tired, she's so beautiful. Her long dark hair is down, and it spreads out around her on the bed. It surprises me how excited I get about making love to my wife.

I quickly strip off most of my clothes as Julia lies there watching me. I stretch my frame down next to her, running my hand up her body to cup her chin, my thumb stroking along her jawline. I could stay like this and stare at her for hours. During my flight, I wondered if our initial time together would be strained, but right now, it seems effortless, and the distance has stoked this part of our intimate relationship. I want to breathe her in and lie like this for hours, but my body starts taking control. Julia leans up and pulls her sweater over her head but then uses it to cover her stomach.

"Let me see you," I whisper, gently pulling the sweater away from her body. She looks away from me as I do this, her hands trying to hide the body I've seen and loved so many times. "You look amazing," I say tenderly as my hand rests against her face, and I make her look at me, "Absolutely amazing."

Julia gives me a shy glance but then looks away again. I pull her face toward mine. I kiss her lips, letting my mouth travel down to her neck and then to her shoulders.

She groans as I move back up her neck to those lips I adore, kissing her deeply, burying my tongue into her mouth. She tastes sweet and like home, and by now, I'm more than ready. I lean down over her as she smiles.

"It's obvious, isn't it? I've missed you," I say, my voice deep with desire. "I hope I can last," I tease. My wife's driving me mad. Weeks of pent-up sexual frustration have built to a boiling point.

Julia responds by kissing me hard and pulling at my boxer briefs that I've mistakenly left on.

"Not sure why you didn't take everything off," she says with a grin.

"I didn't want to presume."

Julia looks at me skeptically, like I'm a big dork. "Really?" Then she asks, "I did wonder if this would be a little weird, but I figured we'd work around that," she says with a wry smile.

Without saying another word, she pulls at my underwear while I strip off her remaining jeans and black lacy bra and underwear, all while our hands keep grasping flesh and our lips find each other haphazardly. It's not one of our most fluid moments, but who cares.

When we're finally naked, I feel Julia tense. We haven't made love since she lost the baby. Dr. Henley told us we'd have to wait several weeks. That time is up, but I'm still not sure she's really ready. I lean up and search her eyes. "Are you sure this is okay?"

"Yes," she says with a penetrating gaze. I can see a bit of fear, but her love shines through. "I'm not sure how it will feel, but yes, I'm sure," and as she says this, she grips my hair and pulls me down on top of her.

And with that, I completely lose it. I frantically run my hands all over her, and if she tenses at all when I touch her stomach, I whisper in her ear how beautiful she is. I want her to feel me. When we do join, Julia tenses up again for a moment, but soon I feel her relax as she lets me enter her all the way, and within seconds I'm doing everything I can not to explode.

Chapter Twenty-Three – Julia

I didn't realize how much I'd missed Raine. It was hard on me mentally, but the physical reaction on my body from seeing him is intoxicating. And although he looks more haggard than ever, to me, Raine's still the tall, gorgeous green-eyed man I married many months ago.

With every kiss and touch, I almost come out of my skin. Although I flinch each time he runs his hand over my stomach, I soon forget about the added flesh I'm still carrying.

When Raine's lips reach my torso and move lower, I lean up slightly as he almost takes me over the edge. He stops, his eyes filled with unmet desire as he moves up, kissing my neck hard. He enters me and as he does, I gasp out loud with pleasure. Raine pauses for a brief moment, checking my reaction. I give him a smile before taking his mouth with mine.

As Raine starts to move inside me, gently at first, then with increasing thrusts, I clutch his back and writhe below him. Raine puts one hand up to my face, stroking my cheek before finally settling one hand in my hair, with his other hand wrapped around me, holding me tight against him.

The first time I come hard and long, and after Raine catches his breath and I relax a bit in his arms, he starts bringing me to an even higher level of release. But this time he can't help himself as he too comes with me, crying out as he does.

Our love and closeness are almost like before. I can't get close enough to Raine as I wrap my arms and legs around him, and he pulls me tight to his frame. I look up at his face. He's staring up at the ceiling, seemingly lost in thought. I reach up and run my finger down his jaw bringing his focus back to me. I didn't think his arms could hold me tighter, but they do. We don't speak and for now, we don't need to. For the first time in too long, we forget about everything but being in this moment, right now.

Chapter Twenty-Four – Raine

For the first time in many days, I'm not thinking about a drink. Julia satisfies me like nothing else. I absentmindedly run my hand up and down her back, and she shudders.

"I could go again," she teases as her head rests against my chest.

"Don't mention it if you can't keep up your end of the bargain," I tease right back, and she laughs.

"God, I'd missed your laugh. It's so good to hear you enjoy yourself."

"I think I'd forgotten how," she says, drawing herself up to look at me as a dark expression crosses her face. For a brief moment, we're both brought back to reality.

I break the sadness by leaning in and kissing her head. "Did I happen to mention how amazing you look? Absolutely beautiful." I look into her eyes. Under my scrutiny, she looks away, but I bring her eyes back to mine. "I mean it. *Fucking* amazing."

"Thanks, I have been working hard to lose ..." she begins, but she stops cold and collects herself before continuing. "I've been going to the gym a lot and eating well," she adds. "Raine, I have to be serious for a moment. You look exhausted."

I'm quiet and I look away. "I know. I'm not doing so well," I say, realizing I must be completely honest with us both. "It's hard for me to admit, but I may need some help."

"We all do, Raine. At times, we all do."

I enfold her tightly in my arms. She rests her head again on my chest.

"I need to sleep," she says softly.

"Go ahead, sweetheart, sleep."

Soon she's snoring, but I'm lying there, staring up at the ceiling. I'm more at peace than I've been in weeks, but then it starts to hit me. The ache for alcohol, especially bourbon, rears its ugly head. I haven't had a drop of anything all day, and a light sweat is breaking out all over my body. I'm determined not to move. I don't want to let her go. But as I lie here holding my one true love in my arms, all I can think about is having a drink.

Chapter Twenty-Five – Julia

I wake up exhausted, but warm and safe in Raine's arms. He'd hardly stirred all night, but the sheets around him are soaked with sweat, and I know why. His body is reacting to the lack of alcohol.

I run my hand over my now almost flat stomach and my chest tightens. Will I ever not feel the heaviness of Jonah's loss in my soul? I stretch slightly, careful not to wake up Raine, and notice a bit of soreness from making love. It was worth every moment. I figure we'll have to take it a bit easy. Sex only once a day until I'm fully healed, I jokingly think. I smile and stretch a bit more.

Raine's eyes pop open and I give him a sideways grin. He smiles back even though his body is clearly going through withdrawals.

"Exactly the way I like to wake up," he sleepily drawls. He leans over and sweetly kisses my lips.

I instantly forget all about my new "sex once a day" rule as I'm entangled in Raine's arms, clutching tightly to him as again, we become one. He's tender with me, but there's still a hunger between us. God, how I get lost with him.

Many minutes later I tease, "You know. We could just stay here, cooped up in this hotel for months. We don't have to leave?" I'm lying on my stomach, with the sheets covering my bare ass as he lies on his back with one arm draped over my backside.

Raine looks down at me appreciatively. "I told Bret I may not come back, and I meant it."

I roll over to face him. "Why don't we find a house to rent and stay for a while? Forget about Nashville for a few months? Everyone would understand. We aren't going broke, we can afford some time off, and, frankly, we need it. What do you think?" I hold my breath, waiting for his answer. The idea just popped into my head, and I have no idea what he'll think.

"I like it. And I know just the spot. I bet we could find a house overlooking the lake outside of town."

I give him a huge smile and then put my head back down on my arms and sigh. I love that lake. It's surrounded by snowcapped mountains and it's one of my favorite spots. "A plan then. What do you think Tracy will say … and the labels, and Bret? You guys are working on his next album."

"I can write from here," Raine says, and then he softly mentions, "Actually, I've been writing a lot back in Nashville. It feels good to get everything out. And I bet Bret would come up here to write. We could make our extended vacation a working one."

I grow quiet. I haven't thought much about writing or even performing since I lost Jonah, and I don't know if I want to do either one again. It's funny. The desire to create anything has completely left me. I know I should be writing songs. After *Next Real Star* ended, my writing was in such demand, I was writing during all my spare time. I'd finished four songs for my own EP, but since the miscarriage, I haven't given that project another thought. I'm glad Raine's writing though and that it's helping him. I look up at him just as he runs a hand across his sweat-soaked brow. He's hurting and doing everything he can to hide it.

I stretch and then bring us back to reality. "It's probably about time for dinner, and I need to feed you." I lean up and place my lips on his.

Raine responds, "I have all that I want right here," as he grasps my head and kisses me long and deep. After several seconds he pulls away from me, "Room service?"

I smile and nod in agreement.

When Raine orders a drink with his dinner, I don't say a word. I don't have to. We both know he isn't able to stop. After we eat and he gets some relief, I hop in the shower as Raine manages the usual calls and texts he's missed. He also sends Tracy a text to let her know he's here with me, and that we plan on staying in Montana for a while. I'm sure that is going to go over like stale bread.

Later we decide we need to head up to Jody's to make an appearance, but it's clear from the way Raine is grasping at me constantly, his vote is to never leave the hotel.

"Since you sent that text to Tracy, she's called me three times. I can't deal with her right now," I tease as I toss my phone in my purse. "She's freaking out at the thought of us staying here for a while."

"Yep," Raine yells from the bathroom. He grabbed his shaving kit and is getting to work. I walk in, sit on the toilet seat, and watch his every stroke of the blade. "I used to watch my dad shave all the time. Usually, it was the only time I got to talk to him," I reminisce.

Raine gives me a sideways glance and smiles. "You can watch me do anything."

I chuckle. "I kind of like your Grizzly Adams look. Very manly," I say with a huge grin, and he gives me one of his famous "bullshit" frowns.

"I look like shit and we both know it," his gruff voice teases. I need to get rid of the whiskers. "Makes me look old."

Something hits me. I grow quiet and walk out. Raine stops in mid-shave with shaving cream on one half of his face.

I go to the bed and stretch out, my eyes closed.

"Jules? What is it?" He implores, following me. "What did I say?" Raine reaches me, sitting down on the side of the bed and grabbing my hand as he does.

One arm is crossed over my eyes, but I move my arm and look up at him, speaking softly, "What if I'm too old to have a baby, Raine? What if that was our only chance?"

Raine's look of despair at my words is obvious as he pleads with me. "It wasn't our only chance," he says bending down and leaning closer to my face, looking straight in my eyes. "If you want to try again, we'll try again."

I can't hold it in as tears stream down the sides of my cheeks. This is the first time we'd even broached having another child, and I completely lose it.

Raine pulls me up into his arms and holds me as I cry even harder. Shaving cream smears across my face, and at any other time I would have laughed at the absurdness of it all, but we hold each other as tears silently roll down our faces and cry together. Our near-perfect night is going downhill fast, and again, it's all my fault.

Chapter Twenty-Six – Raine

It's still early when we drive up to Jody's. We're sitting around the kitchen table with Jody and her husband Jay, making small talk and enjoying a few beers. So far, I'm keeping my drinking in check. Julia lets her sister know we plan on staying for a little while and that we'll need to find a house or condo to rent.

"I can help you find something," Jody says. "Most of the rentals are empty this time of year. Too cold for the southerners," she teases.

"No shit," I say. "But I want to be wherever Julia is." I look at Julia tenderly. Her eyes are still puffy, and a pang of sadness runs through my heart. In the light, it's much more apparent how thin she is. I'm going to have to watch her closely. During our dinner at the hotel, she mainly moved the food around her plate, without much of it actually going into her mouth.

After a few hours, we head back to our hotel room and consider round three, but Julia says she's physically sore. As we lie in bed together, the tension I've been holding finally eases.

"What time is your counseling session tomorrow?" I ask.

"Ten-thirty. I've been seeing Dr. Montgomery every weekday," she says groggily.

"Can I go with you and meet him?"

"Of course."

I can sense some hesitancy in her voice. So I pry, I always do. "Seriously, Jules. I just want to meet him."

"I know ... but I can't add any more to my plate, so just a meet and greet, no more than that, okay?"

"Sure," and I grow quiet as my mind drifts to what she is really talking about. I'm not so sure? Either she thinks I'm going to be a problem with her doctor, or my being here is stressing her out. I soon hear her light snore as I stare, wide awake, up at the ceiling. A light sweat starts pouring out of my body. I really need another drink, but there's nothing in our room and if I move, she'll hear me leave. It's going to be a long night.

The next day, we get up early and trek to the gym. I head off to lift weights, and from the corner of my eye, I watch Julia attack a treadmill and then a spin bike. She's relentless on each machine, fighting her demons her own way.

Later, as we head to her therapist's office, Julia keeps clasping and unclasping her hands in her lap. She's a nervous wreck.

"Honey, are you alright?"

I get a stoic response, "This is not fun for me, Raine. I don't look forward to talking to him."

When we arrive, Julia introduces me to Dr. Montgomery. I size the doctor up right away. He's tall and blonde with some gray, and probably what women consider good-looking. He's also not wearing a wedding ring. *Great.* One more thing to worry about as my jealousy rears its ugly head. I grab an uncomfortable seat in the waiting room. Finally, an hour later, we both walk out to our car in silence, not touching one another.

Julia lets me drive and directs me to her favorite coffee shop. We order and then sit by the fireplace.

"How did it go?" I finally ask, holding the warm cup gingerly in my hands.

"Not well." Her eyes are red and swollen, and she's tense and edgy, but I gently push.

"Do you want to talk about it?"

"I'm not sure you'll understand, Raine. I view the entire miscarriage as my fault. Dr. Montgomery fights me on it. I know how you feel. No one lets me validate what I know in my heart. Then Dr. Montgomery goes over where I'm at in the grief process. Same mumbo jumbo bullshit every day.

It's painful and difficult, and I hate every minute of it."

I look at the fire. Finally, I say quietly, "What if, in some way, it was your fault. You toured too much or whatever, what does it solve? You didn't lose our baby on purpose, so why beat yourself up? It just happened."

She stares at me pensively before speaking. "But I was stupid, Raine. I worked too much, and look at what happened. You even told me … you warned me that I was pushing myself too hard, and I didn't listen. I should have been more careful."

I silently watch her, and I can see she's mulling my words over in her beautiful mind, actually considering them. What does placing blame on anyone solve? Julia looks down at her coffee and rolls the cup in her hands. She's always cold, so I'm sure it's helping warm her hands. She's lost more than thirty pounds since the miscarriage. She weighs less now than before she became pregnant. It's no wonder her hands are cold. I consider taking her hands in mine, but I just watch her in silence.

We finish our drinks, staring at the fire just as Julia gets a call from a local rental agent in town. They've set up appointments for us to take a look at some houses. It'll be a much-needed distraction for the rest of our day. I knew coming to Montana to see her wouldn't be a cakewalk. Physically, we've always been in step, but emotionally, I don't know how we'll get through this. Why is this so damn hard?

Chapter Twenty-Seven – Julia

When we arrive at the first rental on the list, I know it's a perfect fit. The owners rent the house out year-round, and they have an opening for several months through the winter to spring. It's on a secluded lot that overlooks the lake we love.

We're standing in the foyer and Raine looks my way, giving me one of his earth-shaking grins. Clearly, we're on the same wavelength about the place. It has a large open layout, and the back is full of windows that overlook the lake and mountains. It has three bedrooms, more than we'll need, and the room at the edge of the house will be perfect as a writing room. The layout is spacious, but cozy.

I walk into the kitchen. "I could take some time to learn how to cook," I say to Raine, and I laugh as he rolls his eyes. My lack of culinary skills is legendary. Cooking has never been my forte, but I'm pretty good at setting things like hot pads on fire.

"I don't want you to burn down *this* house," Raine says sarcastically. "But it might be good for you to practice. At least it'd keep our home back in Nashville safe," he says with a smirk.

We don't need time to think about our decision as a knowing look passes between us.

Raine says to the rental agent, "We'll take it. How soon could we move in?"

"Tomorrow? I can rush the paperwork," the agent says, obviously pleased. The house isn't cheap to rent and the commission, even for a few short months, is well worth her time.

We head out to a local restaurant to meet Jody and her husband for dinner, and we find them seated in the back with a few of their friends. My sister's friends are cool, and they don't make any fuss about us. You never know how people will react. I love the fact that we can basically go wherever we want in this town, and most people treat us like locals.

After we sit down at the table, I order a beer and Raine does the same. I exchange a glance with Jody, but I nod my head, letting her know it's cool. So far, Raine is keeping his drinking in check. He's having just enough to take the edge off and hasn't gone overboard. I'm not sure if he can keep it up, but so far, he's kept it under control. Raine casually wraps an arm around me as I lean against him.

"Any luck finding a house?" Jody asks, taking a sip of her own beer. Jay leans in to hear our response.

"First house we looked at," I reply. "It's perfect. Three bedrooms overlooking the lake. It has a nice boat dock, so you guys could bring the boat over if it gets warm enough."

Jody nods and then adds, "Do you think you'll stay long enough to do that?"

I shrug at my sister and give her a slight smile as I take a drink of my beer. It tastes good and I realize I'm actually enjoying the taste of something.

Raine must see a flicker of sadness cross my face. He leans in and whispers in my ear, "I could drag you out of here and we can head back to the hotel. Hotel sex is the best sex, *ever*." And he pulls back, giving me a teasing grin and slight wink.

My head falls back as I laugh, then I lean in, kissing him on the cheek, as he pulls me tight against his warm frame. God, it feels good to have his arms around me. I'd love to take him up on his offer, but we need to be a little social.

Jay speaks up, "When do you guys move in?"

Raine jumps in, "Hopefully tomorrow."

"Holy cow … that's awesome," Jody responds. "Is it furnished, or do you have to go out and get a few things?"

"It has the main furniture we need, but you know what?" I pause to look at

Raine before continuing. "I have no idea if it has dishes, silverware, anything like that?"

Raine shrugs, takes a sip of beer like he doesn't have a care in the world, and I smile at him. And we shouldn't care. At this point, with the way we're both thinking and acting, the house only needs a bed.

Chapter Twenty-Eight – Raine

We head back to our hotel, and Julia opts to take a hot bath. I finally take a moment to call Tracy back. I'm sure she's a wreck wondering what in the hell is going on with her bosses. It's time to face the music.

"What the hell?" Tracy doesn't even say hello. "I've been trying to reach you guys all day." She sounds like a worried mother.

"Sorry about that. We've been busy." I pause. "Trace, I'm sure you're concerned about us staying in Montana for a while, but it'll be good for us—we need some time away."

Her heavy sigh echoes through the phone, "Raine, you're walking away from one of the busiest schedules you've ever had, *EVER*. You have three albums due in six months, and one of those is Bret's. You're under contract."

"Well, Bret can fly here to write with me, he'll be cool about that. We already have half of his album pulled together."

"And the other two artists? What do I tell them?"

"Call and ask for a slight delay. If I lose projects, I do. My relationship with Julia is more important."

"I completely and wholeheartedly agree, Julia *is* more important, Raine. I'm just trying to keep your careers from disintegrating. You can go from hero to zero in no time. You know that." I pause as Tracy continues. "Okay, don't worry about it," her exasperated voice relays. "I'll manage the other two artists. You'll have to work your situation out with Bret."

"I'll handle Bret. That's not a problem."

Julia's walking out of the bathroom towel-drying her hair and catches the tail-end of our conversation. She sits on the edge of the bed as I hang up.

"It's settled. A nice long vacation," I say, walking toward her.

Although she looks tired, Julia surprises me by standing up and letting the towel that's wrapped around her, fall to the floor. I give her an enormous grin as I scoop her up in my arms. Julia slides her hands up to my shoulders as I step over to the edge of the bed, kissing her hard on her damp neck. She moans as her hands move up to grip my hair.

It doesn't take much to get me hard as stone. I place her on the edge of the bed, and her fingers instantly grasp the buttons on my jeans. She's sitting as she leans in and runs her teeth on my stomach. My hands are now in her hair as she pushes my jeans down far enough to give me some much-needed relief. I sit down next to her as she straddles me, taking me inside of her. She's fierce as she starts moving on me, and I almost lose it. There was no time to bother with my shirt. I pull her head back gently by her hair, watching her face as she moves on me.

I roll her back onto the bed, push off my shoes, and finally pull my shirt and jeans off. This gives her a moment to catch her breath before I start working on her again.

"You feel amazing," she whispers. I settle myself above her, watching her face as I move. She opens her eyes, looks up at me, and smiles as she lightly arches her back. I watch with pleasure as she' s brought to release.

I move down closer to her and roll over on my back, keeping her inside of me as she rocks back and forth. It takes everything I have to hold back as I watch my gorgeous wife, with her long, dark, wet hair streaming down her shoulders as we move as one.

"I won't … last … if you keep that up," I mutter, grasping her hips. Her head is thrown back and her hands clutch at my chest. I pull her down close to me and she kisses me hard on the neck. I grab her hips and hold her tight against me so she can't move, but I can move inside of her. She groans as she comes again long and hard. God, I love making love to this woman. She can be soft and sweet, yet fierce at the same time.

After a few moments, she starts moving on me again. I pull her down close to my body, wrapping one hand in her hair, the other on her hip as we move together. A guttural moan escapes me as I hear her excitement build.

She whispers, "Don't stop ... don't stop," over and over in my ear until we both explode together.

We make the most of our last night at the hotel. I thought we'd get complaints from people in the neighboring rooms, but so far, we're in the clear. Julia slept fitfully the entire night and at one point she woke up gasping, covered in sweat. She placed a hand on my chest, and it calmed her down.

Our rental agent calls first thing the next morning and we agree to sign the papers with her over lunch. Then the house will be all ours for a few months. It seems like a grand adventure, renting a house in the woods of Montana. My gut tells me we need this. Julia asked the agent about kitchen utensils, and we found out the house has the basics, but Julia wants to buy our own sheets and blankets.

We load up into the car and head to the local Walmart. I grab Julia's hand and kiss it as we head inside. It's like we're a couple of teenagers, spending new time alone together, and I'm relishing every moment. Just as we enter the sliding doors, a young girl standing by the doorway gasps out loud, covers her mouth, and runs back inside. I look at Julia and laugh.

"Oh shit, I forgot. You're famous," I tease.

Julia gives me a huge eye roll. "I thought the sweats, stocking cap, and sunglasses would fool everyone."

We grab a cart and head toward the produce section.

"We're going to have to buy all the essentials if you're going to cook for my ass," I tease.

Julia stops and pulls out a small stack of recipes from her purse. "A temporary gift from Jody—all of Jay's favorites."

"Oh good! I love deer jerky and Elk steaks."

"As a former vegetarian, I am not cooking Bambi," she scowls.

I'm loving this. We're actually laughing and teasing each other like we used to, when all of a sudden, I see Julia's eyes get wide and she stops in the middle of the aisle, her hands tightly gripping the cart. I whirl around and realize we're headed right by the baby section.

"Julia? Are you okay?" I say as I move to her side, peering into her slightly moist eyes.

"It hits me like a ton of bricks from out of nowhere," she says, trying to avoid the tiny, brightly covered clothing to her right. "Dr. Montgomery warned me this could happen, but wow ... I need to get out of here."

I grab the cart and steer it back to the entrance. I calmly push the cart back in place and then lead Julia back to our car. Tears are now streaming uncontrollably down her face.

"I ... think ... I'm having ... a ... panic ...attack." she squeaks out. I settle her in the passenger seat and run around to my door.

"Take it easy, hon, we'll head someplace quiet."

I drive straight to our favorite coffee shop. Luckily, the town is relatively small, and I'm able to find it pretty easily. As I drive, I take quick glances at Julia and see she's fighting to catch her breath and sobbing quietly.

"It's okay, hon," I say softly, covering her hand with mine. We won't sign the papers on the rental property for a few more hours, and we've already checked out of our hotel, so other than the car, we don't have any place to go.

I grab my phone and pull up Dr. Montgomery's number. I get his voice mail, so I leave him a brief message. Just as we pull into the coffee shop parking lot, the doctor calls back.

"Raine? I had a voicemail asking me ..." But I don't let him finish.

"We've got to see you right away. She's having," and I pause to look at Julia, who's still struggling to breathe. "I think she's having a major panic attack or something."

"Sure ...yes, ten minutes is fine."

"We're on our way, hon." I put the car in drive and speed out of the lot straight toward the doctor's office.

I try to soothe Julia with my words and actions, but I can't seem to calm her down and she can't catch her breath. She leans her head against the passenger window and stares at the passing scenery.

As we pull in front of the small office, the doctor walks out and goes to Julia's car door. I quickly get out and go to her side. All at once I'm reminded of that dreadful night at the hospital when we lost Jonah, and once again, I'm drowning in hopelessness.

I take Julia's arm and steer her toward the doctor's door. He looks at me, and I glare at him. I can't help it. All of this pisses me off.

Chapter Twenty-Nine – Julia

I look at Dr. Montgomery but I'm not listening, and I don't care. Something snapped today. Something hit me deep in my psyche that my baby is gone, and the reality that I would never watch my baby grow up blindsided me. The absolute and total realization that Jonah will never be a part of my life has devastated me in a way I didn't see coming. I just can't believe it.

"Julia? Are you listening?"

I look at Dr. Montgomery and nod, but I'm not. I finally stopped crying, but my eyes are itchy and swollen, and the tissue I'm holding has black mascara streaks all over it.

"Tell me exactly what happened today."

"He's gone," I simply say.

"What happened at the store? Did something happen or did you see something?"

My words are hollow. It's like all the life has been sucked right out of me. "Nothing ... nothing happened. We were walking through the store, and then we were standing next to the baby department, and it hit me. He's gone. That's all." I look down at my hands as they continue wringing my tissue. I'm going to need another one as I continue weaving the shredded paper cloth through my fingers.

"Julia, what you're feeling and going through is normal. It happens when we suffer a terrible loss. This is a typical grief response ... it hits people in different ways. You're accepting that the loss happened."

I shake my head "no" at him. I'm not going down this rabbit hole of despair. "No, I was fine and now I'm not. I *have* to be fine for Raine."

"You don't have to be fine for anyone. Right now, we're here to take care of you."

"I don't have time for this," I say, standing up to pace around his sparsely decorated office. The doctor only has a desk, bookshelf, couch, and a few chairs. It's the first time I notice he only has a few pictures on the walls. "Why don't you have many pictures?"

"Not a fan of clutter. Now, let's get back to you."

The doctor watches me pace back and forth across the room. One hand is in my hair as I twist a few strands between my fingers. I stop and stare out the window for a few moments before speaking. "I don't know if I can do this. For the first time in my life, I want God to kill me," I say casually, like we're talking about the weather.

"God wants you right here, right now. He has more plans for you," he replies quietly.

I continue walking back and forth, and I shake my head, hoping it will clear my mind. "I won't do anything stupid. I don't believe in suicide. But I do want to get off this ride. I don't think I can take any more of this ... whatever *this* is." And then I stop in my tracks as my head falls to my hands, and I start sobbing again. All I can think is that I'm totally losing my shit, right here and now, and I really don't care.

Chapter Thirty – Raine

I'm in the waiting area, walking back and forth in front of the door, wearing a hole in the carpet. When Julia walked into the doctor's office, I gave the rental agent a quick call, letting her know we'd be late. I could sure use a glass of bourbon right now. I collapse into an oversized chair and run my hands across my face. Right now, I want a drink more than I've ever wanted one in my life.

I pick up my phone and scan my social media accounts and email, anything to distract me. I need something to keep my mind occupied and distracted. Then I hear her start to sob again. I stand and the pacing continues. *Screw this!* What am I going to do?

I walk out the door into the clean Montana air and take a deep breath. I take the scenery all in for several minutes, just trying to breathe. My soulmate is inside fighting for control of her mind, and I can't do anything to help her.

In despair, I call Tracy. "She's losing it. Right now. I think it's a nervous breakdown."

Tracy instantly tries to calm me down. "It's grief, Raine. She has to go through it, just like you do, and are. Where are you? Are you at a hospital?"

"No, at her counselor's office. Obviously, it's not working," I say, my frustration with the good doctor apparent.

"How does she look? Is she eating?" Tracy asks, her voice rising. She too is worried about her good friend.

"Barely. She's thinner now than before the pregnancy." I can't get myself to say "baby."

"And what about you?"

I sigh heavily, "What do you think? This is killing her and all I want is bourbon. We're both a fucking mess."

Tracy pauses and I figure it's because she doesn't know what to say, until finally she says quietly, "Well, at least you two are together, and if anyone can get through something like this, I'm betting on the two of you. Remember that. You've been through so much. You can't let this tear you apart."

I make my way back into the building right as Julia is walking out of the office, struggling with her coat. The doctor glances at me, giving me a semi-smile. I squint my eyes as I frown back at him.

Dr. Montgomery says, "I'll see you tomorrow, okay?"

Julia nods and walks toward me as I put an arm around her shoulders, guiding her out the door toward the car.

"Dr. Montgomery called my doctor back in Nashville. I need to go and pick up a prescription." Julia gestures toward the Walgreens that's not too far away.

"What for?" I ask.

"Xanex," is all she says.

I nod and start driving toward the drug store.

We go through the pharmacy drive-thru, both relatively quiet. Julia stares out the window pretending to watch the scenery.

"I really don't want to take anything," she says as we drive away. "I hate pills. You know that."

"I get it, but this may help … and it's only for a little while."

"I'll try it because I don't want to lose my marbles next time we go into a store," she says looking right at me, a slight grin on her face. I smile back as this is the Jules I know, sarcastic even when facing her own pain and turmoil.

"I called the rental agent, and she's waiting for us at the property. We'll get those papers signed so we can move in right away."

Julia nods, but I can't tell what she's thinking. Her expressionless face goes back toward the window as we drive on in silence toward the house. I knew being together in Montana would bring challenges, but this is so much harder than I ever dreamed. My heart is in the pit of my stomach.

Chapter Thirty-One – Julia and Raine

After we sign the papers, we walk into the house, and I head straight toward the back of the house. I open the large French doors and walk out onto the deck toward the water. Raine went back to the car to grab our luggage. We still need to get some essentials, but we should be okay for one night.

I walk to the edge of the deck and, despite the cold, sit in a chair by the edge of the lake, staring at the water and mountains in front of me. It's a breathtaking view, but I don't see it. I stare out across the lake and think I must know what it's like to drown above water. I'm suffocating in grief and sadness, and it seems to hit me from out of nowhere. It's all encompassing—like I'm carrying heavy weights across my shoulders.

As I pull the bottle of Xanex out of my coat pocket, I consider pouring the contents into the lake, but instead, I take out a pill, put it in my mouth, and swallow. I don't need water to help wash it down. I want some relief, and the sooner the better.

I watch Julia take her pill from inside the house and my chest tightens. I decide to turn my attention to making a fire in the fireplace. The rental agent made sure we had working water and gas, but I know it's too chilly for Julia. She'll need the room to be warm when she comes in, and this gives me something to do. Julia's heartbreak coupled with my own struggles may be more than any couple can bear. I've never felt more lost or alone.

Julia walks back into the house and tells me she's going to run a bath, her eyes barely meeting mine. Twenty minutes later, I go to check on her and she's stretched out across the bed, fully clothed, asleep. I grab a nearby blanket and cover her up.

By now, the pull for a drink is stronger than I've felt in a while, and it's winning. I grab my keys and, as silently as possible, go out the door to the car. I remember seeing a convenience store down the street on our way here. I figure I should check in with Jody, so I call her on the way.

Jody picks up after a few rings. "We're at the lake, almost settled in," I say as casually as possible.

"Good, I'm glad. How did it go today?" she asks.

"Horrible … no, actually worse than horrible. We went to Walmart and the baby section triggered a panic attack. We had an emergency trip to Julia's doctor, and he prescribed some Xanex." I pause, and Jody breaks the silence.

"I'm not really surprised, Raine. She had a hard time seeing mothers and baby strollers the other day at the mall. Might be kind of a normal response, really?"

"I don't know what's normal anymore, and I don't think we ever will."

We hang up as I reach the small convenience store. Our rental house is in a remote area, and we aren't left with many options. Luckily, the store has a sandwich shop, and right next door is a small liquor store. In addition to my much-needed alcohol, I pick up some wine for Julia, sandwiches, and other snacks. I've got to get her to eat something.

As I'm standing in the check-out line, I glance up at a TV they have mounted on the wall. There's some celebrity trash show on, and I catch the tail-end of a story they're running on Julia, and how she and I have basically dropped off the face of the earth following the miscarriage. Although the host is kind and sympathetic, the story is in bad taste. What do they expect? That Julia would be singing and dancing only a month after we lost our baby?

I growl under my breath as I walk out of the store. My inner bear is waking up. I need to protect all that I love, and that's Julia. Nothing else matters.

As I head to my car, I notice some guy standing outside of his car watching me, so I nod his way. Not unusual. I'm in a rental car with out-of-town plates in a remote area. He nods back and gets in his car.

The house is dark when I pull up. I enter as quietly as possible, put the groceries down in the kitchen, and then walk down the hall to check on Julia. She hasn't moved from the position she was in when I left, and I can hear her snoring. At least she's sleeping. I realize she still has her shoes on, so I pull them off gently, one by one. I tuck the blanket around her, and then lean down and kiss her tenderly on the head. She doesn't stir. She's sleeping more soundly than she has in weeks. I won't be able to sleep without some much-needed relief, and that's found in the bottle in the kitchen. My hands are already shaking as I make my way back down the hallway.

I open a cabinet and find a glass, and then pour it half full of bourbon. I take a few sips, letting it burn down my throat, knowing eventually it will numb my mind along with my heavy heart.

I set the glass down momentarily, put the groceries away, then pick my glass of salvation back up and head to the living room to get the fire going again. I brought one of my favorite guitars with me, so I grab it, tune it, and start to strum. I keep it random at first and play a few favorite covers and a few old songs I wrote. Right now, I'm not ready to go down the path and play the new song about Jonah. I need the bourbon to kick in first, but my fingers will eventually find the chords to that song. I can't seem to get it out of my head right now.

Chapter Thirty-Two – Julia and Raine

I have no idea where I am. I've got all of my clothes on, and they're wet and heavy against my skin. I wipe the sweat from my face, and see an alarm clock that reads one a.m. I slowly come to the realization that I'm in the new rental house, in the master bedroom, being smothered by a down comforter. The room is pitch black, but I can hear the faint sound of a guitar coming from another room.

I get up and trade my now soaked clothes for some comfortable sweats, and then walk into the adjoining bathroom. As I look in the mirror, I jump a little. My hands instantly go to my hair, and I try to make some peace with it. It's everywhere, and what's left of my makeup is smeared across my face. Delightful. I grab a nearby washcloth and try to fix the disaster that is my face.

I'm still a little groggy from my medicine. It did numb my mind, but so far, hasn't done a thing for my heart. I run cold water in the sink and splash it on my face. When I'm finally somewhat presentable, I head down the hallway toward Raine.

As I approach the living room, I pause and listen. He's playing a haunting melody. It's dark and melancholy and it fits my mood. Raine's sitting in a chair facing the fireplace. I can see his profile and his eyes are closed as he plays. He makes my heart flutter. I will never stop loving that face.

Raine must hear me, because he opens his eyes and looks in my direction. I walk toward him, drawn to him like a magnet. He doesn't stop playing as he watches me. I draw closer and sit next to him on the floor, resting my head against his leg. He stops playing, puts down his guitar, and touches my

97

head, running his hand down my hair as I lean against him.

"Are you cold? I started a fire 'cause I don't want you to be cold," he says, continuing to stroke my hair.

I laugh lightly, "I was a bucket of sweat in the other room, so no, I'm not cold."

He runs his hand down my neck and massages my back, which is like a rock under his hands.

I sigh with enjoyment. "That feels amazing. I need to schedule a massage. We both do."

"I'll make us an appointment tomorrow."

"You know what I need right now? Food. I'm fucking starving."

He chuckles, "Good thing I picked up some sandwiches a few hours ago."

"And I see you found some bourbon," I say, glancing down at the bottle sitting on the floor next to him.

Raine pauses.

"Don't worry," I continue. "I'm not coming down on you. I'm 'miss-medication' right now. I have no right."

Raine continues rubbing my shoulders as we sit silently, watching the crackling fire. Finally, after several minutes, I get up and head to the kitchen.

I'm glad Julia didn't walk in earlier when I was singing Jonah's song. I don't want her to hear it until it's done and I'm ready. I follow her into the kitchen.

Julia's searching the cabinets. "I found the food, but where in the heck are the dishes?" I watch in amusement as she opens and closes several cabinet doors until finally the mystery is solved and she finds plates.

"Come here," she says. "Let me make you a plate."

"I got a bottle of wine in case you want something to drink ... and some water and Gatorade."

"I'll stick to water. I'm on a groggy cloud right now and feel like I could fall off at any moment."

I walk up behind her, wrapping my arms around her waist as she cuts up one of the sandwiches. She leans against me and for the first time that day, I feel a sense of peace.

We pull a couple of stools out and enjoy our dinner by firelight. The intimate setting at this house is different than our house in Nashville. It's much cozier here, like we're hiding out at a secluded location where no one can find us. Our Nashville house has so many rooms on our three floors that we seem to sometimes lose each other.

"What is the plan for tomorrow?" I ask.

"Same as today. It's kind of like Groundhog Day up here. Breakfast, gym, I have a crying jag counseling session with a little self-pity, coffee shop, and then back to the gym before dinner and bed."

"Sounds nice, except for that middle part," I say, laughing as I lean in and nuzzle her neck, running my lips down to her collarbone. Julia tenses and I notice.

"What?" I ask, leaning back to look into her eyes.

"Maybe we need to slow the intimacy down a bit. It could be part of why I'm a wreck. It might be too much too soon."

"Is that your idea, or is this coming from the good Dr. Montgomery?" I emphasize my good with hand quote marks. My sarcasm is clearly evident. Julia pauses as I continue, "So, he wants me to lay off making love to my wife, is that it?"

"It's not that. Dr. Montgomery mentioned that maybe the emotional roller coaster we're both on, clouds things, and I need to focus on getting through my grief."

"*Bullshit.* Intimacy brings us closer together and we need that," I say as I swirl her chair around to look at me. "We don't need to pull any farther away from one another. You left and went a thousand miles away, and I started to lose my shit. Please don't pull away from me now."

Surprisingly, Julia leans in and kisses me hard on the lips. I'm not sure if she thought it would calm me down, as conflicting emotions and thoughts are raging in my mind. One minute it's "we have to stay away" and the next she's laying a big one on my lips.

I pull her tight against me and kiss her back. After a moment, Julia stops, leaning back to look at me.

"I almost forgot," she says with a sly grin. "Wait here for just a minute, I'll be right back." She quickly runs out of the room to our bedroom. I have a moment, so I take a long drink of bourbon, hoping it will ease some of my frustration. Dr. Montgomery is definitely at the top of my shit list.

Julia comes back into the room carrying a small, wrapped box. I look at her questioningly as she steps close and hands it to me.

"I've been meaning to get this for you for months." I take the box and then look at her. She continues, her eyes dancing, "You'll understand when you open it."

I tear open the wrapping and inside the box is a wedding ring.

"I got it to replace the ring I bought for you in Napa."

I pull the ring out and smile up at her. "It's perfect. Exactly what I would have picked out for myself." I pull my current ring off and hold the new ring out toward Julia. "Will you do the honors?"

Julia smiles at me coyly as she places the ring on my finger. "With this ring, I thee wed."

"Damn straight," I say, pulling Julia's head toward mine and planting a big kiss on her lips. I reach up and move her down onto my lap, enfolding her in my arms in a tight embrace. My lips go to her neck, sliding the sleeve of her top down off her shoulder as my lips follow the trail. Julia wraps her hands in my hair and sighs.

I stand with Julia in my arms and carry her to the bedroom. In my mind, I'm telling Dr. Montgomery to kiss my ass.

Chapter Thirty-Three – Julia

When Raine picks me up, he helps erase my miserable day and all the troubles from my mind. God, how I love this man. Sex with him is never the same and each experience seems like the first time.

I lean up, pulling at his ear lobe with my teeth, and a deep moan escapes his throat. As he walks, one of his hands is pulling at my clothes. He certainly is a very dexterously talented man. With his large hands, he can hold me with one and take my shirt off with the other.

We step inside the bedroom and Raine puts me on the ground while he pulls at my sweatpants. I'm still self-conscious about my stomach, but he doesn't seem to notice or care. Raine's focus is on one thing and one thing only.

I walk toward the bed, taking my bra off as I do. I sit down on the edge and Raine quickly strips in front of me. I scoot up against the pillows just as he reaches me, his lips devouring mine. His arms are on either side of me as his tongue plays along my teeth. He places one hand carefully along my cheek, stroking along my jawline. I lean up closer to him as he finally rests his body on top of mine ever so slightly.

Raine stops kissing me and pulls back, "I have your words running through my mind … we don't have to make love. I can give you some space and we can just sleep. Maybe your body needs a rest?" His anxious words melt my heart.

"I want you now, in every way," I say, placing both of my hands on the sides of his face, bringing his lips to mine. "To hell with the good doctor."

And Raine loses it. For the next hour, we don't do anything but focus on bringing each other pleasure.

I awake with a start, gasping. This time the dream about Jonah was different, but so vivid. It was like I was watching a scene in a movie. The images were of me and Raine watching Jonah take unsteady steps. It was sunny and my little boy, with his long dark hair, was dressed in overalls as he staggered, giggling, toward his daddy. Raine and I surrounded him, shouting encouragement as he stumbled on. Then I woke up.

I glance at Raine, but he hasn't stirred next to me. My nightshirt is drenched with sweat, so I pull myself out of the bed and head to the bathroom.

As I stand in the shower, I let the hot water soothe my aching body. Tears stream uncontrollably down my face. The dream seemed so real with Jonah's dark hair glistening in the sun, and his little laugh is permanently marked on my brain. He was so joyful and full of life. A life that will never be lived.

I slide down to the tile floor and as the water falls down on me, I continue to cry. I cry until I don't have any tears left.

Chapter Thirty-Four – Raine

I hear Julia get up and, out of the corner of my eye, I watch her walk to the bathroom. Soon, the water is running. Julia had been sleeping fitfully next to me, and she woke me up several times before she headed to the bathroom. Every few minutes, I peer over at the clock, and after thirty minutes when the water is still running, I get up to check on her.

I open the door cautiously. The shower is still on, and I can see her sitting naked on the floor of the shower with her head in her hands as water cascades down over her. I make some noise on purpose, but she doesn't stir. I go to the sliding shower door near the faucet, reach in, and turn the water off. Then I slide the other door open, lean down, and pick my drained wife up off the floor, carrying her back to the bed. I put her in bed, pulling the covers over her tight. I remember to go back and get a towel for her hair or else she'll catch a cold.

I scurry back to my side of the bed. Julia's eyes are closed, and she's rolled away facing the wall. I climb in next to her, placing my warm body next to her, and draping the towel over her head. I pull her tight against me, trying to warm her up.

She doesn't respond. She lets me hold her close, and then finally she takes a haggard breath, expelling hard. Eventually her breath evens out and she falls back into a fitful sleep. I lie there, holding her close against me for hours as my own tears hit my pillow. This loss may in fact kill us both.

Chapter Thirty-Five – Julia

I'm back in Dr. Montgomery's office, and I can hear his voice, but I don't hear his actual words. I'm pissed. Pissed off because I lost it again the night before. When I woke up this morning, Raine's arms and legs were wrapped around my body. My head was covered with a towel, and then I vaguely remembered that I ended up in the shower after my dream. The dream that will likely haunt me for the rest of my life.

"Julia … did you hear me?" Dr. Montgomery asks, sitting across from me, finally bringing me out of the misery going on in my head.

"Actually, no. I haven't heard a word you've said for the past fifteen minutes, and frankly, I don't care." Dr. Montgomery pauses, staring at me intently as I continue, "This shit's not working."

He isn't going to let me off easy, "What's not working? These sessions, your life, what?"

"I'm getting worse, not better … and I'm so fucking angry." My face hurts from the frown I'm sure is permanently frozen on my face.

"It's going to get worse before it gets better. You haven't fully processed the reality of your loss and you're still processing your grief. These are two of the tasks of mourning that we talked about. Specifically, what's making you so angry?"

I pause to look out the window at the beautiful Montana scenery. It's such a contrast to the inner turmoil going on inside my heart and mind. "My own karma. I must have deserved this for something I've done or didn't do. Who knows? God is punishing me in some way."

"Is that what you really think? You deserve to be punished?"

"What else can it be? God doesn't want me to be happy. For some reason, I've pissed God off and he's paying me back."

"Paying you back for what?"

I grow even more exasperated, slumping down in my chair with a heavy sigh. I look down at my feet. "For not living my life right or for having sex too young. I don't know. Maybe for not tipping a waitress enough once … how the hell do I know? But for some reason God has to pay me back," I say as I cross my arms defiantly across my chest.

"I see. And when do you think you've paid enough back to God? What will be enough?"

I shrug my shoulders as I have no answer to that. "It's tearing my marriage apart, so I'm sure that's next."

"I thought you said things with Raine were as good as they could be?"

"Raine found me stark naked having another breakdown in the shower. How much of this shit can he take? He needs to worry about getting himself right, not dealing with my bullshit." I can't help it; my inner sailor is coming out today and I'm letting the four letters fly.

The doctor gives me a look of sympathy, which only makes me feel worse. "Raine is doing exactly what he wants to do and should do. He's being there for you."

"But it has to go both ways and right now, I don't think I have anything left for him."

Dr. Montgomery quickly changes the subject back to exactly what I don't want to talk about and what's really making me angry. My dream about Jonah.

"Let's talk about the dream."

Instantly my face crumples up, but I don't cry. "Fuck you."

"Well, that's a start … talk about it."

My eyes could have lasered a hole right through him. I respond through clenched teeth, "You want me to tell you how he laughed and the little clothes he was wearing? Or maybe how the sun was shining down on his head, and it made it look like he had a halo? What? What do you want from me!"

Dr. Montgomery's eyes fill with sorrow, and right now, I don't know whom I'm angrier with, him or God. I do know one thing. At this moment, I hate them both.

Chapter Thirty-Six – Raine

I'm sitting outside the doctor's door, and I can hear Julia's animated voice, but I can't hear a word she's saying. I want to be here with her, against her wishes. This morning, she seems completely pissed off and won't talk about it, except telling me that it isn't me.

It's only ten in the morning and I'm coming out of my skin. I need something to drink—just a little something to take the edge off.

When the door finally opens, an exhausted Julia walks out, avoiding my eyes. I scowl at the doctor. I don't like anyone or anything that hurts her, especially someone who seems to be pulling us apart.

When we're back in the car heading to our regular coffee shop, Julia finally speaks.

"I'm a real fucking riot, huh?"

"You're exactly as you should be and I'm here to help."

"But who is helping you, Raine? We signed on for better or worse, but you're getting the raw end of the deal right now. I can't keep my shit together."

"For better or worse is exactly what I'm doing, and you are helping me. Being here with you is helping."

"Really? Is it really helping you? The bottle of bourbon was nearly empty this morning. Me losing my shit is not helping you."

My hands tightly clench the steering wheel. Of course I've got a problem, but Julia doesn't need to come down on me about it now. I really can't stand this doctor.

We arrive at the coffee shop, order, and sit by the fireplace across from each other. I'm warming my hands with my cup, not saying a word, while Julia stares at the flames.

Finally, I quietly say, "I know I'm drinking too much, Jules. I know it. I'll get a handle on it. It's only temporary. Right now, my job is to take care of you."

"But who is taking care of you, Raine? Who's going to hold you up? I can't hold myself up right now."

I don't respond.

"Do you want to know why I couldn't get out of the shower last night, or would you rather bury your head in the sand?" Her voice is filled with a callous disdain I've never heard from her.

I reply softly, "My head is not in the sand. I'm doing my best to figure this out, sweetheart." Julia's head drops as she stares into her cup. I continue, "Tell me. I want to know."

She finally looks my way, sets her cup down and answers, her voice breaking. There are tears on her lashes surrounding those breathtaking blue eyes that are filled with so much pain. "It was a dream. It was a glimpse of what our life would have been like. Jonah was walking toward you, taking his first steps as the sun glistened off his thick, dark brown hair, which was so much like yours. He looked just like you."

I look at the flames and slowly back to Julia. "Tell me more. I want to hear it all," I say as I reach out and grasp her hand, looking into the eyes of the woman I love, whose soul is crushed.

Julia squeezes my hand, and tells me how her dream started. From how she was holding him, his head against her face, and how Jonah smelled when she first held him, to his flushed cheeks in the sunlight. And then the way his little arms had stretched out to my arms. As I listen to her words, my eyes glisten. I can't help it.

When Julia finishes, I ask, "Do you believe it was real? Do you think he'll be out there waiting for us one day?" She pauses as her head drops to our hands and she says, "I used to think so, but now I don't know." Then she looks at me. "I hate God right now, Raine. I hate him."

I nod and quietly pull her to me so she's sitting on my lap in my oversized chair. She wraps her arms around my neck and leans in, resting her head on my shoulder. We sit like this for many minutes, staring at the fire and just breathing.

When we've both recovered, we head back to the rental house, change, and go to the gym. From the corner of my eye, I watch Julia on the treadmill and she's running as if she's chasing someone. I'm drained in every way and not really in to working out, but I put myself through the paces. We've got to do something different for the rest of the day and get out of our pity party routine.

Julia walks over to me drenched, and I'm instantly aroused. "What do you think about trying to get that massage. My back is killing me."

I smile and nod. We check with the front desk, and they tell us about a place not too far away. As I drive that way, Julia calls to see if they can get us in and we're in luck. After this, I'm going to suggest a casual dinner away from the house.

The massage seems to ease the evident stress from Julia's face. I suggest a local Japanese restaurant we passed, and as we walk in, I notice a young family sitting by the window and a baby's carrier next to the table. I glance at Julia. She notices the family but quickly looks away.

I ask the host if we can move to the other side of the restaurant, and when our server arrives, I order a beer and Julia asks for a Bloody Mary.

"Drinking in the middle of the day. We're cute," she teases.

"It's five o'clock somewhere. *Damn!* I wish I would've written that song. We'd be at the beach, permanently," I say with a smirk. "You know how many people probably say that same phrase today, all over the world?"

"Thousands," Julia says with a laugh. "I think there's a theme you need to attack," she says with a smile. God, I love seeing her smile.

"Maybe you should write it? We need a female angle. It could be your next big hit?"

"I'm done with writing for a while," she says with all seriousness.

There's an uncomfortable pause as Julia looks out the window, sighing and resting her chin in her hand. The day is gray, cloudy, and cold. I wish the sun would come out. The dreary weather adds to our misery right now.

Julia finally continues, "I heard you playing something the other night. It sounded kinda dark, but pretty."

"Yeah. It's a melody I started back in Nashville. Not done with it though." I silently pray she won't ask me what it's about. She doesn't need to know it's about Jonah. Not yet.

"Have you talked to Bret about coming up here to write? And I bet Tracy is still freaking out. I need to give her a call."

"I sent a text, but I'll call Bret later today, and you should call Tracy. It might help calm her down. She was pissed the other day on the phone with me."

"It would be good to talk to her."

For some reason, our conversation feels unnatural and forced. We're making small talk, and we're not good at it. Thank God my phone rings to break up the awkwardness.

"It's Bret ... his ears must be burning."

When I seem reluctant to pick up the phone, Julia nods at me to take it.

"Yes?" I ask.

"Hey, buddy. What's shakin'?"

"Having a little late lunch with Jules."

"Give her my best. Do you have a minute?" It sounds serious, so I give Julia a look that I'm going to take this outside, and I get up from the table to walk out into the cool air. I give a glance back at Julia and she's picked up her own phone. She never cares if I talk privately with Bret, often teasing me about our bromance.

"What's up?" I ask.

"Tabloids. Have you seen them?"

"No. *God damn.* We don't need this right now."

"They have pictures posted of you two in front of some office, and then at a store and Julia's upset. Headline is painting it as if Julia's having a nervous breakdown."

"Well, she is, but it's no one's fucking business," I growl. When it comes to Julia, my protective nature always comes out, especially when the media is involved.

"True. But clearly someone is trailing the two of you all over town and is painting this worse than it is. The publication has several pictures of Julia. She's really thin, Raine. Noticeably thin. And frankly, you also look like shit."

"I can always count on you for the truth, asshole." Bret's always been known to give me total brutal honesty.

Bret chuckles, "That's what friends are for. By the way, you sent a text about wanting me to come up there to write. What about next week? Our deadline to present songs to the label is coming up, or have you forgotten?"

"Of course not, it's on my radar. Make it happen. There's room at our house, and you can stay with us?"

"No way. I'll get a hotel room. Too much PDA with you two. It becomes annoying after a while."

"Funny," I say, oozing sarcasm. "Thanks for the heads up on the story. Not sure if or when I'll tell Julia, but if she talks to Tracy, she'll find out."

I hang up and instantly my eyes graze the parking lot for anything suspicious. The paparazzi are following us. No doubt it was a "pap" at the store the other day when I was walking out carrying booze, too. We'll have to be extremely careful from now on.

Chapter Thirty-Seven – Julia

While Raine is chatting with Bret, I sent Tracy a text and she told me about the tabloid story. When Raine walks back over, I've got it pulled up on my phone.

"How is your boyfriend?" I say as I give Raine a teasing look.

"Bret sends his best," Raine says, before addressing my remark. "And you and I both know he's not my boyfriend. He's a pain in my ass is what he is. He's gonna head up here next week."

I cut to the chase, "I know the real reason he called. Tracy told me. I have the story pulled up," I say, glancing down at my phone on the table. "It's not pretty, Raine. Makes me sound like I'm one step away from the funny farm."

"*Damn them!* Well, now that we know someone is here watching us, we'll have to be more careful when out in public." I casually look around the restaurant for a suspicious person eating alone, watching us. But other than the young family across the room, we're the only people here.

We're interrupted by the arrival of our drinks, and I order some sushi.

As our server walks away, Raine gives me a funny look.

"What?"

"You should have ordered a hamburger with fries," he says, stoically, and it almost makes me chuckle until I see that he's serious.

"At a sushi restaurant? What the? What's up?"

"Bret thinks you look too thin in the pictures … and I agree with him," the last of his words trail out.

"So, first you have to put the blame on Bret? I know Tracy told you about my problem, Raine. And I'm very well aware." I stop talking and look out the window as we sit in awkward silence until our food arrives. I have no idea how or what to do right now because everything I do seems to be wrong.

"Jules, I think you're beautiful, you're amazingly beautiful. I'm just worried and I don't know how to say it."

I look at Raine sympathetically, giving him a slight smile. "How about if I eat every fucking bite on my plate, will that make you happy."

Raine laughs, "Yes, every fucking bite will make me happy."

That smooths everything over for now.

We have the rest of our day free, so we drive around exploring the area. We go back to Walmart and, luckily, I keep my head together so we can buy the items we need for the house. Raine stops by a liquor store, and for a moment, I think about the paparazzi tailing us. I mention it to Raine, but he goes inside anyway.

We drive by a small mall and Raine asks, "Want to go inside and look for something for you? Some new clothes or something?"

I respond dryly, "You don't like my sweatpants look?"

"You look great in anything. I thought maybe you'd like something new."

"You want me to shop ... and you'll go along?" I dramatically look around the inside of the car. "Where is my husband and what have you done with him?"

Raine laughs, "Touché. Let's go in. I'll let you pick out something for me. You love that shit."

I laugh along with him as we get out and walk in. I saunter around the store, picking out shirts and jeans for Raine, and then I practically push him into a dressing room. I love to buy men's clothes. Raine could care less about such things.

He walks out. "I look ridiculous. I am not made for skinny jeans." Raine scowls as he looks at his butt in a three-way mirror.

I put my hand over my mouth to stifle a laugh. "I wanted to see it. Just once. You're right. You and skinny jeans don't mix."

He twirls around and heads straight back to the dressing room.

"Nice ass," I yell as he walks away.

"You're next," he yells back.

I help him pick out a new pair of jeans, a couple of casual shirts, and one tie. I love him in a suit and tie.

Then it's my turn. I grab a couple of outfits and head into the dressing room. But everything I try on hangs on me. My boobs are practically gone, and you can see every rib.

"Let me see something," Raine yells from outside of my room.

"Nothing is working," I holler back. I walk back out and grab a few things in smaller sizes. "Wrong size," I say to him, and I notice a dark look briefly cross his face before he recovers himself.

"This time I want to see something. You made me wear those damn jeans," he teases. I smile back, but I'm not sure anything will work. Finally, I find something presentable, but it's a long-sleeved, tan-colored, form-fitting dress. Although it looks good with my dark hair, why would I need a dress up here?

"That's beautiful," Raine says the second I walk out. "It's perfect."

"Perfect for what?"

"I've made dinner reservations at a steak place Jody recommended.

"Oh … good," I say but a flicker of disappointment crosses my face and I'm sure he notices.

I walk back to the dressing room, close the curtain, and sigh. I don't want to go out in public at night. Nights are hard and dark, and I really don't want to get all dressed up to go out. All I want to do is stay cooped up in our house and not think about anything.

Later that night, I'm standing and staring at myself in a long mirror. I'm wearing my new dress and a pair of tall, high-heeled black boots. I'm struggling with the finishing touches of my makeup. It seems odd to wear makeup when I've been so used to hardly wearing any. I'm realizing how easy it would be to go back to a private life, before *Next Real Star* ever happened and fame took hold. Fame sure hasn't been great, especially when you're going through any type of personal despair, and it gets posted online for everyone to scrutinize.

I'm finally ready and I head to the foyer. Raine is already there waiting for me, and I gasp when I see him all decked out in a suit and his new tie. I forgot how good he cleans up. He's clean shaven, his signature hair is perfectly coiffed. This is the handsome man I married. As I move closer, his cologne makes my legs wobble. It's one of my favorites.

"You even shaved ... wow," I say, giving him a big smile. "You look great."

"Thank you, and you look beautiful as usual," he says, walking up and kissing my cheek.

Raine helps me with my coat and as we step out the door, I'm hit with a second surprise. A black SUV with a driver is waiting, all warmed up and ready to go.

"I didn't feel like driving, and I want us to relax."

I smile up at him as he takes my hand and leads me toward the vehicle. Although Raine would never drink and drive, risking our lives or anyone else's, I know this is much safer.

We pile into the back of the SUV and the driver shuts the door. After buckling in, Raine reaches over and grabs my hand. I smile up at him and although the ache in my heart is there, for a brief moment, with my gorgeous husband by my side, I almost forget.

We head downtown and arrive at the restaurant located on the city square. The room has an intimate feel and I love it from the moment we enter.

Raine called ahead, and the staff is waiting for us. He made reservations under an alias, but the host recognizes us and thankfully she puts us in a quiet corner, out of the view of the street and any onlookers. Once we're seated and we have our menus, I squint at mine, holding it close to the candle on the table.

Raine chuckles, "We really need to get you reading glasses. You can't read a word on that menu, can you?"

"Nope. But you won't catch me in those things, not yet. I'm just looking for any word that kind of looks like chicken."

He smiles and says, "How about I order for both of us. Luckily, I'm not vain and I have my glasses."

"You usually let me use your glasses."

"I think it's time for you to put on your big girl panties and get your own."

"They'll make me look old. I envision an old lady with her glasses hanging by a chain around her neck," I say dryly. "No, thank you."

The waiter comes by and pours us each a glass of Cabernet. Raine gives him our order: two steaks, medium, with calorie-laden sides.

After the waiter walks away, I tease, "My arteries just clogged up with that order. But it sounds amazing. I haven't had a good steak in eons."

"We're celebrating tonight."

I'm stunned for a brief moment. What on earth could we be celebrating?

Raine quickly explains, "We're celebrating two things. One, you got my ass willingly into a mall today, and two, I tried on a pair of skinny jeans. Thank God you didn't get a picture of that."

I laugh as I hold up my phone, "Who says I didn't get a picture?"

"Give me that phone," Raine teases, reaching toward my hand. I quickly hide it behind my back.

"Never," I say as he laughs. *Damn* ... he looks amazing when he smiles, and I've really missed that smile.

We finish our meal and it's obvious someone will have to wheel us out of the restaurant. We even ordered dessert to take home with us. And although the miscarriage was not that long ago, it seems like years since we've both laughed and let ourselves go, even just a little.

We climb back up into our vehicle, and it's then that I notice lights around the town square.

"Oh my God ... it's almost Christmas."

Raine slowly looks my way and nods. And the terror hits me, hard, right in the chest. With the passing of time, I'd completely forgotten about the holidays. Somehow, we missed Thanksgiving entirely, and now Christmas is a few weeks away.

I rest my head against the cold windowpane and watch the scenery the entire ride home. Raine reaches out and grabs my hand, holding it tight, but I don't move a muscle.

I manage to whisper, "I guess we'll need to get a tree or something."

"We can do that if you want."

"I don't. I don't want to do anything." My mind is reeling. I don't want to be reminded about Christmas, Santa, reindeer, and definitely not about Jesus. I don't want to see any of it. I manage to add, "And I don't want any gifts." My mood has changed on a dime.

"Okay. We don't have to get a tree or decorations. I won't get you anything if that's what you really want."

"I can't have what I really want, so I don't want anything."

When we arrive back at the house, I go straight to the kitchen, grab a bottle of wine and a glass. Raine joins me and reaches for a glass and his bottle of bourbon.

I look at him. "We're a pair, aren't we? Numbing ourselves."

I head to the living room and sit at the end of the couch, wrapping my legs underneath me. Raine follows and sits in a leather chair next to me. He grabs the remote and clicks the TV on. He avoids anything that has to do with Christmas and eventually lands on football.

I sit quietly, staring at the TV, pretending to watch the game. Raine is also staring at the screen and taking rhythmic sips of his drink, but I doubt he's really catching anything that's going on. We've never been in a room like this with one another, and an eerie chill goes down my spine.

How the hell did I forget Christmas? Even though we'd been out, I didn't really notice the decorations in the stores, and since we're somewhat secluded in the country, I didn't see any lights on houses. When I left Nashville, I was in such a fog, and now that I'm taking Xanex, I'm even more numb. I don't like being numb.

I stare at the screen, my glass of wine in hand, and acid churns up my throat. The holidays. How will I get through the holidays? A time of celebration, of faith and family, and all about the birth of the Savior, but I don't have *my* family. As I look at Raine, I'm even more disgusted with God. God has failed me.

"I think I'm going to go to bed," I say, getting up and carrying my glass and bottle with me.

"Can I come with you?"

"No," I say forcefully, and then my voice softens. "No, relax and watch the game. I'm really tired, Raine."

Raine nods, and I can feel him watch me walk toward the kitchen. I look back as his face returns to the glowing screen and he takes another drink.

I set my glass and bottle on the counter, and then drag my heavy body down the hall to our bedroom. After putting on sweats, I climb into bed, pull the covers up to my chin, and stare at the ceiling. Minutes pass as tears stream down the sides of my face, hitting the pillow. I don't attempt to wipe them away, and instead roll over on my side, pulling the blankets up around my face. I want to hide away from the world.

When Raine walks into the room a couple of hours later and gets into bed, I'm still awake but I pretend I'm sleeping as he places his warm body next to mine, draping his arm over me. I welcome the warmth but for the first time since we reconnected during *Next Real Star*, I don't want to make love to him. What if I get pregnant again? I can't risk it. I cannot take another loss like that.

I hear his breathing slow and after a few minutes, he is snoring lightly. I close my eyes and eventually drift off, but my sleep is soon interrupted by another dream about Jonah. Again, in this dream, I'm holding him against my body as he looks up at me with the softest blue eyes that would melt anyone's heart.

When I finally wake up, the sun is shining brightly through the windows. I glance at the clock. Ten a.m. I've been in bed for more than ten hours. I faintly hear Raine speaking in another room. What day is it? Is it a weekday? I fall back against the pillow and pull the covers up. I don't care. I close my eyes, trying to force myself back to sleep. I don't want to face the world.

Chapter Thirty-Eight – Raine

I'm on the phone with Tracy, who's relaying information about my upcoming projects. "I talked with the two labels, and you can start working with the new artists in February," Tracy says. "This should give you plenty of time after the holidays to get everything in order."

"Please don't mention the holidays. We both forgot about Christmas. Julia's freaked out."

"I wondered about that. She was so excited about Christmas and Jonah arriving soon afterward. She used to talk about how pregnant she would be during the holidays, and how she planned on eating whatever she wanted. Is she there? Why don't you let me talk to her?"

"She's still sleeping, and I don't want to disturb her. She had a rough night. One minute she seems fine, and the next minute I get a completely different person."

"Well, considering, I'm sure that's to be expected. And how about you?"

"I'm drinking ... a lot." I've always been straight up with Tracy, so why bother changing now. "It's not something I can't handle, just takes the edge off."

Tracy replies, "What about seeing the same counselor Julia's been talking to? Couldn't hurt?"

"I don't like that guy." I'm sure Tracy notices the animosity with my words. "He's telling Julia to back off from me, like it's too much for her emotionally right now. Complete bullshit."

"Hmm ... well, I don't really understand that, but I'm not the professional. Someone else then? I know someone here, maybe you could talk on the phone?"

"I'm okay, Trace." And I try to turn the conversation away from my drinking problem. "Now what are Bret's plans? You said he's flying in on Monday?"

We finish our conversation about Bret's arrangements, and then I walk down the hall and peep into the bedroom. Julia's still buried in blankets with her eyes closed. I back out of the room and head down the hall to the larger spare room, attempting to mold it into some kind of a writing room.

As I move a couch to a corner and pull a couple of chairs from the living room, I'm dwelling on my conversation with Tracy. Is my drinking under control? Yes, I drink a lot on occasion, but before we lost Jonah, I never felt like I had to have alcohol. It was an option that I could walk away from. But now, it's the crutch that I crave and look forward to. At this moment, I promise myself that I'll try to go a day without any alcohol. I *will* take control of this situation.

Chapter Thirty-Nine – Julia

Two hours later I wake up in my cozy blanket cocoon, and I don't want to move. Raine's in the kitchen; I can hear metal on metal and he's cussing. He can cook, and do it well, but it's not his favorite thing. Between the two of us, it's a wonder we didn't starve back in Nashville. The smell of bacon is soon wafting through the air.

When I can no longer take the clanging of dishes and slamming of cabinet doors, I pull my weary body out of bed on what feels like noodle arms, grab a robe lying on a nearby chair, and head his way. I don't bother to check my hair in a mirror. Who cares?

"My lord ... what are you making?"

"A good kitchen fire, I think." Raine is standing next to the stove as smoke is slowly filling up the room. "It's supposed to be an omelet. At least, it started out as an omelet, now it is a blob of eggs and cheese."

"Let me see." I walk to him, taking the spatula out of his hand. "I think I can rebuild it," I tease.

Raine moves out of my way, letting me take over. He sits on a stool as I crack new eggs into the pan, throw in some mushrooms and cheese, and add his bacon to the mix, making him a decent omelet. He's stunned for a moment, like he's seeing something from me he's never seen before, and it makes me laugh.

I give him a side eye. "What?" I ask, self-consciously running my hand through my hair. "I know ... I'm a disaster."

"You're beautiful," he says grinning, and then he stands, wrapping his strong arms tight around my mid-section.

121

I pull away slightly, going back to the stove just in time to pick the pan up and pour the omelet contents onto a plate. "Here. You have got to eat my masterpiece."

"Impressive," he teases as he takes the plate from my outstretched hand.

We end up sitting on bar stools in the kitchen, eating our late breakfast and staring out the back windows. I missed several calls from Jody, so I send her a quick text letting her know we're okay.

Raine finally interrupts our silence, "What about getting outside today? Take a drive up in the mountains and have an adventure. It's Saturday. We don't have any plans."

"Not sure I want to be out in the cold." This is followed by awkward silence.

"Okay … what about heading to a movie or something like that?"

"I really don't want to leave the house, Raine. I don't want to be around people. Don't you need to get ready for Bret to arrive?"

"Yeah, but he's not coming until Monday. I want to do something together, we have time. Just the two of us."

I don't think I can take going anywhere right now when everything reminds me of the holidays, and in the back of my mind, I wonder about the random tabloid writer, who could be right outside our house … waiting. I don't want any more pictures of us making national news. But I want Raine to be happy, and I know I'm making everything worse. Last night, Raine set up this nice romantic evening, and I blew it. I jump in before he can speak. "Okay. I'll bite the bullet. Let's go out and look for a Christmas tree. I think I can handle that."

"That's my girl!" he says with enthusiasm. "This will be great!"

Raine's warming up the car, and I grudgingly walk out and climb in. Although I agreed to go out, it's like I'm heading to a colonoscopy.

"I have absolutely no idea where we're going," Raine says, looking at me and shrugging his shoulders.

Let's head to that home store not too far from my doctor's office. They'll have fresh trees in the lot. I want a real tree. Nothing fake."

When we arrive, I take a deep breath. I've got to create some normalcy for Raine. I'll drive him further away with my maudlin, mopey bull crap.

I grab some tree ornaments, and then we pick out a tree from the lot. Raine wanted this huge nine-foot monster, but we compromised on a shorter, round tree. Christmas music is playing in the background, and I can faintly pick out "Silent Night." My stomach drops. It's one of my favorites.

"It's time to go," is all I manage to say to Raine.

Raine looks at me with alarm and nods. We rush through check-out and pack up the car with help from an employee, who, as quickly as he can, helps Raine tie the tree to the roof.

We drive toward the rental home in silence until Raine decides to take the plunge. "I think we did well, kid. It'll be a pretty tree," he says, desperately trying to lighten up my mood.

I give him a nod. It's our first real Christmas together. It was supposed to be a time of celebration and relaxation, and the joyful anticipation of waiting for Jonah, not filled with tension and sorrow. I feel like I'm going to jump out of my skin.

When we arrive back at the house, I tell Raine I'm going to run a bath and he starts to grab our supplies and the tree. He's strong enough to manage it on his own, thank God. Every time someone looked at me at the store, I kept thinking they knew, which is ridiculous. No one was paying any attention to us, but I feel like I've got a spotlight shining on my shattered soul and everyone can see my heartbreak.

As I let the warm water soothe me, I think about my amazing husband. Deep in the corner of my suitcase, there is some flimsy lingerie I've never worn for him. Although I worry about getting pregnant, I want my husband, and I want him to want me in return.

Chapter Forty – Raine

I'm setting up the tree, but I can't get it right and it looks haphazard. I keep trying until I finally give up. It's good enough for now. I can hear Julia's water running and I hope the bath helps her. I sigh heavily, looking at the tree, my heart heavy. I didn't realize how sad the holidays would make me feel. Christmas is a time for gratitude and celebration, and all I want is my entire family, but I have a big hole that will never be filled.

After I empty all the bags from our recent purchase, I head straight to the kitchen and pour a glass of bourbon. Even though I wanted to go a day without a drink, I just need a little something to ease the ache. I don't hear Julia enter behind me, but as I swirl away from the counter, she's standing in the doorway wearing a nearly see-through, black lacy negligee and black platform pumps. The glass in my hand almost falls to the floor.

"Nice outfit," I say, casually taking a sip, then I put the glass on the counter next to me.

"Little something I found in my suitcase—needed to air it out," she says, walking toward me and I meet her halfway. We reach each other and I pull her tight against my frame, holding her there, one arm around her waist, and the other goes to the back of her head.

Julia rests against my shoulder. She's slightly shaking, which surprises me.

I lean back and look into her eyes. She's fixed her hair and even has some makeup on, but besides that, I can tell she desires me and that's all that matters.

I scoop her up in my arms and carry her into our bedroom.

"You know, you could have just thrown me against the counter," she murmurs as her lips reach my neck.

I chuckle deep in my throat, "And I would have … but it would've killed my back."

I reach the bed and put her down carefully on top of the covers, then I quickly strip off my jeans and shirt. Soon, I'm stretched down next to her, pressing her body against mine as I firmly place a kiss on her lips.

I pull back slightly. "You look incredible. I think you should just walk around every day in something like that. Forget clothes," I tease, running my lips down her jaw line, and then I move to her neck. Julia moans. I can find her sweet spots so easily, knowing her so well. I revel in touching her but pause as she speaks.

"I have one request before … and she looks down slightly before continuing.

"What is it, sweetheart?"

Julia leans back and grabs something from the nightstand, before rolling back to me, a condom thrust forward. I'm puzzled for a moment before it dawns on me.

"I can't even think about going through that again, not right now," she says. "Even though we haven't been careful before, we need to be. I'm sure you understand."

I pause for a brief moment. "Of course I understand."

And there it is again. Will everything always remind us of Jonah? Will we be tormented for the rest of our lives?

I grab the condom from her hands, look down at her, and smile. She looks as beautiful as ever, but she's still way too thin.

I sit up and pull her into my lap, letting her feel me underneath her. Julia looks at me, running her hands through my hair, smiling with a look I remember well, and in a few moments when I'm ready, it's game on.

Chapter Forty-One – Julia

I'm sitting in Raine's lap, and he's rock solid against me. It's all I can do not to put him inside me immediately, but a little voice inside me tells me to be careful.

I run my hands through his hair, lean in, kissing his neck hard, and then I run my lips to his ear lobe and nibble as he pulls me down hard against him, one hand reaching up to grip my hair as he does. *Damn ...* he feels amazing.

Then he expertly takes the condom I've already opened and moves me up slightly to slip it on. With one hand, he guides me back on top of him and easily slides inside of me. I lean my head back and he kisses me hard on the neck, as one of his hands is under my hip, guiding me.

I think I'll instantly explode. He feels full inside me and it's glorious. It doesn't take long before I'm writhing on top of him, my head thrown back. I lean back up and look at Raine, and he's watching me intently, his eyes full of desire, with both of his hands gripping my waist as I drive back and forth against him.

I smile at Raine and lean in to kiss him, taking his tongue and mixing it with mine. I start moving on him even harder as our ecstasy builds. Raine grabs my ass and holds me tight against him as I come, yelling out as I do.

"That's my girl," Raine whispers in my ear.

It's a long, hard release and it instantly soothes my muscles and my mind.

With determination, Raine rolls me on my stomach and enters me from behind. I gasp with pleasure as Raine grips my flesh, driving into me with skill. Raine knows exactly how to press against me. I'm lying flat on the bed, enjoying the feeling of him against me.

"Come for me … come for me," I whisper.

Raine chuckles deep in his throat, "Not yet, sweetheart. You have a long way to go."

Raine stops, withdraws from within me, and with one hand, rolls me over on my back and enters me again. I gasp out loud as he leans against me, grinding against me in slow, circular motions. It doesn't take long for me to climax again.

I lean up as Raine rolls over on his back, and then I straddle him, pressing against him.

Raine says, "I hate this condom. I want to feel you."

At first I look down, but then I raise my eyes, meeting his as a knowing look passes between us. We silently agree that we can't take any more chances.

As I straddle him, I press my hands against his chest and take control, moving deep and slow as my excitement builds. Raine's body moves synchronously with mine as we reach an even higher plateau. He pulls me down against his chest, taking my head in his hands and kissing me deeply until he pulls away.

"I'm close, baby, come with me," he says, against my hair.

My head is pressed against his neck. I can hear guttural sounds from deep in his throat as he gets close, and we explode with pleasure at the same time. I'm enveloped in Raine's arms as we catch our breath.

He rolls me onto my back, tucking my backside tight against his front. "I am never letting you go," he whispers against my hair. And he's holding me so tight, I believe him.

"You'd better not," I whisper back.

Chapter Forty-Two – Raine

"You're sure this is cool ... me coming up there to write with you?" It's Sunday afternoon and I'm on the phone with Bret.

"Absolutely. I've got a writing room set up, and Julia's looking forward to seeing you. It will be a nice change for us both."

"Seriously though. How's it going? I don't want to come up there and cause any trouble."

"We have good days, but more bad days," I answer honestly. "Yesterday was a particularly good day and night. But it can change on a dime. Having you come up here will not cause any trouble. Julia wants you to visit and I need to work."

"Well, I don't want to be in anyone's way."

"Bret, you're a bull in a China shop. Who are we kidding?" And Bret hears my guffaw at the end and laughs with me.

After I hang up, I check on Julia. After our glorious afternoon, we watched movies all night, covered up with blankets on the couch. Although we went to bed early, this morning after breakfast, Julia went back to the bedroom for a nap and hasn't stirred. Her medication still makes her groggy.

At the bedroom door I peer in and see that she's still under the blankets with her eyes closed. I head to the kitchen to make a Bloody Mary as I try to tell myself it's completely normal to make a drink this early.

Several more hours pass, and my boredom is getting the best of me. I creep back to the bedroom door. Julia has hardly moved from her earlier spot. I quietly walk to the edge of the bed and place a hand on her shoulder. She stirs but doesn't move to get up.

"I'm tired, Raine … can I sleep a little longer."

"Sure, hon … just wanted to check on you. You hardly ate this morning, and it's after three. Your sister will kill me if I don't feed you." She doesn't respond, and I continue. "Speaking of Jody, she called earlier. She wants us to come up to their house for dinner."

"I don't want to. Not tonight," she says, rolling over and looking at me. She looks much more fatigued than she has the last few days.

"What do you want me to do, Jules? I don't know what to do?" I say softly, stroking her hair. She looks up at me with empty eyes, so different from the woman who seduced me the day before.

"Maybe I'm just tired from yesterday. That was a pretty vigorous afternoon we had." A faint smile plays on her lips, but it doesn't reach her eyes.

"Okay," I say with a heavy sigh. "I'll let you sleep."

She nods, closing her eyes as I walk out of the room in total frustration. I'm completely helpless again and I *hate* being helpless. I head straight to the kitchen and pour a glass of bourbon. I grab the bottle, walk to the living room, and plant myself in front of the TV.

Chapter Forty-Three – Julia

The sun is well down on the horizon when I finally drag myself out of bed. I don't bother to shower but instead pull another layer of clothes on as I head toward the glowing light of the living room.

Raine is sitting in a leather chair, his guitar across his lap, with a half-empty bottle of bourbon next to him.

His eyes briefly catch mine as I enter, but he looks back at the TV. "Well, hello, darlin,'" he slurs.

"Hey," I apprehensively reply. The look in Raine's eyes is something I haven't seen since we dated in Nashville many years ago when our relationship was tumultuous at best. He's pissed.

In a slovenly, drunken manner, he picks his guitar up. "You wanna hear a new song I'm working on? You'll love it, I swear," he says sarcastically.

I haven't moved one step closer as I watch him pick up his glass and take a big drink before he starts to play. It's the same melody I heard him play back in Nashville after Jonah died, and that I've heard him play here in Montana. Now he's struggling with the chords, but he can basically put something of a song together. When he starts to sing and I hear the lyrics, my stomach tightens, and I instantly feel like throwing up. It's obvious what the song is about.

I let him continue for a few moments, but after he finishes the second verse, I finally react. I can't take it anymore.

"*STOP IT!* ... Stop singing that song!"

Somewhat startled, Raine's fingers stop playing. With the alcohol, his movements are delayed as he looks at me. "What's the matter, hon? You don't like it?" His voice is filled with disdain. "You need to hear it. Maybe you'll come out of this funk ... or whatever the hell this is."

Now I remember cruel Raine, and how he can be when he's drunk and angry. I haven't experienced cruel Raine for years, and it's not a memory I cherish. He can quickly change into the jerk I experienced many years ago. Raine hasn't been like this since we met back up in Vegas. I hate this Raine; this drunk, angry part of him.

"Raine, you're drunk, being mean, and I don't deserve it."

"Mean? *Bullshit!* I'm trying to wake your ass up! Yes, Jonah died and a part of us died with him. But you have got to get out of bed and live. I need you to *live*," he practically yells, slamming his hand down on the arm of his chair in frustration.

"Live? Like you're living? Covering up your pain with a bottle?" I'm now at his side and I grab his bottle. I lift it over my head and heave it toward the fireplace, watching it shatter into a million little pieces. Luckily, Raine didn't start a fire. That would have been a disaster. My anger has taken over. "Did you ever think that maybe I don't want to live! *Damn you!* It's not that easy to let go," I say, collapsing on the couch.

But Raine ignores my outburst. The alcohol is winning. "Nice," he dryly responds. "You destroyed a perfectly good bottle of bourbon."

I jump off the couch and run to the safety of the bedroom as I cry. I don't want this ignorant asshole to see me like this, but I hear his words as I leave.

"There you go, running away. You're really good at running away," he slurs. From the bedroom I hear Raine pick the guitar back up and he starts playing that song again. The same fucking song.

I slam the door shut and crumple to the floor in a pile of sorrow. Raine doesn't get it and maybe he never will.

I spend the night alone in our room. I don't sleep as I listen for Raine to come in, and when he doesn't, I eventually roll over facing the wall, staring into the darkness, but the tears don't come. I don't have any tears left. I'm all cried out.

Chapter Forty-Four – Raine

I come to, sitting up straight in a leather chair, freezing my ass off. My hand instantly goes to my head, which feels like I put it under a drill just for fun.

I notice broken glass all around the fireplace and a small puddle of liquid. As I rub my temples, it vaguely comes back to me. We fought. Our first major argument since we've been back together and married.

"*Fuck*," I mumble. I barely remember what I said to Julia, but it must have been bad. I remember she walked in, and then I played a little of Jonah's song. She raised her voice, which I should've known would happen, but I don't remember much after that. But I've messed up. That I know. It doesn't take broken glass to prove it. Julia rarely gets angry, and never, ever, in the time that I've known her, has she been angry enough to break something.

I look down at my watch and remember that Bret arrives later this afternoon. I don't have much time to make things right.

Chapter Forty-Five – Julia

I'm staring at the ceiling and wondering if we're headed toward divorce. Although I love him more than anything else on earth, I refuse to live with the Raine who drinks, and is a belligerent asshole. No way, no how. I hear him stir in the other room as his words from last night ring in my ears. And that song ... that fucking song is like a bad dream. I clutch my chest wondering if this is an actual heart attack or a panic attack. It feels like a heart attack ... my heart hurts and my mind is racing. Am I losing it? In my head, I know why he said what he said, and in a way, it's true. I do have to keep on living, but I don't really want to. At least not now, not yet.

I reluctantly swing my legs out into the cold morning air and stumble to the bathroom like a drunk person. I step into a hot shower and let the water run down my head and back, soothing my mind and muscles that are ready to snap.

As I walk into the kitchen, I notice Raine has already straightened everything up. The kitchen is spotless. The broken bottle and living room mess are now gone. Raine's nowhere to be found, but he's made a fire in the fireplace. Bret will arrive soon. I make my way to our spare room, which will serve as their writing room, but he's not there either. And then I notice him out on the deck that leads out to the lake, staring up at the mountains, with his hands on his hips, not moving. I wonder if I should go out there but decide against it. I can't face him yet.

I walk back into the kitchen, find my phone, and call Tracy.

She picks up right away. "Hey girl! I'm so glad you called. I was beginning to think I'd have to send a search party. You okay?"

My light chuckle is strained. "Maybe. Had a rough night last night." I relay the major points of what transpired, including my heave ho of Raine's bottle of bourbon.

"Oh boy … not good. Bret's arriving shortly, what are you two going to do?"

"I haven't talked to Raine yet. He's outside in the frigid air, hopefully freezing his balls off," I joke. "I'll try to smooth this over 'cause I don't want anything to seem weird when he's trying to write with Bret. I can run up and stay with Jody for a few days if it gets to be too much."

"The tabloids may pick up on this if they're following you. Just try to remain steady. I'll call Raine later. We need to talk about this."

"Don't start on him, Trace … he's hurting as much as I am. He just has a different way of showing it." There's a long pause before I continue, "If you heard the song he wrote and played last night, it about killed me. I don't ever want to hear that song again." And I'm serious. It was too vivid and painful, and clearly about Jonah.

"Still, I'm going to talk to him. He needs to get some help."

"True. But you can't make Raine do anything he doesn't want to do. His head is harder than a bowling ball. Stubborn down to his core."

Just then, I hear the French doors open in the living room as Raine comes inside. I give him a sideways glance and he catches my eye but looks away, ashamed.

"I've got to run," I say clicking off the phone and putting it on the counter. Raine slowly saunters into the kitchen toward me. "Tracy, I presume?"

I look at him nodding.

"And she's pissed at me, and rightfully so," he adds sheepishly.

I look at him, my eyes full of love and sadness at the same time. Raine looks down. He takes tentative steps toward me, and I meet him halfway as he gathers me in his strong arms. I lean against him hard.

"You're cold," I tease.

"It's Montana. It's flippin' freezing."

"Did standing outside in the frigid air clear your head?" I say, wrapped up tight in his arms as I start running my hands up and down his cold back.

"Sort of. It certainly didn't help other body parts," he jokes. "I don't think I'll ever get it up again."

I laugh out loud as I pull back and look at him. When I'm not in heels, Raine towers over me. "You were not nice last night," I say honestly, looking up, pulling his face down to look into my eyes. "Last night, I got the Raine I don't like, and don't ever want to see again."

Raine looks away but pulls me back tight against him. "I know. I don't like that Raine either." And then he says words he's struggled with for years. "I'm sorry, sweetheart. I'm so sorry I hurt you. And I'm sorry I played ..."

But I won't let him finish. "I don't want to talk about that song. Ever."

He looks at me, intense sadness filling his eyes, "Got it. I do have to say ... you have one hell of an arm. That bottle shattered everywhere."

"I used to play softball," I say with a slight grin. "I was a pitcher, what do you expect?"

"And now I know. Noted. I'll never have anything around me that you can throw." And he brings his gorgeous lips down, kissing me with a ferociousness that only comes from him, the love of my life.

I finally pull away, "Bret will be here in a few hours. I'll stay for a little while, but would you mind if I head up to Jody's? I want to give you guys some space."

"Sure, but you can stay here, you don't have to leave."

"I want to get out of the house for a while. And I need to run up and see those guys. We've been cooped up here for a few days," I say as I look into his eyes, a grin filling my face. "You've kept me busy."

"And I could keep you busy for the next few hours," he adds, taking my hand and leading me back toward the bedroom.

Although the night before was a wake-up call about the strife in our relationship and the grief we're both still dealing with, all I want to do is love and take care of Raine. He'll have to figure out his drinking, and I have no idea how he'll do that, and my grief is overwhelming us both. But for now, at this moment, we have a few hours to enjoy one another and that's exactly what we do.

Chapter Forty-Six – Julia

I'm sitting at Jody's kitchen counter cradling a cup of coffee. After Bret arrived a couple of hours ago, I drove up the mountain to my sister's house. And I'm reminded that Jody is always good at being honest.

"Seriously … you look exhausted."

"We had a terrible night." I give a slight pause before continuing. "In fact, I may need to come up here and stay with you for a few nights while Bret's here. I don't want to get in their way."

"Are you going to tell me what happened?"

"I'll just say we had a huge fight. We're both dealing with our pain in different ways."

"Do you think the counselor you're seeing is helping at all?"

"I don't know … maybe. He is making me work through my grief and damn, it's a bitch. We're working through this mourning process he talks about. So far, I'm not so hot at accepting the loss and dealing with my grief. He's mentioned eventually I'll adjust to the world without Jonah, and then later, I'll find some way to move forward, but like that will ever happen. I'm pissed and can't get past that. Pissed at pretty much everyone and everything."

"Hmm … since I've never been in your shoes, I'm not sure about the process, but I get being angry. I'd be pissed off too."

I nod as I turn my attention back to my coffee. I probably said too much, but in a teeny tiny way, it feels good to talk a bit about my sessions.

I spend the day helping Jody work around their house. After several texts from Raine, I drive back to the rental house. As soon as I get there, we're all famished and head out to dinner. As we pile into a rented Tahoe with a driver, I notice Raine swivel his head to look out the back window several times.

He whirls back around as deep lines furrow his brow. "Paparazzi."

"*Damn!*" Bret exclaims, turning to look back from the front seat. "I knew I was famous, but this is ridiculous." He gives me one of his gorgeous, dimpled smiles.

I peer out the back window before replying, "Yep, Bret. It's all about you."

We get to the restaurant, ignoring the pap trailing us. We enjoy a nice, leisurely dinner, and after we drop Bret off at his car in front of our house, I grab Raine's hand, and we silently walk inside. The pap's car trailed us the entire way home, and I don't want to give them any reason for speculation.

I have no idea what will happen when we're inside alone. Nighttime is the most difficult for us as we face our demons. Raine held it to two drinks at dinner, but his palm is sweaty in my hand.

"I'm gonna take a bath, and I'm sure you need to relax in your own way," I say, gesturing to the kitchen.

Raine quietly nods and drops my hand as he goes in search of a glass of comfort. I watch him for a few moments before making my way to the bedroom. After my bath and a much-needed pill, I climb into bed. I can hear the faint sound of a guitar coming from the main room. There is no way I'm going out there to listen.

Chapter Forty-Seven – Raine

I strum a few chords of the song I'm working on with Bret, but after a few minutes my fingers automatically go to Jonah's song. The chords are pulling on my fingers like a magnet because I can't get the words and melody out of my head. As I play, a single tear rolls down my face for what we've lost, and what I may still lose.

Several hours later, my weary body staggers to the bedroom. I go to Julia's side of the bed and stand there, watching her sleep. She's talking lightly and she seems tormented. Another one of her bad dreams, I'm sure. Even in my numb stupor, I realize we're both in a bad dream we can't seem to escape. I crawl in next to her, but I don't touch her. I don't want to wake her.

I feel Julia wake up with a start as she sits straight up in bed. I open my eyes and watch her run her hands over her face and sigh. She looks down at me and sees my open eyes.

"Sorry ... didn't mean to wake you," she says, embarrassed.

"It's alright, honey."

She settles back down on her back, pulling the covers back up to her chin. I roll closer to her, draping my arm over her. Normally, she would melt against me, but she's stiff against my frame. After a few minutes, the tension in her body eases and she falls back into a fitful sleep.

The sky is gray and dark as I creep out of bed and into the shower. I'm quietly leaving the bathroom, toweling my damp hair when I almost run smack dab into Julia. She jumps.

"Jesus ... didn't see you there," I exclaim as I drop my towel and my hands instinctively go to her shoulders.

"Didn't know you were still in the room."

"Did you sleep at all? I could feel you moving all night."

"Barely."

And here we are, having an awkward morning conversation like two strangers who've just met.

"Bret will be here in about an hour. You have a counseling session, right?"

"Yeah. Then I think I'll head back to Jody's. Maybe I'll even stay over there tonight. Let you two work."

My hands drop to my side in frustration. "I'd rather you didn't stay there ... but suit yourself." I briskly storm back into the bathroom and slam the door. She'll have no doubt how I feel about her leaving.

"She's staying at Jody's tonight. Just us again today, buddy." Bret's been around long enough to know what's up. Although we sometimes try to hide it from our good friend, the tension is palpable.

"Maybe you should go up the mountain and get her, Raine? Fight for this!"

"No. She's still angry with me about the song, she just won't admit it. And I don't know what to do when she's this depressed. I don't know how to handle it."

"She still looks thin, Raine. Too thin."

"*I know it*! Damn! What do you expect me to do? I can't make her eat."

Bret tries to break the tension with humor, "Well, I'm hungry, shithead. Go make me a sandwich."

I scowl at him but let out a slight chuckle. "You can make your own fuckin' sandwich. You're such a demanding rock star." I sigh. "C'mon, I'll show you where everything is." While we're in the kitchen, I pour myself a glass of bourbon. Bret doesn't say a word as he grabs a beer from the fridge. At least Bret doesn't judge me.

139

Chapter Forty-Eight – Julia

"You think it's a good idea for you to stay at Jody's?" Tracy asks, her voice clearly filled with concern.

"When we aren't having sex, I literally have nothing to say to him. It's like we've never met ... it's awkward. I hate it but I don't know what to do."

"Staying at Jody's is not going to help. It'll probably piss him off even more."

"My counselor seems to think it's okay. Distance may give us some needed perspective and we'll fight harder for our relationship."

"I don't think it's a good idea, Jules. Not with Raine. His mind doesn't work in a typical way, and you know it."

My gut knows she's right, but I can't face him right now, not with this underlying anger going on between us. And Raine has every right to be angry with me. After everything that's happened, I'd be angry too.

We keep this charade going for a few more days. I call and text Raine every day, but I'm staying away from the house while Bret's here working. I can't be in the same space while they write, it's too difficult, and frankly, right now, I don't care about songs. All I want to do is work out, talk to my counselor, and try to ween myself off of my pills. Bret is flying out on Friday, and then I'll have to go back to the house. We'll have to face each other then.

Friday arrives and as I stop my car and turn the ignition off in front of our rental house, I let out a loud and heavy sigh. I miss Raine terribly. It's not that I don't want to see him, but it's late afternoon and I figure he's already drinking. So I'm about to greet that "Raine," and I hate that "Raine."

I enter and the house is eerily quiet. I find Raine in the bedroom, sitting in a chair, staring out the window at the lake.

"Hey ... how'd it go with Bret?"

His head swivels to me, but he doesn't say a word. He stands and walks toward me and I'm frozen. The room is dark, and I can only see an outline of his face. He's halfway across the room and almost to me when I take an automatic step back.

"Don't. Don't move," his voice is deep and quiet. He's inches from me now in the darkened room, but with the light from outside, I can see he's shirtless and only wearing pants. Nothing else. He places his hands on the side of my arms, and my purse drops to the floor. I'm breathing hard and my heart skips a few beats. He moves closer and puts his face next to mine. I can breathe him in, and his scent makes my head spin. He smells like sweat mixed with my favorite cologne. He pulls me tight against him, pinning my arms against my side, my head thrust against his chest, and he holds me like this for several moments. Finally, his grip loosens slightly, and I can't take it as I free my arms and slide them up his chest, encircling his neck as I lean up and kiss him hard on the mouth. Raine's hands are instantly all over me, one hand on my ass and the other in my hair, kissing me back with such ferocity it takes my breath.

His hands are quick as he pulls at my clothes, and in kind, I tug at the button of his pants. When I'm left in only a bra and underwear, he grabs me and pushes me against the bedroom wall, his mouth insistent as his tongue mixes with mine, and his hands squeeze my eager flesh. I let Raine take me away from everything. We're hungry for each other. He pulls at my remaining clothes until they're gone, and then he picks me up, setting me directly on top of him. He fills me up and he feels glorious. My legs encircle him as my arms wrap around his neck.

Raine doesn't waste any time. He carries me to the middle of the room, drops to his knees, and lays me down on the floor, never losing me from inside of him. He's hard and fast, and it feels amazing. I didn't realize how starved I'd been for his touch. No matter if the world is falling down around us, we can make love well, anywhere, at any time.

He brings me to release quickly and as I catch my breath, he starts again, covering me with his body, his head next to mine, growling low in my ear, "You're mine … you're mine."

He takes me to sweet release once again, and then he picks me up and places me on the bed, stretching his body lightly on top of mine. I'm quiet as he looks into my eyes. There are no words as we make love. We watch each other reach a higher plateau and explode together, both yelling out as we do.

Chapter Forty-Nine – Julia

I wake up exhausted, my arms and legs heavy with fatigue. But it's a good fatigue and I roll on my back and smile, thinking about the night before. Our relationship is more fire and ice than ever before. I reach next to me for Raine, but he's gone.

I throw on a robe and as I reach the kitchen area, he's sitting at the table, staring out at the beautiful, snow-capped Montana mountains.

"Good morning, beautiful," he says gesturing for me to come closer, and I instinctively walk into his arms.

The look of him sitting with the sun blazing in through the windows, shining on his dark black hair, makes my insides stir. I sit on his lap and look down into those gorgeous green eyes that soothe my soul. "Good morning, love. Did you sleep well?"

"I did." And he pauses as he looks away before cutting to the chase. "I've been doing some thinking. It's time for us to go back to Nashville. We have to find a way to move on."

I instantly stand, worming my way out of his arms and backing away. "*NO!* I'm not ready, Raine." I'm instantly filled with panic.

A frown overtakes his face and a stern look fills his eyes. "You can't keep running, Jules. We have to face our lives back in Nashville."

I jump in, "What if I never want to go back? I like it up here with Jody and her family and, frankly, the real world. I don't know if I can go back." My voice continues to rise, my arms outstretched emphasizing every word, "I don't know if I *ever* want to go back … I can't face him … I mean it. I just can't!"

Raine skims over my Jonah reference, but we both know what I'm talking about. "Bullshit! You're a songwriter and an incredible performer at the peak of your career. You have to go back. Not just for you, but for us. We need to rebuild our lives … Jules, this is the only way." Raine's tone is firm and forceful.

"I don't know if I want that career or life anymore," I whisper. "I don't know if I can handle a public life."

"You're just depressed and rightfully so. We both are." Raine stands and closes the distance between us, but I stiffen. He's not listening to a word I'm saying.

Raine pulls my reluctant body into his arms, the tiny muscle along his jaw pulsating and his green eyes are fierce, as he calmly states, "I am not losing you, and staying here doesn't help one damn thing. We need to go home. Our careers and lives are back in Nashville. I've got to finish my project with Bret, and I've got two other artists waiting. We can't keep running. We have got to face this."

I start to break down. Although his arms are usually my safety, right now I'm terrified as my pulse races when I even consider going back to Nashville. A light sweat covers my body. It's just too soon. I struggle out of his arms. "NO! I'm not going!"

Anger crosses Raine's face. He's not in the frame of mind to lose this battle. And that's what we're having. A battle for my soul; for both our souls.

He looks me in the eyes as he stoically replies, "I've already booked the flights. We leave tomorrow morning." And without a glance, he walks straight out the French doors that lead onto the back deck.

I walk to the couch and collapse against the cushions, my head falling into my hands. I can't leave. I can't go back when all I see is Jonah's grave in my mind. By now it will have the gravestone we ordered for him. I can't do it. Not yet.

The day passes by in a blur. I went to the gym and tried to ease some of the anxiety about leaving, but it didn't help. When I was leaving the house, Raine was packing up his clothes, clearly more than ready to go.

It's dusk when I finally get back to the house. Raine is sitting in the living room staring at the fireplace. A glass of his familiar brown liquid in his hand.

I'm a few feet away from him when he speaks, "You're not coming with me, are you?"

I stop dead. "No. I'm not."

His head slowly looks my way, and his intense gaze strikes my heart. "If you don't leave with me now, you may never come back. This is a choice, Julia. You're making a very big choice."

I pause, staring at the fire for several minutes. "I can't go back and see that house ... his room ... his grave," I whisper. "I can't."

He nods and his head goes back toward the fireplace as he takes another drink of bourbon. I spin out of the room straight to the bedroom and collapse on the covers, fully clothed. Raine doesn't join me as I lie there, tears streaming down my face until I finally fall asleep.

The next morning when I stagger to the kitchen, he's gone. Our rental car is still in the driveway, so he must have called Uber or something. The ache in my chest makes me fall to my knees. Why couldn't he understand that I just need more time? I'm frozen like this for what seems like forever until I finally pull myself up off the floor.

I pace around the house restlessly. It's Sunday and Dr. Montgomery isn't available. I have got to talk to someone right now. I call my one confidant who I know can help. Tracy picks up after a few rings.

"He left. He left me this morning and is headed back to Nashville."

Tracy doesn't miss a beat. "I know. I helped with the flights. I'd hoped you would be on the plane with him."

"You do understand why I can't go back," I say, pleading my case. "You get it, don't you?" My voice is rising with despair.

"I think so, but honestly, I have no idea what you two are going through. He loves you, Jules, and he's scared to death. Scared that you'll never come back to him, and you guys won't find a way through this. In a way, I agree with him. You need to come back."

145

"But he won't lose me if he can just be patient. I don't care about my career. I don't care about any of it. I'm just numb," I say, and the sobs start. I can't help it. I'm losing the one thing that matters and the only thing I have left. Raine.

I'm able to squeak out over my sobs, "Promise … me … one thing," and I take a deep breath. "Watch over him. He's drinking … a lot," I manage to get out.

"I will. Jules, try to consider coming back soon. I miss you."

"I miss you, too."

I hang up and with my phone in hand, I stare around the empty house we just shared as tears stream down my face. Even though the view this morning is spectacular, with a low cloud line reaching the mountains in the distance giving everything a blue hue, I don't see any of it. I head back to our bedroom and climb into the big king-sized bed, roll up into a ball, pull the covers nearly over my head, and stare outside. And that's the last thing I remember.

Chapter Fifty – Raine

I'm boarding the plane feeling lower than I've ever felt in my life. Some of the other passengers recognize me, make eye contact and smile, but all I see is pity in their eyes. I'm on the plane alone.

Bret arranged for a car to pick me up at the airport. Thank God. I don't need to think or stress about anything else. I had way too many glasses of bourbon on the flight, and now I can barely see what's in front of me. I'm numb and everything around me is a hazy fog.

When I get to our empty house, it's dark and musty. I should walk around and air it out, but instead I go to the master bedroom and fling my suitcase on our bed. I glance in a nearby mirror, but I don't see myself. I see a scared, empty stranger with hollow cheeks and blood-stained eyes. Who is this creature standing before me?

The door of Julia's new closet is ajar. I walk to that door and open it wide. They did a marvelous job and Julia would absolutely love it. Even now in my buzzed stupor I acknowledge that she may not come back, I drop to my knees in the closet and sob into my hands. It's a hard cry I haven't let myself feel for weeks, shit, maybe even years. I'm losing everything and I'm powerless to stop it.

I don't recall how I ended up fully clothed lying on top of the bed. I stagger to the bathroom and stare long and hard at the haggard, unshaven mess before me. My typically olive skin is taut and pale. I vow from this moment on that I'm going to live again. I don't know how, or if, Julia will be a part of my life, but I'm not giving up.

I clean myself up and after making a strong pot of coffee, I head straight to my studio. I have work to do and if that's all I have left, I'll give it all I have. I'm scheduled to start on a four-song project with a new artist, and we'll start recording Bret's ten-song project soon. I don't have time for bullshit. Not that Julia is bullshit, but I don't have any more time to waste. Although I still can't face Jonah's loss and now the possibility of losing Julia, I'm going to surround myself with work.

I'm relentless all day, working non-stop. But that night when I'm alone again, I'm pacing around every room with nothing to do, and no one to talk to. I finally give in. As I'm pouring my favorite brown liquid into my glass, I know I should eat, but I'm not hungry. This isn't a good combination, but what the hell?

This pattern continues for days, and I only take breaks to meet with Bret or other artists. I've had to cut some tracks with musicians outside of our house, and that at least gets me out, but Tracy is good about not scheduling anything too late. Night after night, I'm at the house drinking until I'm buzzed enough to sleep. And every morning when I look in the mirror, I see how it's affecting me. I'm losing a ton of weight, but at least I'm being productive.

Julia and I send texts, but it's more like a formality. We never stray from the simple "how are you" or "are you eating." Nothing real. I'll have to face it sooner rather than later. She's not coming back and we're over.

Chapter Fifty-One – Julia

I grab my phone from the nightstand, but there are no messages, no calls, and no texts. Raine's been back in Nashville for several days and all I get are a few texts from him during the day.

I roll over and stretch my legs and arms, realizing how much my body hurts from the tension, sadness, and anger. When I get out of bed and make my obligatory cup of coffee, I instantly start to clean. That's how I'm dealing with this crap. I clean when I'm stressed so I have some sort of control. You could eat off this floor.

Midday comes and I force a sandwich into my tired, weak body. I pick up my iPad and log in. I hit a news page and almost drop the device in shock. What the hell? They have a story up about Raine leaving me in Montana and that we're headed for divorce. Paparazzi followed Raine to the airport and there are pictures of him boarding alone, and then more pictures of him at the Nashville airport getting into a black Suburban, looking disheveled and distraught with his phone up to his ear. I look at his pictures and suddenly I can't breathe. I let the love of my life walk away and I've done nothing to get him back. I run to the bathroom and vomit.

I'm on day ten of my routine, which is exactly what I'd been doing in Montana before Raine came to visit. I'm burying myself at the gym and with counseling believing it's helping, but it's no use. One day I broke the cycle and stopped by a church for a good cry. Although part of my heart is still angry with God for taking our son, I no longer blame anyone, not even myself. Church is actually becoming a comfort for me, and I stop by and talk to God on a regular basis.

The paparazzi continue to follow me around town, snapping pictures of me coming and going to the gym, the grocery store, and all my regular places. I waved at them once. My routine is comforting in a way with no surprises or turmoil, but at night, that's when the Raine wave washes over me, and I walk around our now empty rental house, barely breathing, barely living.

Tracy calls one night, and I ask, "When was the last time you talked to him … is he eating?"

"Yesterday, and Bret is with him almost every day."

"But is he eating … and the drinking. What's going on, Trace?"

There is silence on the other end for just a few moments. "I don't think he's eating much, and from what Bret says, the drinking is about the same."

"*Damn.* Does he ask about me? We text some, but he's not saying much to me right now."

"Of course he asks about you. He misses you, that's a given. But he's angry, Julia. He believes you've abandoned him."

"But I haven't abandoned him! I wasn't ready to go back to that city."

"What about now … are you ready now?"

"I don't know. I'll never be the same. And I don't know if I can walk back into that house … I really don't."

Tracy doesn't mince her words, "Your home and your life are back here in Nashville, Jules. Your true love is fighting for his life, and as much as you don't want to hear it, he needs you and you need him. You need to come back."

The force of Tracy's words and the fierceness in her tone surprise me. Up to now, she hasn't been so firm in her opinion. I trust my best friend, and her words sink in. Maybe it's time for me to fight for Raine and our love. And God, how I miss him.

I can't help but sigh and my stomach acid churns as I say these words, "All right. Book a flight for me the day after tomorrow. Don't tell Raine. I don't want him to hide how he's doing. I want to see it for myself."

I hang up and go into every room in our big, empty rental house. Every room seems so much larger without Raine to fill them up. My mind is telling me this is the right thing to do, and part of me will be glad to leave this empty space and go back to Tennessee, but there's an ache in the pit of my stomach knowing everything will remind me of my loss; everything will remind me of Jonah. I stare out the back windows at the gorgeous snow-capped mountain view as the moon illuminates the lake. I'll miss the serenity and the little bit of peace I've found here. I hope I can somehow feel like I'm headed back home, and not to a dark, sad place. My hand instinctively clutches my chest as I think about Jonah; an ache that will never go away.

Chapter Fifty-Two – Raine

I pull my now slender frame from under the covers and begin my routine. After a cold shower, I get some eggs and toast down, but coffee is all I want as my mainstay. Often this is my only real meal, so I make a point of eating every bite. I won't be hungry later, I never am.

In just a few short weeks, we've already finished half the tracks for Bret's record. We'll record a few more vocals and then take the roughs to the label for approval. I don't want to get too far into this project without letting the head of Bret's label hear what we're doing. This project is different, and it's even harder to make a living writing and recording songs with all the clutter of social media. We've got to get this project right. Even though I've had a great deal of success with Bret, and he's a major country superstar, the business gets harder every day as we compete against major label artists and independents.

The night before, we finally put a great vocal down on Jonah's song, which we're calling "Born by Song," and we may have it right. The song is basically how Julia described her dream, picturing our young son alive and growing up but then questioning where he is now. It's hopeful and haunting at the same time. The song is my way of letting my son live through the lyrics. I think it's beautiful; it's very ethereal and like a lullaby. I talked Bret into cutting the vocals and including it on his project, which wasn't easy to do. Bret thinks it's too personal, but I love it. I'm hopeful Julia will love it too if she gives it a chance.

I force the rest of the food down my throat and instantly head to the refuge of my studio. I'm relentless. Work is the only thing that gets me through the day, but a bottle of bourbon is never far from reach.

Chapter Fifty-Three – Julia

I step out of the rental car at the airport and wave at the photographer capturing my every move. I don't care. One day the circus will stop, but for now, I'll play my part.

Several hours and two planes later, I finally land in Nashville. I get into my waiting car and head home. I didn't say a word to Raine about my arrival, and as far as I know, Tracy has kept the secret as well. My apprehension grows as the car gets closer to our neighborhood. I have no idea what I'll find at home. Will Raine be there? And if he is, will he be sober? Will I walk into my house and lose it? I have no earthly idea.

As we pull up the driveway, I see Raine's truck in the garage. It's midday on a Friday in January. Even though the sun is out, it's cold, and it seeps into my bones. I grab my bags and, filled with dread, I enter the house I once loved.

As soon as I open the front door, I hear music coming from Raine's studio. There are no other cars here, so he's working by himself. Good.

I drop my bags in the foyer and cautiously make my way to the open studio door. I consider making a lot of noise so he'll know I'm here, but the music is so loud he'll never hear me. Even if I broke dishes right outside the door.

My heart is in my throat. I have no idea what he'll do when he sees me. I take a deep breath and peek inside the room. Raine's back is to the door and he's messing with dials on the mixing board. Bret's voice rings loudly through the speakers. At least it's not that song I heard in Montana. Standing behind him, I can tell he's thin … and he needs a good haircut, I think with a smile. My chest tightens with longing. I didn't realize how much I missed him.

Finally, when there's a break in the music, I knock lightly on the frame. Raine jumps around in his chair, his eyes wide. When his shock subsides, he quickly rises, staring at me from across the room. Now I can really see how much his clothes hang on him.

He makes a guttural noise and crosses the room in a few large steps, picking me up in his arms and burying his face against my neck. He's holding me so tight it's hurting my ribs, but I don't care. Tears form on my lashes as his lips make their way to mine. He pulls back and looks deeply into my eyes before kissing me hard again on the lips, one hand holding my head to his.

When he finally pulls away and lets my feet slowly fall to the ground, he says, "What the hell? I didn't think you were ever coming back," and with these words, his voice breaks.

My heart flutters, "I missed you. I had to see you." I raise my hand up to his face to brush his hair away from his eyes.

"I know … I need a haircut."

I smile up at him, my eyes dancing. "I like it. Very bohemian."

"You look better … I mean good. You look good," he says with a sigh of exasperation, which I'm sure is with himself. His words are stiff, and it strikes me as adorable.

"I know what you're trying to say," I say, smirking. "I actually can't believe I'm here with you, right now." I pause and my honest words just come out. "You're thin, Raine. I need to go right to the kitchen and make you something to eat," I say, my eyes teasing but serious at the same time.

"The only thing I'm hungry for right now is you," he says, a mischievous grin filling his face. And he doesn't say another word as he scoops me up and carries me up the stairs toward our bedroom.

When he reaches the second-floor landing, he gently puts me on the ground, and instead of continuing what he started in the studio, he leads me through the bedroom to the room that would have been Jonah's nursery.

I put on the brakes and pull back hard against his grip. "No … Raine … I can't go in there." I won't take another step.

"It's okay … really," he says soothingly. "Please let me show you. It's not what you think. I have a surprise for you."

He takes my hand and gently pulls me to him. As I look at his hand, I see he's still wearing his wedding ring—the one I bought for him in Montana.

"Please?" Raine says, smiling. "Come see what they've done."

I reluctantly let him lead me to the door that adjoins our bedroom. Raine gives me the sweetest smile as he opens the door wide, gesturing for me to look inside. As I peer in the doorway, I gasp, and then I smile at him. The small room that I was sure would bring me such sorrow has been transformed into the most beautiful closet I've ever seen. A full wall-sized mirror greets me at the end of the room, and the walls are lined with my clothes and shoes. Raine has somehow managed to get every pair of shoes into its own spot. A feat I thought would have been impossible.

I cover my mouth in amazement. "Oh … my …it's perfect," I say, walking to his side and leaning against him. "It's beautiful. I never thought this room could be beautiful, but this is amazing."

Raine smiles down at me. "I've wanted you to see this room ever since …" and he stops. I lean against him hard, my arms wrapping around his waist, letting him know it's okay. Raine found a way to take a simple room that would have caused me so much heartache, and turn it into something useful that I may be able to stand, although it will still bring me pain.

"It's perfect." I lean up to him, taking his face in my hands to kiss him softly, but with longing. My longing becomes insistent. We need to finish what we started downstairs.

Raine takes me in his arms and kisses me back, embracing me tenderly, as he walks me backward to our bed. We both lie down on the bed, fully dressed, facing one another. Raine places his hand lightly on my face, and then runs a finger along my jaw line as he looks at me tenderly.

"You have no idea how I've missed you."

"I think I do," I whisper back as Raine continues lightly stroking my face as if he's memorizing every line. He's studying me hard, and I get flustered under his gaze.

"What?" I say, my eyes darting back and forth between his.

"You have a little touch of gray at your temples … it makes you look wise."

I grimace as my hand goes to my hair. "With everything, I forgot to get my hair colored. I'll take care of it tomorrow."

"I like it … kind of Emmylou Harris, she's hot."

I chortle, "So, you find gray hair attractive … good to know," I say, my ironic grin lingering.

Raine leans in and kisses me deeply as his hands move on my body and we finish what we started earlier.

Chapter Fifty-Four – Julia

I'm next to Raine, twisted up in bed sheets through the early evening and into the night. After making love twice, I should be exhausted, but I can't sleep as I listen to his steady breath. Earlier Raine made us a light snack and a drink for himself. I could smell the bourbon on his breath, but right now, he seems to be in control.

I wriggle free from his arms and slide out of our bed. I go to the new closet, open the door, and flick the light on. It's a beautiful room, but my heart is in my throat as I can picture the tiny baby furniture that used to fill this same space.

I grab a robe hanging next to me, hit the light switch, and spin out of the closet. I pause at the foot of the bed and watch Raine sleeping. Even dreaming, his brow is furrowed and serious. It makes me remember long ago when we first started dating. He's more handsome to me now, but his face always shows his everyday stress and now the sadness we're both going through.

I go to the kitchen and as I'm staring out the back window, the night sky is incredibly dark. I can see so many stars from these windows that overlook our back property. A shooting star flashes off to my right and I know it's a sign. Jonah is letting me know he's up in heaven and he's okay.

I pad through each room getting used to this house again. Each space holds so many memories, good and bad. I know I have to find a way to get over the pain of what could have been. I head to my private office, which is more like my sanctuary. Raine hardly ever comes into this room.

I walk over to a couch that has a small trunk in front of it. I sit down, my hands shaking as I open the lid of the trunk. I stare at the contents on the top, a tiny ball cap and glove. I pull these two items out and tenderly place them on my lap. I look back down at the little clothes and shoes I'd been collecting for years. I'd always wanted children, and I'd secretly bought and stored away baby clothes for the children I'd hoped to someday have.

I thought seeing these items would bring me to tears, but I'm surprised by my strength as I take out piece after piece, marveling at how tiny they are in my hands.

It's right at this moment that a wave of inner peace crashes over me and I vow to myself that I won't let this house, these items, or Nashville get the best of me. I will somehow survive this. I have to. I have to do it for Jonah. I have to go on and cherish the memory of my little boy. And now I understand a little of what Dr. Montgomery was trying to help me figure out. I'm finding a way to live through this loss.

I pause as I come to the very last item in the trunk, his baptism outfit. I remember the exact place and time I bought the outfit. It was when Raine and I were in Napa, and he surprised me with our impromptu wedding. I hurriedly went shopping for a few last-minute items, and this baptismal gown was in one of the local stores. I had to have it. The dressing gown was so light and beautiful, and I couldn't pass it up. I hold the tiny outfit up to my chest and relax against the couch pillows, clutching the tiny cloth against me. I stare out the window at the night sky and let exhaustion overtake my body and mind.

Chapter Fifty-Five – Raine

My hands instantly reach for Julia. I sit up straight when I don't feel her next to me. After so many nights apart, for a moment I wonder if last night was a dream, but I see lights on in the hallway, and I know that Julia is really back home.

I roll out of bed and grab a robe. The air in the room is chilly. I'll need to turn the heat up now; she's always cold.

I search the house and find the light streaming from her private office. It's a room I rarely enter, but I'm drawn to wherever she is, and I don't want to let her out of my sight.

I enter the room and my eyes go right to her sleeping form on the couch as my breath catches. Baby clothes are strewn all around, and she's fallen asleep with a tiny outfit clutched in her hands. I stand there for several minutes unsure if I should wake her. For the first time in a long time, she looks peaceful, and I want her to sleep. Yesterday, the fatigue in her eyes was so heavy it tore at my heart. She must hear me, because she blinks and finally opens her eyes.

"I didn't want to wake you," I whisper, entering the doorway.

Julia gives an embarrassed glance down at the clothes all around her and then back up at me. "You had no idea I had all of this stuff, did you?"

I take two long strides and I'm by her side. When I reach her, I kneel at her feet. "I'm actually not surprised. You've always been a planner," I tease, and she gives me a gorgeous, sleepy smile. "I like the dress you're holding … very pretty."

She gently touches the lapel on the gown. "It's actually a baptismal gown," she says with a sideways smile, knowing I have no idea what she's talking about.

I reach out and touch the fabric in her hands. "Well, whatever it is, it's beautiful." I pause, looking down at the trunk at her feet. It's then that I notice a familiar blue Tiffany's box—the gift I gave her many months before. I reach down and pull it out of the trunk.

"I wondered what you'd done with this."

Julia watches me as I run my fingers across the silver rattle. It was a gift I gave her to try and make up for hurting her feelings.

"Raine … do you ever think we'll ever need these clothes … or that …" she says, reaching toward the rattle as her voice catches. She's doing all she can to stifle her tears.

I put the rattle down and take her face in my hands. "I have no doubt we'll need these one day, and one day, we'll display this rattle in our baby's room. For now, we can put everything in a special place in your new closet." I then reach down and grab her hands. "If it's what you want, we'll have a baby in our arms. I believe … no, I *know* it will happen."

I say these words with such conviction that I almost convince myself, but a flutter of doubt crosses my mind. I just hope it didn't show on my face.

Julia reaches out and touches my face before she starts to pick up the tiny clothes, putting them back in the trunk as I haphazardly help. When we're finished, I take her hand in mine as we walk back up to our bedroom. Once inside, we climb into our big, king-sized bed and wrap ourselves up in each other's arms, silently clinging to the hope in our hearts.

Chapter Fifty-Six – Julia

The next day, Raine heads to his studio and I realize I have nothing to do. My mind goes into overdrive. I've got to find something to get me out of this house. It's a Sunday, so I decide to try a local church down the road from our house. I've passed the little building many times and I always wondered what it was like. There is no way I could go back to the church where we held Jonah's funeral, so I'll give this one a try.

As I'm picking out something to wear from my new closet, I'm thrilled by the new space—any woman would love it—but the room still causes a sharp pang in my heart. I grab something warm to wear for the cold winter air. Before I go, I poke my head in the studio, letting Raine know where I'm going. I know there's no way he'd go with me.

My car reaches the church parking lot, and as I stare out at people entering the church, doubt seeps into my mind. This church has a small congregation. Will they react when they see me? Do they know the story? I get out of the car and slowly walk toward the doors, where I'm greeted by the pastor, an elderly man with stark white hair who warmly takes my hand, welcoming me. I take a seat in the back row at the end. Several other visitors snag a quick look back at me and smile, but most don't pay me much mind.

Before the pastor starts his sermon, a small choir sings a hymn I remember hearing when I was a young girl. I let the music soothe me. This is the first time in months that I miss having music in my life. Music was always my first love. Today's sermon is about forgiveness, and it makes me wonder if one day, I will truly ever forgive myself.

I leave the church and decide to drive around the area near our house.

Why not? I don't have anything else to do. I stop at a small diner to pick up something for our lunch. As I walk in. I notice a stand with magazines, and I pause, knowing we're likely on some of the covers. On one cover, they have pictures of me looking gaunt, walking to and from places in Montana with a bold headline, "Julia Tate and Raine Wagner Headed for Divorce." They're ruthless. I quickly swirl back out the door embarrassed. But is it true? Raine and I can play the part of a married couple in the bedroom, but what happens during the day is a different story.

I reluctantly head back to our house. What am I going to do with the rest of my day? Raine will work, that's a given. My breathing becomes labored at the thought of having nothing to do. I grip the steering wheel with full force. I've got to come up with something to keep me busy. I press the phone in my Jeep and call the one person I can count on in times like these.

"How'd the reunion go?" Tracy asks before I can get a word in.

I take a deep breath, instantly calmer with her on the line. "So far so good. Did he show you the new closet? That was a welcome surprise."

"Who do you think put all of your shoes away? Took me days," Tracy jokes. "I know Raine is busy with a project, but what about you?"

"That's why I'm calling. I want you to set up a couple of writing appointments for me. I need to start working again."

"Jules! That's fantastic! I've had a few calls from people wondering what you were up to. A couple of new artists are looking for songs. Your own EP sold well, and it might be time to get you out there singing a few of your own songs too. Your fans would love it."

"Not sure I'm ready for that. And honestly, I don't know if I ever want to step on a stage again. But writing ... that's different. You think you can find something for me tomorrow?"

"I'll sure try. I'll call you later."

I hang up relieved. Now I'll hit the mall near our house. I've got to keep my mind occupied.

Chapter Fifty-Seven – Raine

I finish the songs I've been working on and glance at the clock above my head. It's well past three in the afternoon and Julia's not back yet. I stand, stretch, and there's a familiar ache in my muscles I haven't felt in some time. A smile overtakes my lips knowing she's the reason. I can't wait for her to return.

There's a text from Tracy letting me know she's setting up writing appointments for Julia. Good. I'm glad she's working again.

I head to the kitchen and start to fill a glass with ice for my favorite liquid. I usually have one or two glasses during the day, and then several more later to help me sleep. My hands shake as I reach for the bottle. I pour my glass full, and then I let the liquid run down my throat. Instantly my mind eases. This is a problem, I think, looking at my half-empty glass, but for right now, I need bourbon to keep me from drowning.

I walk to the front of the house with my drink in hand just as Julia's red Jeep pulls up the driveway. Since the miscarriage, she won't go near her black Jaguar. She gets out, struggling with a couple of shopping bags, and I smile watching her. No doubt she bought more shoes. I quickly set my glass down and run to help her. I get to the door just in time and open it as she approaches.

She steps in and her head drops with some embarrassment. "Went to the mall today." And she raises her arms as she shows me her multitude of bags, her eyes meeting mine.

I give her a huge grin. "I see that. Get anything interesting?" I say, pointing at the pink Victoria's Secret bag in her hand.

"Of course you'd go to that one. My surprise," she says, her eyes dancing.

I lean down and give her a light kiss before replying. "I can't wait. At least let me help you get these upstairs. And when do I get my surprise?" My eyes drop back to the pink bag.

"Mr. Impatient … you'll have to wait." She pauses, taking a quick look at me. "Did you eat anything today?"

I realize I'm starving. "No. Forgot."

"Okay, then you go make us something to eat, and if you do that, I'll change into my surprise."

Julia laughs as I sprint toward the kitchen, leaving her alone in the foyer to carry her many bags up the stairs. *"Men!"* I hear her say with mock frustration.

Our fridge is pretty sparse, so I make her the only thing we really have, bacon and eggs. In no time I'm yelling up the stairs, "Honey, it's ready."

A few moments later, she's at the top of the landing, "That was quick."

"What do you expect? I want my surprise."

Julia laughs as she walks down the stairs and I lead her to our late lunch. We sit together at the kitchen counter, and she watches with amusement as I inhale my food.

Upstairs, Julia lights a few vanilla candles and then takes a quick shower. I stretch out on the bed completely nude, waiting for her. Minutes later, she boldly comes out wearing a red lacy negligee with nude platform pumps. She has her hair pulled up and I notice that she looks a little heavier. Thank God. Her breasts are filling back out. She looks healthy and fucking amazing.

"Wow," is all I say. I quickly stand, walk to her, and pull her tight against my body as my lips drop to her neck. One hand goes to her breast and caresses her nipple through the soft fabric. I press against her body, and she can feel me hot between her legs. Her hands clutch my shoulders pulling me in tighter.

I run my hands up her sides, underneath her negligee as I press my lips against hers, my tongue darting into her mouth. Julia takes her hands from my shoulders and runs them through my hair, pulling her face to mine. She's eager and clearly persistent in her need. I back her up toward the bed, and then I stop and sit down on the edge of the bed, my hands resting on her lower arms as I stare up at her.

"You need to take that off," I say, my voice deep in my chest. Julia gives me a sly smile as she pulls the tiny garment over her head, letting it drop to the floor next to her. It's still daylight, but we didn't bother to shut the blinds. The scent from the candles wafts all around us. Julia can see that I want her more than ever.

I take her by the hand and pull her to me. When she reaches me, I gently guide her to the bed to lie down on her back. I crouch down at the foot of the bed and work my way up her body with my lips and tongue, lingering between her legs, and it leaves her breathless. My hands follow my lips, and I caress her firmly until it brings her to release quickly the first time. Finally, I bring my face close to hers, lightly grasping the sides of her face as I enter her, watching her reaction. Julia gasps and arches her back as she lets me all the way in. Although I'm still a little sore from the night before, I nestle lightly on top of her body, holding myself up on my forearms.

Julia clutches my back, but I stop her arms and lift them up and over her head, holding them there. I won't let her touch me as I move my hips against hers, driving into her with a practiced skill. As her excitement builds, I lean down to kiss her, taking her tongue in mine, savoring every ounce of her. Julia moans underneath me, arching hard, and I finally release her arms as she grabs my hips, exclaiming out loud as she reaches sweet release again.

Julia looks up at me, and I smile down at her. "I think it's your turn," she whispers.

"Not yet, you're not even close to being done," I say huskily as I roll over and pull her on top of me. As she straddles me, she takes me again fully. Julia leans her head back hard, feeling all of me as I hold her by her hips.

"Come for me," I urge as Julia moves on me slowly and sensually, back and forth, clutching my chest. It doesn't take long for her excitement to build again, and as she gets close, I pull her against me, my lips near her ear, one hand wrapped in her hair, the other on her hip, guiding.

"Oh ... my ..." she begins, but she doesn't finish her sentence as again she comes long and hard on me as I hold her tight against my body. I roll her onto her back. Moments later, I'm holding myself above her, I enter her again and she gasps feeling how hard I've become. She wraps her legs around my hips as I bury myself within her. A few minutes later, we explode together as I yell out.

Spent, I drop by her side on my back. As Julia's breath eventually slows, she rolls over, facing me. She runs her hand lightly down my chest to my hip, and then back up my chest. I catch her hand, bringing it to my lips, as my head rolls to look at her.

"I know it's cliché to say it after making love, but I love you," I say. "More than anything on this earth ... I love you."

Julia smiles, placing a hand on my cheek, repeating my words back to me, "more than anything."

Chapter Fifty-Eight – Raine and Julia

It's dark when I look at my sleeping wife, lit only by the candles in the room. She looks so peaceful. I'm careful not to wake her as I slide out of bed, placing the covers back over her form.

I need at least one drink before I can fall back asleep. I hope one drink will do the trick, but I don't know if it will be enough. I pour the brown liquid straight in the glass and give it a swirl, then lift it to my lips and I down the glass. I pour another, followed by a third. My latest ritual before Julia came back home was to work on a bottle through most of the night, but now that she's returned, I'm hopeful I can just have enough to take the edge off and relax my tormented mind.

Finally, I put the lid back on the bottle, shut off the lights, and make one pass through my studio to make sure everything is turned off. At least now my hands have stopped shaking.

##

I'm standing at the top of the staircase, peering into the kitchen as I watch Raine drink glass after glass. He woke me up when he left the room and I silently followed. His drinking will be a battle for us. I quietly pad back to our room, climb back into bed, and pull the covers up to my face, even more worried for us both.

##

The next morning, I hear Julia in the kitchen moving things around, but what surprises me the most is that she's singing along with a song on the radio. I haven't heard her sing in months, so I lie there, relishing the sound of her voice. She has an amazingly pure sound, which captivated the world when she won *Next Real Star.* I didn't know how much I missed hearing her sing.

I quickly dress and head her way. When I reach the kitchen, I'm struck by the smell of bleach. Julia's wearing workout clothes and is using all her energy to clean our now spotless kitchen.

"Smells kind of like a hospital in here," I say with a laugh as I stroll into the room, catching her in mid-song.

"We've left this room alone for far too long. It needed a good cleaning, Raine. It was gross," she says with a look of disgust.

I laugh with my response, "What can I say, I'm a typical bachelor."

"Careful, my dear, you're a bachelor no more," she teases as she heads to me wearing yellow cleaning gloves and holding a towel in her hand. She leans in and kisses me hard on the lips. "Good morning, love. Breakfast?"

"I think it's closer to lunch," I say catching the time on the stove.

"True. I've been up for hours. You clearly needed your beauty sleep."

"Ouch." I pause before continuing, "What are your plans for the day?"

"I don't have anything today, but I have a writing appointment here at the house tomorrow. Tracy can work wonders. I'm writing with a young girl who's had a few major country hits. We thought it would be easier if she came here to the house instead of writing downtown. Today, as you can see, I'm cleaning."

"Good. I think I'm meeting with Bret and the label downtown today," I say, looking down at my phone to confirm my schedule. "It says 'Bret at one' on my phone."

"Well, you'd best get your 'you-know-what' upstairs and shower if you're going to make it," Julia teases, flicking her cleaning towel at my ass.

"Only if you'll join me," I say leaning closer to pull her against my body.

"Not this time—I have a man-cave to clean," she replies, gesturing toward my studio. "I'm actually afraid of what I'll find in that room."

"I'm afraid of what you'll find, too," I say over my shoulder as I scurry back up the stairs.

Chapter Fifty-Nine – Julia

In my mind, I'd hoped cleaning the house would clear out some of the bad energy I'm feeling. I also hope to gather as many liquor bottles as possible. I want to send a clear message about Raine's problem and our future. I'm determined to find a way to save him, and in the process, our marriage. I honestly have no clue exactly how to do that, but maybe if I pull the proof together in one room, it'll send a message.

I enter the studio and let out a long, heavy sigh. It's not as bad as I thought, but it definitely needs some airing out. The room is perfect for sound, but with no windows, not so great with odor. I grab an air purifier we have in another room and turn it on. The room smells entirely too manly. I can't work my magic in a day, and I'll have to use my office for my upcoming writing appointment.

As I walk through the studio, I look at the small bar. I know I'll find traces of Raine's problem there. There are three large empty bourbon bottles in the trash can, and two more full bottles in a cabinet. I grab them, but I won't throw them out. I'm going to pull them all together and ask Raine to make a choice. He's so stubborn that I figure he'll have to make the decision. There's no way I can force this on him.

I hear Raine walk down the stairs.

"Bout done in here?" he says, casually strolling into the room. His eyebrows are raised and there's a huge grin on his face. He knows this room is a mess.

"Right … from now on, you're cleaning your own man-cave. Never again," I reply in mock frustration as I drop my yellow cleaning-gloved hands to my waist for added emphasis. But I'd never really give him this duty. Cleaning helps clear my mind and relieve stress. I'm way too type A to let anyone else do it.

Raine walks up and wraps his arms around me. "I've offered to hire a cleaning team how many times? You won't let me."

"Due to the way this room smells, I'm rethinking that," I say as my face scrunches up to let him know how bad it stinks.

Raine pulls back and kisses my forehead. "Your wish is my command. I'm off to meet with Bret. Shouldn't take long."

I hug him before letting him go. As he walks out, I realize how much work I have to do before he gets back.

While cleaning the studio, I find one of Raine's notebooks lying on a table. I don't usually read through any of his writing. It's personal and I wouldn't want to betray his trust, but something inside drives me to open it up. Maybe I'll find the lyrics to the song I can't bear to hear, and my intuition is correct. The lyrics are written just a few pages into the book. I stop and sit on a nearby couch reading his words, and my hands start to shake.

Words have been crossed out and different lyrics are written in the margins in several spots, but I can clearly make out the verses and the chorus. It's simple, beautiful, and devastating all at the same time. In Montana, I only heard part of the song, which completely broke my heart. But after reading all the verses, I'm beginning to understand why he wrote it. Raine paints a picture that is eerily similar to what I visualized our life would have been like with Jonah. He even added parts of my dreams.

I sit in this same spot, reading his lyrics over and over again for more than an hour as silent tears roll down my face. The melody I heard in Montana is playing along in my head. A sense of calm overtakes me, which surprises me more than anything. The song has some of the best lyrics Raine has ever put down on paper.

Chapter Sixty – Raine

The sun is still up when I return to the house. As I pull up, I notice most of the blinds are closed from this morning. It's only a little after four, so too early for Julia to be asleep.

I walk in and call Julia's name, but there's no response. I search the kitchen, studio, and all the rooms on the main floor, but she's nowhere to be found. My adrenaline starts to climb just as I notice a large box sitting on the dining room floor. I open it up and inside is likely every bottle of liquor I had in the house. My temper starts to get the best of me until I see my notebook lying on the table near the box. It's open to the lyrics of Jonah's song and next to the notebook is a glass half full of bourbon.

I scamper up the stairs calling Julia's name, but every room is empty and dark. I hadn't bothered to check the garage, believing she was at home, so I race outside toward that building. Her Jeep is sitting in its spot, but the Jag is gone. The same Jaguar she miscarried in and hasn't driven once. Tracy had the car cleaned up, but neither one of us have gone near it.

My heart is coming out of my chest. Where could she have gone? Is she drunk? Julia would never drive if she'd been drinking, at least not in her right mind. But she read the lyrics to that song, the song she couldn't stand. I have no way of knowing if it has taken her over the edge.

Then it hits me. Julia's at the cemetery.

I grab the keys from the front pocket of my coat and rush back to my car. I don't bother to lock the house back up. I don't care if someone robs us blind. I have to find Julia and fast as fear races through my veins.

Chapter Sixty-One – Julia

After reading the lyrics, I carry the nearly full and very heavy box of liquor to the dining room, and then I grab a glass and pour it half full of bourbon. Usually, I'm not one for heavy liquor, but I want just enough to stop the pain searing through my heart. Raine's words, while beautiful, are tearing a hole right through me, and it feels like nails are driving into my temples.

I'm standing with shaking hands, and I start to take a sip, hoping it will warm me up. I've never felt so cold in my life. But then it hits me, I have to talk to him. I have to go to Jonah. I set the glass down on the table and run out of the room.

I grab my purse and fiddle for the keys. I don't want to take my Jeep. I want the full torment and pain of taking the car I lost him in. I don't want to numb myself; I want to feel the absolute loss. I deserve to feel as bad as possible.

As I climb into the car, I almost throw up. The memories of that fateful drive to the hospital are overwhelming. I stoically pull myself together, start up the car, and the engine roars to life. I hastily back up and speed down the driveway to make the short drive to see our son.

Chapter Sixty-Two – Raine

I'm glad there is still some light outside. The sun is starting to set over the horizon, which gives me about thirty minutes before it's dark.

I drive toward the cemetery filled not only with fear, but with dread. I haven't been able to visit the spot since the day of Jonah's funeral, and I can only imagine the torment my beloved wife is going through. And it's all my fault. I wrote that damn song.

When I pull through the iron gates, I know where to go. Jonah's grave is like a beacon, and I'm relieved to see Julia's car parked a short distance from the site. And then I see her. Julia's not wearing a coat and she's kneeling in the cold January weather by his grave. I park the car and sigh as I pull the keys out of the ignition. She must hear me, but she doesn't move.

I get out and walk toward her. Her arms are wrapped around herself, and she's slightly rocking back and forth. When I reach her, she still doesn't look at me but continues to stare at the stone. She's not crying, but I can see dried streaks running through her makeup.

"I thought I'd find you here," I say softly, kneeling down next to her but not touching her.

Julia doesn't look at me, or say anything, she just nods.

"I found the box … and the notebook. Talk to me, Jules."

Julia stops rocking and collapses further on the ground, her head in her hands. I reach out and put my arms around her shoulders. She feels cold in my arms.

"If only … if only your lyrics were true. I don't know if my heart can take this, Raine. I want him here with me … with us," she says, letting out a soft sob before continuing. "And I don't know how to save you. You're drowning and you don't even know it."

For a moment, I'm quiet, lost in her words. "Did you read all of the lyrics?"

She nods. "I get why you wrote it … it's beautiful."

I pull her in tight, hoping my body heat will warm her. Julia leans hard against me.

"You've got to get help, Raine. I can't make you do anything you don't want to do. But we will never get better unless you stop drinking."

I sigh heavily next to her. "I don't know if I can," I reply honestly under my breath, but she hears me.

"For us … and for Jonah. You've got to quit."

We're both quiet as we sit there, my arm around her as we stare at the tombstone in front of us.

We sit like this until the sun is completely gone. Julia is shivering hard now. I help her up and to her car. I can tell she hasn't been drinking, so I get her into the car and then follow her home. I have no idea what will happen when we get there. Can I stop drinking? I know she's right, but the thought of losing my crutch sends a wave of nausea through me. I look down at my hands and they're shaking. It's past my time for a drink.

We pull in and Julia drives into the garage, and I park out front. She meets me and we both walk into our dark, empty house.

She's exhausted, so she heads up for a bath. I go to the dining room and the looming box. What am I going to do? Can I quit cold turkey?

Chapter Sixty-Three – Julia

I'm relieved Raine found me at the cemetery. I didn't think through what I'd do once I got there, but I was able to talk to Jonah. I crossed a milestone by being able to sit at that spot and talk to my son.

I sit in the hot bath, resting against the back of the tub as I let the cool porcelain soothe my aching head. I can hear Raine moving around downstairs, and I wonder what he'll do. Will he drink, or will he just stop?

And is it right for me to ask him to stop? I realized at the cemetery that it's not fair to ask him to stop when I haven't changed. I'm still pissed, mainly at myself, but also at God, the moon, the stars. I'm mad at everything, and everyone. Somehow, I've got to give up my anger and forgive, just like I'm asking Raine to give up bourbon. We both have to do our part, but I still feel like I need my anger. It gives me something to hold on to when I'm drowning in grief.

I step out of the tub, wrap a robe around my tired body, then head to the kitchen, not knowing what I'll find. As I round the corner, Raine is standing by the sink with the box of liquor bottles by his side, and he's pouring the alcohol down the drain. My hand goes to my chest. He's actually doing it. Raine is making the decision to fight. He hears me and looks my way, setting an empty bottle on the counter.

"I have one left and it may be the hardest one to pour down the drain. Not only because it's the last, but it's also really expensive," he says, casting a sly grin my way as he tries to hide his pain with a dose of humor.

I walk to his side and put my arm around his waist as we both stare at the remaining bottle on the counter.

"How about one celebratory drink for us both," he says, teasingly.

"I'm proud of you, Raine. I realized upstairs that I have to do my part too," I say quietly. "I'm angry and using it as a crutch. If you're quitting bourbon, I need to lose my anger, or it won't work."

"You're right, darlin'. You're absolutely right." With his words, he picks up the remaining bottle and with shaky hands, he opens it up and pours the contents down the drain.

Chapter Sixty-Four – Raine

When all the bottles are empty, I take Julia's hand and lead her back up the stairs. No words are spoken. I'll need her to help me get through the next few days, which I know will be some of the hardest of my life.

When we get to the bedroom, Julia drops her robe on the floor and stands in the center of the room, lit only by the hallway light. She reaches her hand out to me.

I walk to Julia, and she envelops me against her. I raise my hand and place it against her head, running my fingers through her hair.

"It's still wet from my bath."

"I see that," I whisper.

These are the only words spoken as she sits on the bed and I sit beside her, kissing her gently on the lips. My addiction could easily transmit to her. She may realize this, but we need each other now more than ever.

At first, I'm soft, but soon I'm clutching her body with an intense longing, trying to take the edge away from my mind while she lets her body soothe me the best way she can. My lips move from her lips, grazing her neck, and I nip at her as I quickly join my body with hers. After we finish making love, Julia rests her head on my chest, and I concentrate on taking long breaths in and out. One second, one breath, and one day at a time.

Later that night, I roll on my back and let out a heavy sigh. I'm now shaking, and sweat is soaking our sheets. Julia is sleeping soundly at my side, her hand still clutching mine. I give her hand a slight squeeze, but she doesn't stir. God, how I love this woman. I must love her, or I never would have agreed to quit drinking cold turkey in the middle of a shitstorm.

I pull my hand free and sit on the side of the bed, running my hands through my now sweat-soaked hair. I walk into the bathroom and run some water, dousing my face and neck. I'm so hot and unsteady. I think this just may kill me.

After toweling off and drinking at least a gallon of water, I stare at my reflection. Taut skin and hollow eyes stare back. I should take a shower, but I'll just continue to sweat, so what's the use?

I walk back to my wife, and although she's sleeping somewhat fitfully, she's the most beautiful thing I've ever beheld. I reminisce about the night, remembering her gripping me hard as we made love. It has been a night of redemption, lust, and a little bit of desperation, as if we're both hanging on for our lives.

With shaky legs I climb back into bed, lying on my back. Julia must have sensed me. She snuggles closer, putting her arm across my stomach. I lie there staring up at the ceiling, just trying to breathe. It's all I can do. My mind is all over the place and my heart is racing. My heart doesn't seem to be keeping the right pace. Both my body and mind are urging me to get in my car and head to the nearest bar or liquor store. There has to be something open? I'm not sure I'm going to win the night as I close my eyes, trying with every ounce of my being to keep the train on the tracks.

Chapter Sixty-Five – Julia

I wake up several times and look at my husband. I can see the sweat on his brow in the moonlight. So far, he's hanging on, but his breath is labored, and even though he's never one to keep still for long, his body is twitching as he tries to sleep. I sit up and take a long drink of water, and then I reach over and grab a nearby towel and spill a little water on it. I try to dab his forehead lightly, hoping it won't wake him up.

His body feels wet and warm. Carefully and quietly, I douse the towel with some water and start to wipe him down. The water is cool, and I hope it'll help him. I look at his face and jump when I see his eyes open, watching me.

"That feels good."

"I didn't want to wake you."

"I'm not really sleeping. Just lying here sweating through the sheets. We may need to get a new bed," he says dryly. "I'm probably ruining this one."

"Hush. It'll be fine," I reply softly.

"Come here."

I set the towel down and crawl up next to his side until I'm facing him.

"We may have to have sex at least twice a day until I get past this. It may be the only thing that helps," he says with a sly grin, but there's truth in his words.

"Your wish is my command," I tease. "You don't have to ask me twice."

I lean in and kiss his hot neck, running my hands down the front of his chest until I find him, hard and wanting. I hear his intake of breath as my hands start to work on him, hopefully soothing his body and mind.

"I knew I married a very talented woman," he mumbles.

"You haven't seen anything yet." And I make him gasp as my lips follow my hands, eventually taking him over the edge to sweet release.

The next day starts with fury. Raine was already out of the bed when I got up, and I doubt that he really slept at all. And I'm worn out, not only worrying about him but about myself. My songwriting appointment begins in a few short hours. I don't know if I can get back into the creative realm, but at this point, I don't have a choice. I run down to my office to make sure everything is presentable. As I pass the kitchen, the empty box that used to be filled with bourbon still sits on the counter as a reminder.

After readying my office, I head back upstairs for a shower. Raine is sitting on the edge of the bed, staring at his shaking hands. I sit down next to him and notice how pale he is, and that he hasn't bothered to shave.

"Well, I hope this stops soon," he says holding his hands out in front of him. "It's too noticeable."

"It will. It'll get better," I promise. "Maybe we should check with a doctor to see if there's something that can help."

"I thought of that, but the instant I visit with a doctor, the tabloids will find out."

"What if we beat them at their own game? Come clean and tell the world you quit drinking cold turkey, and that we're still together, working on our marriage. Screw the tabloids."

"Hmm … it's a thought. But not sure I'm strong enough yet. Give me a few days to think about it."

"Fair enough. I've got to hurry. My co-writer will be here soon. What have you got today?"

"I'm going to try to stay out of your hair. I don't have much planned, which is a problem. Tracy needs to keep me as busy as possible for the next few days."

I nod, kiss his cheek, and hurry into our bathroom to fix myself up. I try not to think about how hard this is for him, and what I will have to do to get better myself. Maybe songwriting will help, or it could make it worse. I have no idea how this session is going to pan out.

Chapter Sixty-Six – Raine

I struggle to get my clothes on as waves of nausea hit me, sparking more anxiety. I'm barely keeping my shit together.

I dial Tracy. "Yes?"

"Schedule as much as you can for me in the next week or two."

"What happened?" Tracy instinctively thinks something happened between me and Jules.

"Not what you think. I quit drinking last night and you can imagine how that's going. I need to keep my mind busy.

"First, I'm glad. Second, I'll place some calls. What about Bret? Have you checked with him yet?"

"Haven't, but he's my next call."

I hang up and dial Bret. Thank God he picks up right away.

"Hey, buddy. What's up?"

I cut to the chase. "I quit drinking and I need you to keep me busy."

"We could write, or do something? It's too cold for golf, but what about playing pool? We haven't done anything like that since your big almost brawl," he says, laughter filling the phone.

"Good plan. In an hour?"

"I'm there."

It's like we have a secret code. We don't have to tell each other where to go, we just instantly know. We'll head to our favorite country club. The only problem is that the club will be filled with other people, and they'll be drinking. But the owner knows us really well and we usually get a private room.

I run my hand over the stubble on my face. There is no time like the present. I have to face this challenge one day at a time.

When I arrive, Bret's sports car is already there, so I walk to the entrance of the club. He meets me at the door.

"We're all set," he says. "The room in the back. And don't worry—I'm buying."

"Wow … what did I do to deserve this? I usually end up paying even though you're the rich and famous star," I jeer. Of course Bret will pick up pool, that's not expensive. But not our golf games. Somehow, I usually end up paying for all of those.

"You keep this shit up and I'm never meeting your sorry ass again. Some friend," Bret replies. A semi-pissed off sneer crosses his face, but he's kidding. I know him too well.

I give him an eye roll as we head straight to the back room. Thankfully, Bret's early arrival was to make sure we weren't plied with booze. My friend understands the seriousness of my situation and is trying to help. The most difficult part for me was walking through the club and seeing everyone with their cocktails and beer. If I thought I was struggling before, it hit all my senses like a wave. What I wouldn't give for one drink.

During our third game, the sweat starts to pour, and my hands won't stop twitching. If Bret notices, he doesn't mention it, so I beat him to it with jokes.

"Look at my shirt, soaking wet, and we just started. If I'd known I'd lose this much weight by not drinking, I'd have stopped years ago," I say with a slight smile as I casually set up the table for another game. So far, Bret's kicking my ass. With my hands and mind, I can't get the balls to do anything I want them to do.

"I was going to tell you how pudgy you were getting, but I didn't want to hurt your fragile feelings."

"You're all heart, asshole."

Bret stops and puts his cue down, taking a serious turn. "How's Jules? Is she any better?"

"This is between you and me. She found my notebook with the lyrics to Jonah's song, and she went to the cemetery yesterday. That's where I found her and it's the reason why I quit drinking. We both have got to do something, or we won't make it."

"Whoa ... that's heavy."

"Yeah. It was pretty brutal. It was getting dark and cold, and she didn't have a coat. You know Julia, for one thing, she's practical."

"Yep. She's the level-headed one."

I sneer at Bret as I pick up my cue and pull back, and I hit the balls with such force, everything around us rattles. Several balls roll into holes. Now I'm winning.

"I certainly can hit the right buttons to help your game," Bret jokes.

"True. Remember when you said I should take up professional golf? Maybe I will, and I want you to be my caddy."

"Not in a million years, dickhead. Not in a million." Bret continues, "So what is Julia doing now?"

"She's actually writing with Candace Taylor. The girl who wrote a couple of recent Jerrie Simpson hits. I have no idea how it will go. This is the first time she's written anything ... since he died."

"Wow ... that is heavy."

I look at my good friend. "What is this, the sixties? You keep saying heavy?"

Bret looks at me and laughs, and then takes a drink of his Gatorade. I pick up my own Coke, take a hard look at the bottle, and down it.

Chapter Sixty-Seven – Julia

I'm pacing back and forth across our foyer when Candace arrives. I haven't been this nervous since I first appeared on *Next Real Star*. The thought of trying to write songs again is freaking me out even more than I thought it would.

When Candace is a few minutes late, I'm about to come out of my skin. I walk outside to greet the young girl. She's taller than me with lighter brown hair and brown eyes. I shake her hand and welcome her inside. I hope I don't come across as desperate as I feel on the inside.

Candace exclaims as she enters the foyer, "Your house is absolutely gorgeous!" And then she turns back my way with bubbly enthusiasm, "Thank you for inviting me over to write!"

"I should be thanking you for coming all the way out here. I know it's not the most convenient location."

"I was honored to get the invite. Is it just us today or are any other writers coming?"

"It's just us. I thought it would be good for me to start back slow. You must know what has been going on with my family. It's been all over the tabloids," I say as I somewhat nervously gesture down the hallway, and we both start walking toward my office.

Candace hesitates. "I've read a few things," she says, looking down at the floor as though she might hurt my feelings. "How are you holding up?"

I can tell she's being sincere, so I decide to be honest with her, "Not great, actually. This is the first time I've tried to write anything since we lost the baby, and I'm not sure how it will go. I guess I'm trying to warn you in case this turns into a big waste of your time. I may not be ready."

Candace doesn't hesitate, "I'm happy to get to write anything with you. I followed the show and everything you've written. I'm a fan."

"Let's hope you stay that way," I joke. Already I'm at ease with her. Candace seems straightforward and easy to talk to. If anything, I may end up with another friend. I enter my office and settle on the couch. Candace puts her own guitar and other gear down next to a big, comfy chair. I took the time to prepare a few snacks, and we have some fruit and vegetables laid out for us, along with water and a big pitcher of tea.

Candace reaches for an empty glass and starts to pour. "I don't imagine this is sweet tea?"

"Nope, I'm a Yankee," I reply. "Regular, unsweetened tea, but I've got sugar if you want some?"

"This is good. I'm a Yankee as well. I'll never forget the first time I took a sip of sweet tea and wasn't prepared for it. Wow! What a shock."

"I know! I remember exactly where I was when that happened to me. Hey … what if we write about being transplanted Yankees in the world of the south, and make it funny?"

"I like it, but we definitely have to be careful about how we write it."

"Exactly! I love it here, but it sure is different."

We start to banter ideas back and forth and before we know it, we have a decent start to a witty, up-tempo country song called "Down South," which seems to fit both of our personalities.

When we're done with a fairly good work recording and Candace is heading to our front door to leave, she casually mentions that she's working on her own record.

"I don't know if you'd be okay with this, but I'd like to take a stab at recording our song," she says. "I could really use another up-tempo song, but I don't want to overstep if you're working on material for your own project?"

"Of course you can record it! I haven't thought much about recording any new songs. We finished the first four songs for my EP and maybe one day I'll add more, but for now, I'm okay with letting others record my songs."

Candace smiles and gives me a quick hug before heading to her car. She waves as she makes her way down the drive, and I smile back and wave. The session went better than I'd expected, and I am relishing the mentor role. During our session, Candace had so many questions about my world and navigating the business, we could have talked for hours.

As I'm returning to my office to tidy up, I notice Raine's car pulling up the drive headed to the garage. I've been worried about him all day and anxious to know how his day went.

I meet him at the front door. Right away, I notice how tired he looks. I open the door with a huge smile, startling him, but he quickly recovers, smiling back sheepishly.

"I know … I look terrible."

I gesture to him, "Come here, sweetheart, let's go upstairs and get you in the shower. Let me guess … you were with Bret?"

Raine just grimaces.

"Thought so." By now, I've grabbed his hand and I'm leading my frazzled husband up the stairs. I don't want him to think about anything right now, I just want to take care of him.

As we reach the landing, I pull him into the bedroom. I keep him talking while I pull off his coat, which is damp with sweat, as is his furrowed brow. As Raine stops and puts his things down on the bed, I go into the bathroom and turn on the shower. Raine is pulling his shirt over his head when I reach him with a towel that he runs across his face. As I watch, I notice his hands are still visibly shaking.

I take his hand. "Come on, darlin', let's get you in the shower."

"Only if you are coming with me."

"You know we can't always shower together." But I'm already stripping in front of him, and his eyes follow my every move.

"I could watch you do that every day."

"Well, guess what, we're married. You're gonna have to," I say, chuckling, taking his hand, and leading him toward the soothing water, which God knows will help.

Chapter Sixty-Eight – Raine and Julia

After a slow, sensual shower, all I want to do is nap. I've never been so exhausted in my life. I was relieved to see Julia smiling when I got home. I'd been worried that her writing appointment might put too much pressure on her, but judging from the look on her face, it went well.

Julia has forced me into bed and is applying some oil into my too tense muscles. What she's doing feels amazing.

"I think I need to sleep a bit," I say, reluctantly rolling on my back.

"You've got it. I've got a few more things to do downstairs," Julia says as she lightly places the covers over me and leans down, giving me a sloppy kiss. She shuts the light out as she leaves.

I close my eyes, trying to soothe my body and especially my mind. My head is aching more than I can take, and I grab some Tylenol. I need something else to take my mind off of my nausea and racing thoughts. I didn't want Julia to see how much I'm hurting. Bret noticed and tried to cover it up all day with his terrible jokes. Between the jokes and my aching head, I haven't experienced a tougher day out with my good friend.

Then reality hits me. From now on, everywhere I go, every party, event, awards ceremony, and special occasion will be marred by my problem. I can't get up the nerve to say "addiction" yet. It has a ring to it that I'm not ready to accept.

##

I hit the kitchen, heading straight for the recipe book I've barely opened since we got married. It was a wedding gift from an acquaintance who obviously had no idea I could barely cook. I want to make something to take Raine's mind off how he's feeling, and it has to be easy on his stomach.

I find simple recipes for baked chicken and mashed potatoes. There is no way in God's green earth I could mess something this easy up, but I send Tracy a text for some pointers. The last thing we need is a kitchen fire, and I've been known to set off a few smoke alarms.

As I work on our dinner, my mind drifts to my sleeping husband and where we are in life. We're both so blessed that I feel guilty for feeling sorry for myself, but it's hard not to go there. On this day, we should be preparing for the arrival of our new little baby boy, not fighting our demons. It's the first time I let myself think about Jonah all day. The ache is always there, and it always will be.

I look out the back window at our property. We have a huge, empty pasture that I hope to fill up with horses. In a few short months, after the weather warms up a bit, I want to fill the land with animals. Working horses and having animals to care for will give me something to do.

An hour later, as I sit at the table messing with my iPad, I hear Raine's feet pad down the stairs, and I watch him enter the room.

"Something smells absolutely amazing," he says, forcing a smile. He's wearing a robe and he looks a little better, though tired. I rise to meet his arms and hug him tight.

"I thought we both could use a good, quiet meal. The chicken is almost done. I just need to mash the potatoes," I say, letting him go and giving my attention to the stove.

"I don't know whether to be impressed or shocked," he says incredulously, and I laugh in reply.

"I know. And I haven't torched anything, not even one hot pad. At least not yet," I say, lightly laughing as I reach to lift a full pot of potatoes off the stove, but my two unsteady hands struggle to carry the pot to the drain.

"Let me help," Raine says, jumping to my rescue as he carefully takes the pot from my hands, pouring the hot liquid down the drain while holding the lid on the pot as steam rises around us.

"How many do you have in here?" he teases. "This pot is heavy."

"I didn't know how much to make. You know me, I have no idea what I'm doing," I say, shrugging my shoulders and rolling my eyes with my words. He laughs.

As I watch him drain the potatoes, his hands seem fairly stable. I think the shower, back rub, and nap did him a world of good. So far, this night is going like any natural, normal evening a couple would share. I grab some butter for the potatoes. Raine takes it from me and becomes chef as he mashes them with an electric mixer. I go to the stove and take the piping hot chicken out of the oven. And it does smell good. I actually managed to make a regular meal without burning our house down. Absolutely amazing.

We sit at the small table in the kitchen eating quietly, likely afraid to talk about anything serious. I realized earlier today that it's a month from Jonah's due date. Before Jonah died, we had the date circled in red on a calendar that was stuck to the fridge. I look at that bare appliance now and a lump fills my throat. I set my fork down.

"Had enough?" Raine asks inquisitively. searching my face and settling on my eyes. I've been trying to fight it, but the tears come.

"I don't know what it is … I see something or am reminded, and it just hits me from out of nowhere."

"I know," he responds, grabbing my hand. "Kind of like a wave washing over you." We both silently stare out the kitchen window, trying to keep it together.

Raine finally speaks, "It's okay to miss him … we'll always miss what could have been."

I nod, letting my head fall against Raine's shoulder. After a few minutes, Raine pulls me up and leads me out of the room. Not toward our bedroom but to the living room. He drops my hand for a moment and reaches for the remote that controls our stereo system. Raine has the room rigged for sound in any room we want. He turns the TV to a station that plays old standards and, luckily, a Nat King Cole song is playing. He pulls me into his arms as we start to dance to "Sentimental Reasons." I cling to him with my head resting on his shoulder. We slow dance together for what seems like hours, both content to be in each other's presence, lost in the music, propping each other up.

Finally, I pull away and Raine must see that my eyes are moist.

"Let's go upstairs."

Raine nods as we walk silently, hand in hand, up to our room to give each other the kind of relief we both need.

Chapter Sixty-Nine – Raine

I've turned to songwriting to help my tortured mind, but I'm not sure Julia has really found anything to help her. As she leads me up the stairs, I run my free hand up her back, massaging her shoulders, and she groans in response. She's wound so tight that my hand feels like it's rubbing a brick.

We reach the top of the stairs, and I startle her by picking her up and carrying her the rest of the way to our bed. After I set her down, she instantly starts removing her clothes and I do the same. Once every stitch is gone, I lean down and silently roll her onto her stomach, pushing her up to the middle of the bed. I grab the massage oil she used on me earlier, straddle her midsection, and rub the oil between my hands to warm it up.

As soon as my strong arms touch her back, she lets out a loud groan of pleasure and I smile. It's music to my ears. I rub her tense and tight shoulders, easing my way down to the middle of her back, and then slowly reach her lower back just above that gorgeous, bulbous ass.

"Damn ... I'm always amazed by this view."

Julia chuckles as I caress her lower back, and when I reach lower, she sighs in response. My hands continue to rub one of her greatest physical assets down to her thighs and lower legs.

"You keep this up and I'll fall asleep," she says groggily. "You won't get your happy ending."

"I'm happy with any ending, even if it means I have to wait."

But Julia moves to her side and looks me directly in the eyes, and I know she's ready. I move my body above hers.

"Show me," is all that I say.

Julia reaches up and grabs me by the hips as she pulls me down closer to her. I pull back, watching her as I tease her with my hands, letting her excitement build. I enter her and she exclaims loudly. After she catches her breath and relaxes again, I lean down and kiss her hard, then I roll over onto my back, pulling her with me.

She straddles me, again taking me inside of her, and I hold her hips still as I move underneath her. She moans with pleasure as I take her higher and higher. When she can no longer take it, I release my hold on her and watch her move on me hard until she comes. It's all I can do not to join her, but I don't want this to end. We have a hunger that can rarely, if ever, be satisfied.

I roll her onto her back and press myself between her legs. She smiles up at me, spent, but I can tell she's loving every minute as much as I am.

I smile back and slowly place myself inside of her again, and we carry each other to a level of bliss we so frequently enjoy. Julia raises her hands above her head, and I follow, grasping one of her hands in mine as we both release a day filled with angst into a world of love.

Chapter Seventy – Julia

Raine seems to have had a much better night and didn't sweat as much. I think back on the night and try not to stress-out about how reckless we were.

We've sort of been careful about not getting pregnant, but as I replay the night in my mind, I'm more than a little worried. I know I can get pregnant.

Raine rolls over, opening his eyes to look at me. He catches my furrowed brow.

"Now what's worrying your pretty little mind?" he whispers, rolling closer and putting his head near mine.

I look at him sheepishly. I don't want to tell him the real reason I'm troubled. "You know me ... always worried about something. Nothing new."

And I'm right. I've always been a worrier. I roll toward him and put my head against his chest while Raine enfolds me in his arms. I'm sure he's wondering what I'm really thinking as we both lie there silently lost in thought.

It's another weekday and we both have work plans. Raine takes off for a meeting with a new artist, while I head to my office to do some research. After we lost Jonah, I read some about my miscarriage, but I didn't really want to know. Today, I log onto my computer and search for "placental abruption" so I can find out what actually happened to my body.

One web page relays that I'll have a higher chance of it happening again, but most medical websites state I'll have to talk to my doctor. I consider calling Dr. Henley right away, but I change my mind. It's best to keep any thoughts about another baby to myself at this point. I'm clearly not ready, but I want to be prepared just in case. At any rate, it's too soon for my body—it's experienced too much shock, and my mind is still lost. Just the thought of being pregnant makes my pulse race and a wave of sadness flows through me. I'm not in any shape physically or mentally to try and carry another child.

Tracy has booked another writing appointment for me later today, but this time, it's at a studio downtown. I hop off my computer, change, and grab the keys to my Jeep. I call Tracy during my drive.

"About time you called me!" Her semi-frustration is evident. "Relying on texts from you both is not a good way to run a business."

Yeah … yeah. You're always harping on me," I tease. "You need to lighten up."

"I hope you're headed downtown. Raine was a half hour late to his appointment."

"My fault and, yes, I'm on my way downtown right now."

"And how are things?"

"One day at a time, but better. I don't think we can hope for anything more. I know Raine wants to drink. He tries to hide it, but it's there, and I'm sure always will be."

"Well, I'm proud of you both. I know this has been incredibly difficult."

I murmur under my breath, "You have no idea."

Tracy didn't hear me, because she continues with all seriousness. "After your appointment, you wanna grab a late lunch? I have a few business items we need to discuss."

We agree to meet at one of our favorite restaurants in the Midtown section of Nashville. Anxiety spreads through me. We haven't had a formal lunch together in months, so this has to be important.

Chapter Seventy-One – Raine

I instantly apologize when I walk into my meeting. I'm working with a new male artist Bret heard one night at a club. I thought I was doing Bret a favor by giving this kid, Wayne Carson, a look, but so far, it's been worth it. In my opinion, he's the next big country superstar, complete with hat and swagger. This kid puts on one hell of a live show. Wayne has it, whatever "it" is: an amazing voice and movie star looks. Even Julia was struck by his presence. She claims he has charisma, and he has something that matters most to her: deep down, he's a really good guy. And he is a kid. He's barely twenty years old, studying music business at a great school in town, with supportive parents. He has the entire package. Now it's my job to find the right songs for him for his first project and put everything together in the right way.

I've already recorded one song with Wayne, and we're working on a new one. My usual plan is to have the best musicians in town lay down the instrumental tracks, and now we're working on a good lead vocal. Then I'll fill in with other instruments and lay some background vocals. Typically, vocals are my least favorite part because I'm dealing with so many variables that are out of my control, usually related to the health of the singer. But this kid is good, and he makes my job easy.

Wayne is already warmed up and ready to go, which is another reason why I like him. He's professional and doesn't need a lot of coaching. Wayne also doesn't smoke or drink, and right now, I'm especially grateful for that. I do wonder if he has any fun though. One thing I've learned over the years is that you can take what you do seriously, but you can't take yourself too seriously.

Those are completely different things. You have to have something to live for, and my mind instantly goes to Julia. She's my life.

I roll my chair in front of the control board, and we get to work. I prefer to record lead vocals in one of Nashville's premiere studios. They have amazing microphones, and the right one can make or break a song.

I hit a few buttons on the panel and check with Wayne in his sound booth to make sure he's ready. A trio of fiddles greet my ears, and I smile. I love my job.

Chapter Seventy-Two – Julia

After my writing appointment, I pull up to the valet station at the restaurant. It's a quiet afternoon in the city, and they aren't very busy. Thank God. I'm still getting used to my real life back here, and I don't need to see any more looks of pity on everyone's faces.

Tracy is seated at a table near the back, her face buried in her phone. With her long, curly blonde hair, I can't miss her. She gets up as I approach and gives me a huge bear hug. We haven't seen each other for weeks.

"How'd the appointment go? Write a hit yet?" Tracy says, half-serious.

"You know, it wasn't as good as my session with Candace, but we had a few good ideas flowing." I wrote with a songwriting duo made up of a young guy and his female friend, but they were just friends. He made that perfectly clear; he only talked about other women during our session. It got old. I continue, "It'll take a few more sessions before I'm fully back on the horse. Got to get my groove back."

"Well, your groove needs to write a hit," she teases.

Even though I love how seriously Tracy takes her position, sometimes it would be good to not always think about our careers and making money. Raine has done a great job of making and saving his money, and with my winnings from the show and my initial songwriting, we're doing well. We can't retire yet, but we aren't in a poor house either. But I get where she's coming from, this business is hard enough that you can't afford to drop out for any amount of time.

Our server arrives and we both order. I ask for a glass of white wine, and Tracy raises her eyebrows as she looks up from her phone.

"What? Raine quit cold turkey, not me. And you know this isn't a problem for me. Plus, we haven't scheduled a lunch together in forever and I'm sensing from your body language and tone that we need to talk about something serious. This isn't a 'let's hang out with my best-friend' lunch, is it?"

"Pegged. You pegged it."

"I'm all ears."

Tracy puts her phone down and plays with the wrapped silverware on the table. The hair on the back of my neck goes up.

"Just spill it," I add. "I can take it, I promise."

"Okay…" but Tracy takes a long pause before finally speaking. "There's a rumor a story is coming out in a major magazine, and oh God, Jules, it's not good."

I throw my hands up with exasperation, and a look of disbelief takes over my face. Here we go again. "What could it be about, Trace? Raine and I have hardly been out of our house for days. We're keeping a low profile. They couldn't have captured much while we were in Montana either," I exclaim, my voice taking on a higher pitch with obvious frustration.

"I got a call from a friend, a former editor. He says they have very intimate details about you and Raine. Stuff that only a few of us know about. I knew I had to tell you right away and I want you to know, it wasn't me."

"Well, of course it wasn't you, and what kind of stuff?" I say in a hushed tone, trying to control my rising pitch.

"It's rumored they know about Raine's drinking problem … and about your battle with anorexia. I'm hearing they'll paint it as verified the two of you are on the brink of a divorce. He says the article has some intimate details about your life, and about the argument you had with Raine in Montana … about not wanting to come back to Nashville, and about wanting to quit the business."

"*Oh, for fuck's sake!* Who could have told them that stuff? Only you, Bret, and Jody know about any of this, and no one knows everything that's been happening with me!" But then I stop short. There is one other person, Dr. Montgomery. But he's bound by professional confidentiality and would lose his license if he let anything out. It couldn't be him, could it?"

My face must have instantly gone white. "What is it, Jules? Is there someone else who could have talked to a reporter?"

I quietly nod my head "yes." No one truly close to us would ever reveal anything to a reporter, but the doctor knows everything. I don't know if there is any way to prove it was him though. The magazine may never tell us who it was.

"Who?" Tracy asks, leaning in closer to me. "Who would do such a thing?"

"Maybe a certain doctor for the right price."

Tracy leans back in her seat, covering her mouth. "No way. Really?"

"It has to be. He's the only one who knew the truth about what was really going on in my head and my heart, and his office was never really busy. Maybe he needed the money?" And I wonder if that's also why his office was so sparsely decorated without pictures—he had no ties and was planning on leaving.

"Raine's gonna blow a gasket," Tracy says, her eyes wide.

"You think," I say, my words filled with heavy sarcasm. It's grown colder in the restaurant, and I pull my coat up over my shoulders. I'm no longer hungry. After the server puts my glass of wine on the table, I down it. Tracy continues to look at me with shocked sadness.

What in the world am I going to tell Raine? He'll want to hop on a plane and find Dr. Montgomery. Never in a million years did I worry about discussing my life in a setting I thought was strictly confidential, but we didn't do any real research on him, other than a reference from someone in Montana. Jody isn't to blame. If it's true, the only person I can, and will be, angry with is Dr. Montgomery.

How in the world will I tell Raine? Will this take him over the edge, and he'll drink? Although we talked about going public, he was apprehensive about telling the world he has a drinking problem. He feels vulnerable, and who wants to admit that to the world. Not only could this hurt our careers, but he'll feel humiliated too.

Chapter Seventy-Three – Julia

I pull up to our house and turn off the ignition, but I sit in my Jeep for several minutes. Raine's car is in the driveway, and lights glow from several windows. It's almost time for dinner and he'll worry if I don't show up soon.

After I left lunch with Tracy, I called Jody and gave her the high points. Jody offered to do her own detective work to find out more about Dr. Montgomery, and if he's still in town. My gut tells me he's already gone.

I pull myself out of my car and slowly walk to the front door. I have no idea how to deliver this news to Raine.

I open the front door and I'm engulfed by an amazing smell coming from our kitchen. Despite everything, I smile. I love it when Raine cooks. He's also much less likely to start a kitchen fire.

"Oh. My. Word," is all I say when I find him at the kitchen stove.

"That good, huh?" he says with a satisfied grin spreading across his rugged face. He's recently shaved and looks good and happy. It tears at my heart when I think about my news. He continues, "I thought it was time for more steak … you know, the protein and all."

"Right. And the cholesterol, and fat," I tease as I walk up and wrap my arms around his waist. He drops one hand, placing it on mine.

"Hush," he says, looking into my eyes. "You need some iron."

"I need to hit our workout room, that's the only iron I need. Do you realize I haven't worked out once since I came back from Montana? I'm gonna start again tomorrow after this meal." I notice mashed potatoes, warm bread, and some kind of pie cooling on a wire rack by the stove, and I silently groan. Everything looks amazing, but my mind screams fat and calories. I know, it's something I have to get over, but I can't help it. Raine goes back to tending his steaks, and I'm glad we have a temporary distraction from the magazine story. I'll wait until after dinner to tell him, or maybe I'll wait until we're in bed and catch him in the best possible mood.

Raine has set the table, so I carry some of the food over. He follows with our steaks, and when everything is ready, he pulls my chair out for me.

"Nice touch," I tease, with a quick glance and a smile. "Really, hon, this is amazing. I didn't eat much at lunch, and this is perfect."

"Cooking keeps my mind off of 'you-know-what.' I may end up gaining a hundred pounds, but at least I'll be sober," he says with a laugh, but a tormented look crosses his face, giving him away. So much of our world revolves around socializing. Living without alcohol will be a hard adjustment for both of us.

After our amazing meal, we're both relaxing at the table and talking about our day, except I'm omitting my dreaded secret. I'll muster the guts to tell him soon, but I don't know when that right moment will be. But I have to tell him before he sees it in print or someone else tells him.

"It sounds like it went well with Wayne today," I mention before adding, "I really like that kid."

"I do too. He makes my work easy," Raine says, running his hand through his hair. A sign he's getting tired.

I reach over and grab his hand, but I don't say anything. We just sit in each other's presence, and I realize I've got to jump.

"Raine ... there is something I need to talk to you about."

"Uh oh. I don't like your tone," he says spinning toward me, suddenly giving me his full attention, his brow furrowing. "I'm not going to like this, am I?"

"Nope. You're not." I sigh heavily, pausing to look down before I continue. "I had lunch with Tracy today," I start but I just can't get the words out.

"That's not unusual, and?"

"She talked to a friend, and a story is coming out." I hesitate, and I sense his frustration that I'm delaying this.

"Okay, the look on your face is scaring me. A story is coming out about

… what?"

"Us," is all I say. I can't seem to tell him everything.

"Us … *what*? What about us? Good lord, the whole world knows about what happened, what else could it be?" he asks, his tone rising.

I decide the best approach is to put the blame on myself. After all, I'm the one who talked to the doctor. "Well … it's really me and my big mouth," and then I sigh realizing I have to let it all out. "The source knows some details that only a few people would know. Intimate stuff about what happened in Montana and things we're still going through. They know about our problems."

The look in my eyes must be enough, because Raine picks up on what I'm trying to tell him without my having to actually say the words.

"They know I have a drinking problem," he states, his voice slightly cracking.

My heart is crushed knowing how much this hurts him. Yes, many people in the entertainment industry have been up front about their similar problems, but they often have a choice about publicly coming clean. Not always, but it's often under some sort of control. We have no control in this situation.

"The source seems to have relayed everything. My problem with food, panic attacks, our fight in Montana, and that I thought about quitting the business … *everything*."

"How in the world would anyone know about that? Was our rental house bugged?"

"I think it may be Dr. Montgomery. I don't have any proof yet, but it makes sense. You know Bret, Tracy, Jody, everyone close to us would never say anything. So, unless the house was bugged or someone tapped our cell phones, it *has* to be him."

Raine silently stares out the dining room window. A tiny muscle in his jaw moves as he clenches his teeth. He takes a deep breath before responding. "First, I'm okay. I know I seem angry, and I am, but I'm holding it together."

I must have a look of extreme fright or worry for Raine to instantly allay my fears. "Second, I'm calling my lawyer to try and stop the story. He may be able to come up with something to at least delay it. And third, we need a plan of attack. We're going to publicly address any rumors or stories out there. No more hiding. I won't let my issue, problem, whatever you want to call it, have any negative impact on our careers. And lastly, if it was your doctor, I'm going to make him pay."

I nod as Raine reaches his hand out and grabs one of mine. We sit like this for several minutes, watching the sun go down outside of our dining room window. Neither of us say a word, but I'm trying to calm the storm raging in my mind. Will this shit ever end?

I don't really care what the press has on me, I can't be concerned about the skeletons, or the perceived skeletons they will drag out. I have to stay as focused and healthy as possible. Back in Montana, I was slowly able to stop the Xanex, and now that I'm home, I think I'm better. I'll be damned if I'm going backward.

After dinner, we quietly cleaned up, and then I went upstairs for my regular nightly bubble bath while Raine grabbed his phone and called his lawyer and Bret.

I'm in bed when Raine comes upstairs and pours himself into bed next to me. He wraps his arms around me tightly. He's edgy and I offer many ways to help, but he's too preoccupied. I know that any perceived weakness released publicly will hurt his ego. Raine's proud, and although he has rare moments of public display, he keeps his private life private.

I remember an interview a celebrity recently gave where he talked about how releasing your secrets can set you free. I hope it's true. If we can't stop the story from going to print, we're about to find out. Maybe if we come clean about everything, we'll ultimately be in a better place? I hope our friends and fans will be able to relate to our struggles without judging us too harshly. Raine quit drinking cold turkey, which is one of the hardest things to do, and I'm so proud of him, but am I proud of myself? So far, I've survived one of the greatest losses imaginable, but that's all I'm doing, barely surviving.

I lean against my husband's frame. Like me, he's still awake. Raine responds by pulling me tight against him. Feeling him against me makes me feel safe and protected, and no matter what, we'll get through this.

I whisper quietly, "I'm proud of you, Raine. I don't think I've told you how proud I am of you." In the moonlight, I see him look down at me as I continue, "You're the most talented person I've ever known, and you have such a kind heart. It took guts to quit drinking. I love you very much. I just wanted to tell you that."

Raine leans down and kisses my forehead as his free hand lightly runs up and down my back. "Thanks, sweetheart, and thank you for saying that. I'm proud of both of us. We're gonna make it, and no matter what happens, we vowed for better or worse. I will do everything in my power to take care of you. No one is going to bring us down. No one."

He leans over and kisses me softly on the lips, and then pulls back slightly. "I love you," he says, and it's enough as we eventually fall asleep in each other's arms.

Chapter Seventy-Four – Raine

I wake up with a pounding headache. With the bullshit going on, I forgot to take anything before I went to bed. *Damn.* My body is still reacting to the sudden loss of alcohol, and my system is a mess. I wonder if I should talk to a doctor. The whole world is about to learn about my "issue," so it doesn't really matter if I talk to someone.

I reach for Julia, but I only find cold sheets. I pull myself up and grab a couple of Tylenol from the nightstand, and then eventually make my way down the stairs. Julia's brewed a pot of coffee. Thank God for this wonderful woman, I think as I pour a cup, hoping it will help my head. As I take a drink, I notice my hands are still shaking. This coffee won't help.

I search the house for Julia and finally find her in our exercise room. I remember running my hands over her now voluptuous body two nights before, and a familiar tingling courses through my body. The torrid article will probably make her exercise even more. I hope it won't make her lose her breasts and that ass. She has her beautiful soccer ball derriere back, and I want it to stay that way.

I step into the room, coffee cup in hand, and watch her on the spin bike. It's her favorite form of exercise, and I also like what it does for her assets.

"Thanks for the coffee," I say, raising the cup toward her.

Julia nods but doesn't stop. "I'll be done in a few," she says rather loudly, yelling over the music in her ear buds, which makes me grin. She continues, "Got a good hour on this thing this morning."

"Good," I yell back. "I don't want you to lose that ass."

Julia shakes her head in mock embarrassment as I give her a big thumbs up. She continues to pedal, standing up and shaking her ass as I laugh out loud.

I walk away, cell phone in hand, and see several calls from Tracy, as well as several numbers I don't recognize. My guess is the story went to print and we're getting media calls. I reach out to Tracy.

"Finally," is all she gets out.

"Let me guess. The story is out, and several media outlets want a statement from us or from me?"

"Hit the nail on the head."

"Don't suppose we can get away with 'no comment.'"

"Doubtful. Did you guys talk about what you want to do?"

"We want to tell our side. Can you reach out to a couple of major morning shows and see if they're interested? And please call those who've been relatively good to us. As for a statement, let me talk it over with Jules. She's better at dealing with a media crisis."

I hit the off button on my phone and sit at a kitchen barstool, looking out at the cool, crisp morning. A light fog settles over our property and the early morning sun is quite beautiful. Julia, sweating heavily, walks into the kitchen, heading straight for the cupboard with coffee mugs.

"Had a bunch of calls this morning and just got off the phone with Tracy."

"They published it this morning?"

"Yep. Tracy said it went online this morning and she believes it will be in the February issue."

"They sure didn't waste any time. I'm surprised they didn't ask us for a comment before going to print."

"Probably too hot, and I'm sure they've already paid their 'source.'"

Julia's quiet as she comes over and sits down next to me. She gives me her hand and I take it in both of mine.

"What did you tell Tracy?"

"I told her to get in touch with a couple of morning shows. Maybe we can get on right away?"

"Are you sure this is what you want to do? I'm not sure I'm ready."

"Jules, we're both doing much better. It's time to come clean. I know our family and friends understand, and we need to give our fans credit. They'll still be there."

Julia takes a sip of her coffee, sets the cup down, and leans against my shoulder.

"After watching you on that bike and now leaning against me, I may not be able to control myself."

Julia chuckles and then looks down toward my boxer briefs. "I think you're already out of control."

I look down and laugh. "The cat is out of the bag ... literally." And then I jump up and head toward the stairs, running. "You had better bring that gorgeous be-hind up here with me."

"Can't I finish my coffee first?" she yells after me.

"*NO!*"

"Well, all right then!" She continues to yell up the stairs, "Can I at least take a shower?"

And I yell back, "NO!"

"Men!" she exclaims out loud as she runs up the stairs after me.

Chapter Seventy-Five – Julia

We've discussed everything with Tracy and she's finalizing all the details, putting everything in motion. We'll tell the world our side of the story, share our grief, and the issues we're dealing with personally. We'll lay it all out there. Tracy's also added our names to the list of presenters at the upcoming Academy of Country Music Awards show in Vegas. Now that we're at the end of January, we'll have a short amount of time to recover from the story and get our heads clear before we head back to Vegas, where our second chance at love began.

I won't sing at the awards show; there is no way I'm ready for that, but Bret is scheduled to perform. The song I wrote with Trent Austin for *Next Real Star*, called "Leaving Ashes," is up for Vocal Event of the Year.

The magazine article is all we expected and more. Somehow the publication landed a few Montana locals to go on the record about seeing us out, and supposedly we didn't look happy. Maybe they were at Walmart for my near breakdown—that must be what they're talking about. They even got a quote from the young girl at my favorite coffee shop. She didn't relay anything earth shattering, except seeing me in tears, which was true.

Likely with help from Dr. Montgomery, the article portrays me as grief-stricken, having a nervous breakdown, and suffering from anorexia. Raine is portrayed as an angry drunk, and they have pictures of him coming and going from the local liquor store with what appears to be brown paper bags. They insinuate he's suffering from a major addiction. And they end with pictures of Raine at the airport alone. The article seems to fill the public in on all the gory details of our lives.

From the moment it's posted, we're bombarded with requests for a statement and interviews, and I'm reminded of Raine's public reveal of our relationship on national TV. So far, we won't comment. We'll get our chance to tell our side of the story. We just have to get through the next few days.

Paparazzi are now staked out down the street, and we can't really leave the house. Thankfully, our local police planted a few officers out front to make sure no one gets too close.

Since I'm basically homebound, my co-writer Candace still has to come to me for our next appointment. Candace never pries into our situation, and I feel like I can trust her. We've become fast friends.

Raine, on the other hand, is out of the house every day, as defiant as ever. God love him. He's fearless. One day as I watch footage of him posted on social media, I smile when he stops and poses for pictures but doesn't respond to questions. He's so strong, and even though he's doing really well and hasn't had one drop of alcohol, he started seeing a doctor to help him through the process. Raine wants to make sure he's doing everything he can do to tackle his problem head on. I've never been prouder.

Just as I'm finishing up my writing session with Candace, my sister Jody calls. "Dr. Montgomery left town a few weeks ago without a trace," she says right away. "It has to be him."

"But we need proof. How are we going to get that? We'd have to hire a private detective." I pause. "I bet Raine's already done that," I reply, letting a heavy sigh of exasperation out with my words. In my mind, I hope Raine will drop the whole thing. But knowing him, he's probably already working on this and doesn't want me to worry.

Jody asks, "You think Raine hired a private detective?"

"Yep. He won't let this go."

"So, what's the next step?"

"First, we're gonna address the story head on. Tracy has arranged some high-profile appearances for us next week. We aren't going to run and hide from this."

"Good. I knew you both would handle it. People want to hear the truth from you."

"That's the plan."

I hang up and think about calling Raine to ask about a private detective, but I don't want to know. He'll tell me eventually. Knowing that Dr. Montgomery, someone I trusted, is the person who likely betrayed that trust makes my head spin. A familiar pang of sadness makes my stomach churn. I want Raine to drop his vendetta because I don't want to rehash everything ... not after we've come this far.

Speaking of Raine, as I glance down at my watch, I see he'll be home soon. He's been great about being home around six every night. He's finishing up Bret's new project and I can't wait for the world to hear it. Bret put Jonah's song, "Born by Song," on it, and I'm honored that he recorded it.

The song has become a source of comfort to me, and I listen to it every day. Although it brings back the pain of losing Jonah, the song gives me a sense of peace, as if he's here with me in some way. It's one of the most beautiful songs Raine has ever written, and I can't wait for Bret's fans to hear it. He's done an amazing job with it.

I'm checking on my pot roast when I hear my beloved husband walk in. I'm now used to and enjoy our new routine.

"I smell a pot roast and it's fantastic," he yells out as I hear him drop his keys on the credenza in the foyer.

"You're right, my dear," I yell back before he swoops me up into his thick arms and lays a big kiss on my neck.

"Damn. You smell good. To hell with the food," he whispers against my ear.

I look up into his dancing green eyes. Since he's quit drinking, his eyes are so much clearer and brighter. I easily get lost in them. Raine's always cut an imposing figure, but now he's working out with me every morning, and I can feel his muscles rippling under his shirt and my insides ache.

"I had to sweat for a good five minutes putting all this stuff in the crock pot," I joke, wiping my brow for added emphasis. "You're eating first ... and then ... maybe later, you'll get something more. Maybe," I add, pressing my backside against him hard as he groans.

"You cannot tease me with that thing," he says, staring down at my derriere. Raine reaches out and runs his hands over my hips, sighing as I pull away out of his arms.

"The table is set, and we're having a nice, normal meal like every other couple across the country. No more sex at all times of the day and night." But I'm kidding and he knows it. An added perk to his not drinking is that he can last much longer, and our sex life is going to an even higher plateau, which I never could have imagined. We're like newlyweds. We still have our moments of sorrow but we're learning to live with our grief.

Since that one day when I visited Jonah's grave site, I've been able to go back, and the police won't allow anyone to follow me. I've been able to sit and talk to my son, and it helps.

Raine checks the food in the crock pot and then dishes up our plates. I've set two places for us in our kitchen nook, which gives us a great view of the sun going down in the pasture. I'd mentioned to Raine that I want to fill the pasture up with horses, and we've started to look.

"I talked to Tracy today," Raine says, then takes a big bite.

"And?"

"We both think you need to start performing again. You've written several new songs with Candace, why not get out in front of an audience and try them out, Jules? You're too good of a singer not to be out there."

"Nope. Not ready."

"Okay ... but promise me you'll think about it."

I nod and then stare down at my now half-empty plate. I really don't have much guilt about eating or working out constantly. I've been able to keep my eating disorder in check. I think it's because Raine is here and we're trying to work it out as normally as possible, if there is something called normal.

Raine pushes his plate back. "Dessert?"

I laugh. "I picked up some fruit and whipped cream at the store today?"

Raine frowns dramatically. "I'd rather use the whipped cream in another way," he says with a grin, his eyebrows rising, waiting for my response.

"And there's some Rocky Road in the freezer," I say with a laugh as he jumps up. He has so much more energy now that I have a hard time keeping up. I realize how lucky I am to have such an amazing man by my side, taking care of me as I take care of him.

"Grab a bowl for me too."

"Good girl! Keep that ass."

And I laugh out loud as I pick up our dishes. We're such a good team and our love is obvious. I hope our strength and our love will get us through next week's talk shows.

Chapter Seventy-Six – Raine and Julia

It's Sunday morning and we're flying out to New York before our big appearance on two major news networks. We've got a room at the Ritz-Carlton, and we've talked about hitting a Broadway show, but we decide to make it a low-key night before we have to get up at the ass-crack of dawn.

As we head to the airport, I realize this is one of the first times we'll be seen publicly since we've returned from Montana. The paparazzi picked us up at the end of our street and they are trailing our SUV. We don't have any security, or a driver, and I hope I can lose them, but it really doesn't matter. We'll be seen together, which is a good thing.

I give a quick glance at my wife as she primps in the visor mirror, finishing up her makeup. "You have never looked more beautiful."

"I don't even have mascara on," Julia teases as she leans over to tenderly kiss my cheek.

"I mean it. I am the luckiest S.O.B. on earth."

"You got that right," she says with all seriousness, sliding back over to her side.

For a moment, I'm caught up in a different memory with her in the passenger seat and feeling her ice-cold hand on top of mine. I quickly shake the thought from my mind, but Julia didn't miss it.

"What?" she whispers.

I don't want to upset her, so I just smile. "It's nothing." And I take the back of her hand, bringing it to my lips.

We pull up to the valet entrance at the airport. They're quickly at Julia's door, but she pauses until I reach her side of the SUV. A car quickly pulls up behind us and someone jumps out to take pictures. Shocking.

I open Julia's door and help her out as we both look at the camera, and she gives a slight wave. As has been our protocol, we don't say anything back to the questions shouted our way.

The valet grabs our two small bags and gets us quickly inside. A few onlookers stand and watch, but everyone basically leaves us alone. We've already checked in and we only have carry-ons with us. We make our way to the Delta Sky Lounge. We typically don't care about privacy at the airport, but this time, Tracy has arranged for us to have downtime in a private room, and we'll get on the plane last. Everything has been set up with security.

We arrive at the VIP room and take a couple of seats by a window. It's early, so we both order coffee and something to eat. Luckily, this is a direct flight. We'll have time in New York to relax and have a good dinner.

When it's time to board the plane and we make our way to the gate, a few people stop and take pictures, and we both acknowledge them. After getting our bags into the overhead bins, we settle into our first-class seats and prepare for take-off. The flight attendant asks if we want anything, and we both order some orange juice.

Julia is sitting by the window, and I lean in as she looks at me, planting a big kiss on her lips.

"What was that for?" she smiles, taking my hand.

"Just that I love you."

Julia looks down at the ring she purchased for me in Montana as it glistens in the sunlight. "Best decision of my life."

"What decision?"

"Auditioning for the show. Best decision ever."

I lean back in my seat as the flight attendant brings us our drinks. We take our glasses and toast each other. I take a big gulp and it's all I can do not to spit it out all over the place. It's not just orange juice. The attendant brought me a Mimosa. An honest mistake, I guess, but a big mistake, nonetheless.

The alarm on my face is obvious. Julia looks at me, her eyes wide.

"My drink has champagne in it, does yours?" she asks under her breath, but she knows my answer.

I put down my glass and look at her. Julia calls out to the attendant and relays our problem. The poor girl looks like she may vomit and cry at the same time when she learns of her mistake.

"I'm so sorry, Mr. Wagner. I'll fix this right away."

Julia gives her our glasses and orders a bottle of water. I press hard against my chair. Although it was a tiny sip, it was alcohol. My first taste in many days.

"Honey ... it was one small sip," Julia says soothingly. "You're going to be okay."

But one drink of alcohol was like fire in my veins. I just hope it won't burn out of control.

##

I spend the entire flight in panic mode watching for any reaction from Raine, but after the champagne incident, he seems to have calmed down. He put his headphones on and appears relaxed in his seat. We land in New York and once outside, we find the car and driver that's been reserved for us. Raine is quiet for most of our drive, madly typing away into his phone.

"Bret says hi," he says.

"Tell that big lug he needs to come by for dinner one night."

Raine nods at me but he's silent for most of our drive.

After we check into our hotel, we hurry up to our room and I hold his hand the entire way. That one sip has been so distressing to us both. I can only think of one thing to get our minds off of it. I hope it will work.

We have a nice-sized suite with a TV room, kitchen area, and bathroom in the main section of the room, and a master bedroom and another bathroom. Raine walks in, shuts the door, and runs his hands through his hair.

"I think I need a shower."

"Sure, babe. Whatever you need." Raine must sense my worry.

"I'm fine, Jules. I just want to relax a bit before dinner."

"Do I need to change?"

"We're going someplace comfortable. No worries." He manages to give me a sweet smile.

I nod as he heads to the master suite, and when I hear the bathroom door shut and water running, I hastily put my plans in motion. Before we left, I took the time to order a few new things and slipped them into my bag. I thought I'd bring them out at the end of our trip, but this is an emergency. We need a distraction, now.

##

I'm standing under the hot water, letting it soothe my aching back. I've never been so tense on a flight before in my life. It really isn't because I want another drink, but the taste won't leave me no matter what I try. Gum, food, nothing seems to help. I know it's not that big of a deal, but technically, I've fallen off the wagon. If someone asked me if I've been able to stay away from alcohol, what could I truthfully tell them?

As I clean up, I think about how sweet the last few weeks have been. My mind is clear and more focused than it's been in years. And talk about creativity, I'm writing and producing some of the best work I've done in years. I don't want to fall backwards. Not now.

I shut off the water. I know this is tormenting Julia too. I could see it in her eyes. I towel off, wrap a towel around my waist, and open up the door. What greets me is an amazing, beautiful Julia surprise.

She's draped across the king-sized bed in a black, skin-tight lace bustier, with matching thong, thigh-highs, and tall, black knee-high boots. She's fluffed her hair up, and her makeup is fresh. The room is dimly lit, but there is enough light to see her in her full glory.

I instantly drop the towel and walk naked to the bed, looking down at her as she rolls onto her back, her legs at a seductive, relaxed angle. Instantly, I'm hard as a rock. Her bustier makes her now voluptuous figure even more appealing as her breasts overflow and the curve of her hip is literally driving me mad.

"I knew there was a very good reason why I married you," I grumble, my voice filled with desire.

"I told you, best decision ever," she replies as she sits up, eye level with my engorged member.

I watch her take her hand, and then she grasps me with just the right pressure, running a finger from base to tip as I groan, and then she leans in and takes me in her mouth. I put my hand on her shoulders as my head tilts back, letting her have her way with me. She has such a good touch and her tongue, damn, she's talented.

Julia stops, looking at me expectantly as I quickly kneel on the bed, pulling her underneath me. My hands are all over her body as I pull one of her legs up, running my hand along her stocking-covered leg and pressing against her suggestively. Julia is wearing my favorite perfume, sweet and sensual, which is so distinctly her. I press my lips against her neck and then run them up her jaw line to those lips that are mine.

I'm decisive, bold, and we both are loving every moment. I'm taking command of her body, playing it like a finely tuned guitar as my fingers find just the right spots at just the right time. Somehow, I manage to rid her of her binding clothes. When we finally join together, Julia groans loudly, leaning hard against the pillows.

"Damn," is all she says as I lean down close to her, my face against the side of her neck, breathing heavily as I thrust deep inside of her, and then I hold myself there for a moment. Julia puts one hand behind my neck and the other on my hip as she holds me, daring me to go even deeper. I move slightly as she arches her back, coming hard and long.

I chuckle against her neck.

"It's not funny," she says with mock frustration.

"But I barely moved, and you lost it ... imagine what this will really be like." And that's all I say as I roll over, carrying her on top of me. This time I let her move and as she does, we're both writhing with pleasure as I watch her come long and hard, gasping out loud as she does.

"I want to do it again," she says huskily. And I let her; again, and again, and again, until she's spent. I let her catch her breath and then I roll her on her back. But now I'm soft and tender. I want every touch and every movement to show how much I love her. I press against her, my lips just above hers as we look deep into each other's eyes. A lone tear rolls out of her eye as I make love to the one woman I've loved for so many years and can't live without. For both of us, it's a precious moment as we slowly and sensually come together as one. Happily, we never make it to dinner.

Chapter Seventy-Seven – Julia

As our driver pulls up to the back entrance at the first TV station, I'm clutching Raine's hand with such force, I could break a bone.

Raine says with such confidence, "It's going to be okay. I'm all right and so are you. There is nothing anyone can do to us; we just need to tell our truth."

I nod but even with his bravado, I'm not convinced. If Jonah's name comes up during our interviews today, I'll likely lose it, and the thought of displaying all my sorrow, emotions, and fears on live TV has me more than petrified. Sure, I can sing for millions of people, but this is so different. This is about exposing the greatest kind of loss. A loss I'll never get over.

A security officer opens the back door of our SUV and helps me out. A few onlookers greet us, and we smile and wave. The station has a live camera crew outside capturing our arrival for the millions already watching.

We're led to a greenroom, and once inside, Raine grabs a towel and dries off his hand while giving me one of his gorgeous smiles.

"I know … I'm sweating like a whore in church," I say with downcast eyes, but a huge grin fills my face.

And with that, Raine leans his head back and laughs out loud. "Don't you dare say that on camera," he says, grabbing me in a bear hug, careful not to mess up my hair or makeup. The stylist who arrived at our room at four in the morning to try and make me presentable would not be amused.

There's a knock at our door, and the show's main host peeks her head in. Emily Hamilton, the tall, green-eyed goddess of morning show news, is not only known for her quick wit, but also for her down-to-earth nature.

She's the reason why I agreed to appear on this show. She catches us in our embrace.

"There you are! I wanted to meet you both before you came on the set," she says, entering the room with her hand outstretched to me. "We're so excited to have you join us today."

I speak first, stepping away from Raine as I take Emily's hand. I've never met her, but I'm a huge fan. "We're the ones who are excited. We're so thankful we get the chance to tell our side of the story."

Emily smiles and nods before chiming in, "Well, I know one thing, this will be a *huge* show. Your upcoming appearance has been trending on Twitter for hours."

"I'll bet," Raine jumps in. "Millions waiting to watch the car crash," he says with a sarcastic smirk. He's right, everyone will want to watch the drama, but we've decided that above all else, we will remain united, solid, and strong.

Emily responds, "I think you'll both be pleasantly surprised at how many people are pulling for you both and care about you. I know I do, and we've never met!"

I give Emily a hug before she heads out the door. I swing back to Raine, giving him a "what were you thinking" look.

"I was just kidding," he says, like he's a kid in trouble at recess.

"I know that, but she may not," but I'm laughing at him. We're driving this car, and we'll make it safely to our destination. We will not crash.

Chapter Seventy-Eight – Raine

As I'm sitting under the hot, bright lights preparing to go on live TV, I'm the one sweating. Earlier I was making jokes as a comical distraction, but now that the shit is about to hit the fan, the reality train is coming down the tracks. I'm going to admit on national TV, in front of millions of viewers and our fans, that I'm an alcoholic. I glance over at Julia, and she's as cool as a cucumber. She has a calm, serene look on her face, and her hands are loosely clasped across her lap as she makes small talk with the crew.

The line producer starts to count down—five, four, three, two, and then she points at our small group seated around a small white table. I have a cup in front of me and I stare at it for a moment, wishing bourbon were in it and not water. I take a deep breath, swallowing hard as Julia grasps my hand, likely sensing my distress.

Brian, one of the hosts, leads off the segment, "And we're back with the talk of the nation, Raine Wagner and his lovely wife, Julia Tate. Julia, we know a certain article gave viewers a slice into what supposedly has been going on in your life after the sudden and very sad loss of your baby."

The camera flashes to Julia, and she smiles at Brian, nodding along with kind consideration as he continues, "We haven't heard a word from you or Raine in response to what was written, and now you're here with us today. What is the truth? Is the article factual?"

Julia gives my hand a light squeeze and a smile before weighing in, "Yes, Brian, the article is factual. Every bit of it. From my panic attacks to my battle with an eating disorder, to the struggle between Raine and me over the loss of our son, Jonah," and she looks at me as she says this, visibly lifting my hand up slightly.

And then I join in, "And my issue with alcohol is also true. I'm an alcoholic. I have quit and I've stayed sober since the day I decided to give up drinking."

Both hosts seem slightly taken aback by the frank and forthright words coming out of our mouths. Emily responds and is obviously not following the prewritten questions prepared by the show's producers.

"Every word was true?" she asks.

Julia and I look at one another like a couple deeply in love, and then back at Emily as we reply in unison, "Yes."

"How did the publication find out about what was going on with you both?" Emily starts to take over our questioning. As a mother herself, she's bound to take it easier on us, especially Julia. At least I hope so.

"That is a good question," Julia replies, "and one day we hope to get to the bottom of it, but we know it wasn't any of our closest friends or family. We know they wouldn't have relayed what was going on privately, but, you know, I don't think it really matters. The truth sets us free, and that's what it has done. Raine and I have nothing to hide. We're human, and hopelessly flawed, and working on ourselves and our marriage, and maybe in some way it will help others." Julia pauses, looks at me and then down for a brief moment before she looks back at Emily. "Losing our baby son Jonah was the hardest thing a person ... a parent will ever have to endure. And we are enduring," and her voice cracks at the ends as she chokes up.

I jump in. "And we're thriving." I grasp both of her hands in mine as I continue, looking from one host to the other. "I loved Julia with every ounce of my being before our loss, but I love her even more now, and I didn't think that was possible. She is my rock and I'm hers. Nothing, and no one, can tear apart this bond. And it really doesn't matter who the source was for the magazine article. It happened, and maybe it's better this way because the truth is out. It is what it is."

I smile at Julia as if we share a secret joke. "That's one of Julia's least favorite phrases, but it's true. God gave us a hand no one should ever have to play, but it's the hand we've got, and we're going to do the best we can with it."

Brian jumps in, "And your drinking problem, you think you'll be able to stay sober? So many celebrities struggle and are in and out of rehab. Are you sober for good?"

"Definitely. We're both working a ton, and Julia has started cooking more, which is slightly dangerous as she's known for starting minor kitchen fires," I say with a laugh, looking at Julia tenderly. "But it's for good. I'm more aware and more present than ever before, and my work. Wow. Writing and producing has never been more fun. I'm in the best place creatively that I've been in a long time." Julia leans in and gives me a kiss on the cheek.

Emily cuts in looking straight at one of the cameras, "Well, there you have it, straight truth from Raine and Julia. We'll be back after this short break."

And we're done, at least with this segment. The next segment may be a tougher interview. The second station is known for more hard-hitting journalism, but we've made it through the first TV show, and it went very well.

We both stand and shake hands with both hosts. Julia gives Emily a quick hug, and Emily comments on how proud she is of us both. Now we'll hear what the world thinks.

As soon as we're in the privacy of our SUV, I grab my phone, searching Twitter and my messages. For the most part, the response is favorable. The hash tag #RaineandJuliaR4Real is trending, and from what I'm reading, most people are supportive, especially about the loss of Jonah. Most fans have been kind, but hearing directly from Julia as she talked about our loss struck a nerve across the country. People are defending her with a ferocity I haven't heard before on social media.

I look at Julia as she tries to relax against the leather seats, and we head to our next destination. This time, hard-hitting former prime time news broadcast journalist Diedre Sampson will ask the questions. Julia's brow is furrowed, and I can see the worry all over her beautiful face. Diedre has specifically requested to handle our morning interview, and I don't know if we should be glad or terrified. Julia has long admired her skill, and Diedre is one of our favorite broadcast journalists, but she's known for her straightforward interview style that goes for the jugular ... there will be no sugar-coating and likely no hugs with this visit. We'll be in the hot seat, playing a very different game, more like chess and not checkers.

I'm holding Julia's gloved hand and I give it a slight squeeze, bringing her out of her reverie. I notice tears glistening on her lashes.

"What is it, hon? You were great on that show," I say, leaning toward her with obvious concern.

"Thanks," she squeaks. "But it never gets any easier, Raine. Every time I talk about him ... it doesn't get any easier."

I reach over and pull her tight against my frame. "And it may never get easier, but we endure. We endure together." And it's all we say as we hold each other, steeling ourselves for round two.

But we have nothing to fear from Ms. Sampson. She's kind, welcoming, and although she cuts right to the chase, we manage this interview as well as, if not better than, the first.

As we head back to the hotel, we're both spent from the stress of two painful live interviews. We decide to stay in New York for another night to give ourselves one night of fun and relaxation. Julia makes plans to see Aubrey Wilson, one of the other contestants of *Next Real Star,* and one of her closest friends from the show. Aubrey moved back to New York and has landed a role in the hit Broadway musical *Chicago.* We both can't wait to see her show, and Julia can catch up with her old friend.

Chapter Seventy-Nine – Julia

We arrive back at the hotel and as soon as we hit our room, Raine heads straight for his suitcase, digging inside. I take off my winter coat and watch him with amusement as he lifts a small jewelry box out of the side pocket, giving me the sweetest look.

"Last night, you squashed my plans with your little black outfit," he says, his eyes dancing. "I had planned on a nice intimate dinner, and then I would surprise you with this, but I think now is the perfect time."

I go to him, and we both sit on the edge of the bed as I take the small box from his hands. I give him one of my questioning glances as I open up the box, then my eyes pop open with delight at the contents. Inside is a gorgeous amethyst stone necklace surrounded by diamonds. The center stone is bold, but the necklace is delicate at the same time. Raine takes the box from my hands, and I pull my long hair back to let him drape the necklace around my neck.

"Oh Raine ... I love it," I exclaim. "But why?"

"Amethyst is the birthstone for February."

It's all he needs to say as a silent understanding passes between us. Jonah would have been born in February. I put my hand up and hold the center stone gingerly as I nod at him. Raine leans in to kiss my cheek and pulls me close. We hold each other like this for several moments, neither saying a word.

I'm literally speechless. It's a gift I'll treasure, and as the stone lies so close to my heart, it'll serve as a reminder that Jonah is always with me. After several minutes, I realize that we had such a busy morning, we didn't bother to eat.

"Let's get out of here and enjoy the city until it's time to head to Aubrey's show. We could use some fun."

"Fun coming up!" And Raine jumps up, grabbing my hand and our coats in such a fluid motion, it's all I can do to hang on and enjoy the ride.

We spend the day shopping, eating, and talking. Talking is something we haven't done a whole lot these past few months. We make it to Central Park and even though it's February, the sun warms us as we walk. If people notice us, they don't let on. It's a lot like Nashville, no one cares about two famous people casually enjoying a leisurely stroll in the park.

"You know, we do need to call Jody and let her know everything is good."

"I'm pretty sure she watched the news this morning, darlin', that ship has sailed," Raine teases as we stroll along.

"I know. But a personal call to let her know we don't hold her responsible for our betraying doctor. Last time I talked with her, I could tell she blamed herself. It'd be good to put her mind at ease."

"Speaking of your betraying doctor ... they brought it up today on the show. You haven't asked me anything, but I thought you'd want to know. I hired someone to find him. He left the country and is living in Canada. He admitted to it. He said he was approached by a reporter after we left his office. After we left the state, he gave the reporter some of his notes. We've reported him to the licensing board, and he'll never work in the U.S. again."

I've been walking along with my head down, holding Raine's hand and listening. A gnawing sensation has hit the pit of my stomach, bringing up a familiar pang of guilt. My actions caused us turmoil, but I'm trying to push it out of my mind.

Raine continues, "Which brings me to a question for you. Do you want to pursue legal action against him? I'm leaving this up to you. I know what I want to do, but it will likely make headlines. So, whatever you want to do, hon, is what we'll do."

I lift my head up and look out over the park, silent for several minutes as we continue walking along. "He did help me, Raine. Even though in the end what he did was despicable, he ended up helping me through my grief and pain. I want that part of our story to end."

"You got it. We could head back up to Montana though for a few days to see your sister and relax?"

"No. Not yet. I have some more work to do back in Nashville."

Raine smiles at me. "What work specifically?"

I keep talking but I don't look at him. I'm purposefully trying to be nonchalant, casually messing with the hat on my head. "My full album. I need to finish it."

"That's my girl," Raine says, grabbing my hand and pulling me against his side.

We walk in silence for several moments before I continue. "I've been thinking about something else, Raine." And I just blurt it out. "Another baby."

He stops in his tracks and faces me as he reaches up and pulls my sunglasses from my eyes. "Did I hear you right? A baby?" The little muscle on the side of his jaw starts to twitch, and now I regret bringing it up.

"Raine … I … don't mean to …" I begin, but he cuts me off.

"Julia, it's okay." His strong features relax as he searches my eyes. "I was just startled. That's why I had to look in your eyes. I had to see what you're feeling. But honey, it's probably too soon."

"I want us to consider and research the options. If I can't carry another baby, maybe there is another way? I just wanted to mention it," I continue to spew out my words, unable to stop.

Raine chuckles softly as he puts my glasses back over my squinty eyes and leads me to a welcoming park bench. After I vomited those words to him, my knees almost buckled.

He settles me down, takes my hands, and looks directly at me.

"Okay. You have my full attention. Talk."

"I've been doing some research about what happened … the placental abruption … and I think I can try again. There's a chance it could happen a second time, but it's actually lower than I thought. And there's always a surrogate."

Raine looks at me questioningly.

229

"Someone else would carry our baby. You know, you've heard of other people who have someone carry the sperm and egg of the mother and father," I say casually, trying to lighten up what has become a rather serious mood. "I even thought about asking Jody, which is why we need to butter her up." I clutch his hand hard and laugh nervously. Raine always wears those impenetrable mirrored sunglasses that give me no indication of what is going on behind his bold green eyes. His face is stoic as he listens to me intently, and I can't read his emotions at all.

Raine squeezes my hand as he looks away. My breath catches in my throat. I hadn't really thought how this would go down, and it doesn't seem to be going the way I'd hoped.

"I can't say I haven't thought about it," he says softly, still not facing me. Jonah's song is part of keeping his dream alive. I just didn't know, or thought you'd want to consider another baby right now. I'm kind of in shock."

I nod and lean into the crook of his arm as we relax against the back of the bench. Raine drapes his arm over my shoulders, and we sit in silence, both lost in our own memories and hopes.

"I'm not saying tomorrow," I finally whisper. "I've just been thinking about it."

"I'm glad," he says, pulling me in tighter and his gloved hand runs along my arm. "But for right now, I think my balls are starting to freeze off."

I laugh out loud. "Let's go back. We need to get ready for Aubrey's show anyway," I say, standing and reaching out my hand and helping pull him off the bench. "Dang ... I do think you've turned to eating since you stopped drinking," I tease as I groan loudly with emphasis, pulling his frame to a standing position.

"Bullshit. I'm two hundred and some pounds of muscle," he tosses back at me, laughing.

"Baby, you are two hundred and some pounds of wonderful."

"That's more like it. You know, we may have time for a quickie back at the hotel before the show?"

"You're reading my mind," I say, giving him a smile in agreement. And we grab hands and quickly run to hail a cab.

Chapter Eighty – Raine

After Aubrey's fantastic show, we meet her for a drink and end the night on a high note. Aubrey and Julia fall back into their friendship as if they'd never been apart, and I relish watching my wife have some fun. She needs it. Damn it, we both need it.

I'm still somewhat floored by our earlier conversation, and as I watch the two women get lost in chatter, I think about Jonah and trying to have another child. I'm more than concerned that trying to have another baby is Julia's way to cope with the loss, but is that such a bad thing? It's way too early, we both know that. We're still in the throes of grief, not to mention my recovery, but it definitely gives me something to think and hope about.

We stay up late with Aubrey, and we finally say our goodbyes at close to two in the morning. When we arrive back at the hotel, Julia excuses herself and heads straight to the bathroom while I check my phone.

I'm reading through texts from Tracy, and I can't wait to share some good news with my wife when she finally opens the bathroom door, casually wiping the makeup off her face.

"I can tell something is up," she says. What is it, hon?"

"Tracy got a call today from the ACM Awards. We're still set to present an award and they've announced the performers. They've invited Bret to sing since he's up for three awards."

"Hon, that's great! He can sing one of the songs from the new album."

"That's the plan. He may actually win an award this year, at least he'd better fucking win one. Jeez. It's about time!"

"He will, love. I'm so proud of you!" she says putting her towel down and walking to stand next to me. My face is still buried in my phone, reading messages. She stands patiently next to me, but I'm too caught up in messages until I hear her loudly exclaim, "Uh, um!" And then I finally take a look up at my makeup-free wife, standing in her PJs, and she takes my breath. The sight of her in basically anything makes my heart burst. Always has.

Julia leans down close to me, reaching around my neck. "So, 'Mr. Award-Winning, Hot Shot Producer,' what's a girl got to do to get your full attention?"

I throw my phone down on a nearby table. "You've got it, and you always will," I say, cupping her face in my hands. I stand, lean down and kiss her tenderly as my arms wrap around her waist. I stop and whisper against her lips, "Did I happen to mention how amazing today was?" My lips slip down to her neck, and she groans softly. "I had so much fun hanging out. It was a wonderful day."

"Uh huh," she whispers. "And I know one way to top it off and make it the best day ever."

Julia slips her hands to my pants and already has them unbuttoned as she slides them down. She's wearing pants that easily slip down and I effortlessly take them off. I pick her up as her legs wrap around my waist, and she quickly pulls her top off in the process.

"I wondered why you even bothered with clothes," I say, my lips against her neck and then they find her lips. I carry her to the bed and I sit down with her straddling me. Julia has pushed my shirt up, and I pause to pull it over my head as her lips go to my neck, her teeth grazing the skin. With one hand, I pick her bottom up and place her on top of me. It's fluid and easy as if she weighs nothing.

"*Damn*," she murmurs. "Always a good fit," as her lips move from my neck along my jaw line to my waiting mouth.

I pick her hips up and pull her down hard, one hand has found her hair and I hold her still as we both moan. We cling tight to each other's body, meshed against each other so perfectly. It's hard to tell where one begins and where the other person ends, chest to chest and hip to hip.

I continue to hold one hand in her hair as she moves on top of me, slow at first but then her excitement builds to a breaking point and we both come quick and hard.

Julia lays her head against my shoulder, and I laugh.

"What?"

"I didn't last long at all," I say as I continue to laugh, chiding myself.

"It worked long enough for me," she says dryly. "It doesn't always have to be a marathon, you know, and the one thing I like is that it's never the same. It's always a new experience. I learn something new about what turns you on every time."

"Same, but c'mon … that was short, and you know it."

"Enough. It was perfect. A perfect end to a perfect day."

Julia rolls off me and I pull her down next to my body. Our arms and legs stay entwined as I lean down and kiss her head. Eventually, we crawl under the covers and we both drift off into a sound and blissful sleep.

Chapter Eighty-One – Raine and Julia

Several weeks later, we've met our SUV at the Las Vegas airport and are heading to our hotel. After our New York trip and big national TV reveal, we both have been working nonstop. I finished Bret's new album, and Julia is writing and recording enough material for her own record that we hope to release in the spring. But first, we've got the ACM Awards to attend.

As we settle into our room at the MGM Grand, I'm standing in the doorway, my arms stretched across the door frame as I watch my wife put her things away.

"Have I told you how amazing you look today," I say, scanning her appreciatively.

"Right," Julia responds with a sideways glance filled with sarcasm. "I've hardly slept these past few weeks, and you know it. I'm not sure I'm ready for a red carpet and limelight." Apprehension is written all over her face. She's been basically freaked out not only today, but for days. I tried to build her up the entire flight, but it hasn't helped much.

"I mean it, you look great," I say as I walk up and lightly place my hands on the sides of her upper arms, looking deeply into her sea of blue eyes, which light up as she gazes up at me.

The past several weeks have been like a second honeymoon. We have a newfound ease with one another, and although the pain of our loss flares up and my struggle with alcohol is constant, we've been able to manage it. I attempt to change the subject.

"Remember this hotel," I say mischievously, knowing she'll remember. She remembers everything.

"How could I forget … lots of great memories in Vegas, and what happens in Vegas …" she says with a snort. Julia leans into me and I wrap my arms around her waist as she rests her head against my chest.

"I have a surprise tonight that I think you're gonna like."

"You and your surprises," she says, drawing back to look at me with her best "don't mess with" me look. Julia knows better than to pry me for details, so all she asks is, "What do I need to wear?"

"I'd prefer your birthday suit, but a dress will have to do. I don't think Tracy or anyone on our publicity team would appreciate anything less."

Julia gives me a huge grin. "All right, a dress it is, but no other surprises. I don't think my nerves can take it.

Later that day as I'm relaxing in a hot bath, I think back on the past few weeks since we left New York. Luckily, we haven't had to deal with too much press or paparazzi after we revealed our truth. Most media and our fans have left us alone, giving us space to live our lives. Raine is staying sober, and I'm coming to grips with reality more and more every day. The ache of losing Jonah never leaves me, but somehow hope has reentered my life as we learn how to love each other through it.

I'm still exercising regularly, but I'm managing my food, and I look better physically than I have in months. We've arrived in Vegas a few days before the awards show so we can get our bearings and relax. The town holds many special memories for us, and we've been looking forward to the visit. It's just the actual show that's freaking me out. Even though I won't perform, the pressure of walking down the red carpet and then presenting is making me more anxious than I thought it would.

I carefully dress. I figure Raine's taking me to a nice dinner, and we'll celebrate the fact that we're back where our second chance started, and where we fell back in love.

I step into the main room of our suite, and Raine's standing in front of a mirror messing with his tie. Seeing him in a suit makes me unsteady on my feet. He catches me staring at him.

"What?" Raine asks, looking down and pressing his hands against his coat and pants before he checks himself again in the mirror.

"You look great in a suit, and I love that tie. Matches my dress," I say with a huge smile.

Raine stops and gives me an up and down look. I'm wearing a dark purple dress that hugs me in all the right places and sets off my dark hair and blue eyes. My new amethyst necklace is lying close to my heart. "And you, my darlin', are stunning."

His words make me blush as I smile back demurely. In two steps he's in front of me, taking my hand. "Are you ready?"

"Ready as I'll ever be," I say with amusement. "Now will you tell me where we're going?"

"Nope," he says smiling like a little kid.

We step into the elevator. Rather than hitting a button to go down, Raine hits the very top floor, which is where one of their most exclusive penthouse rooms is located. I eye him suspiciously, and he's still silent, smiling at me with his secret. He runs his hand up my backside and I shiver. I hear a ding as we hit the floor and when the door opens, I'm amazed by what I see. Candlelight greets us along with several huge vases filled with tulips. I can hear string music playing, and Raine takes my hand, leading me through the foyer into the center of the room, where I see a string quartet playing in the corner. Several hotel staff are on standby, and our table for two is set up in the center of the room.

Raine stops near our table and swirls me around to him. "It was almost one year ago that the good Lord brought you back into my life. We had an amazing dinner that led to the most blessed year of my life. I thought we should have a dinner like that one back in my hotel room but make it a little extra special.

I look at him and smile warmly, but a deep ache enters my heart, and it must show on my face.

Raine looks deep into my eyes. "I do mean blessed, Julia … even with all that has happened, this year has been the most precious to me, I hope you believe that."

Raine takes my hand and leads me to my seat as memories come flooding back to that dinner we had in his hotel room.

He takes my hand from across the table. We haven't talked much after our New York trip about moving forward with another child, but I've been thinking about it nonstop. I want to bring it up, but I don't know how.

"You're lost in thought ... what's up, Jules?"

Raine can peer into my soul, and he knows when something is weighing heavily on me.

"I've been thinking a lot about New York, and, you know ... a baby. I think it's time we pursue a surrogate. I'm ready." Raine's watching me intently as I stagger over my words, hoping I can convince him. "I've done some research on companies, and there is a good one in Atlanta I think could help us find the right person."

"What about you? You don't want to try again? You said there is some risk but that we could try again?"

"I talked to Dr. Henley about it, and she doesn't have any reason to believe I can't carry another child. But I don't know if I can put all of our hopes on me again. Too much pressure."

Raine doesn't say anything but glances down at my hand wrapped up in his fingers. "Okay, well what can you tell me? Not that it matters, I'd spend anything, but how much do you think it will cost?"

"We'd have to pay the surrogate's fee, all her expenses, and the hospital costs. It'll be quite a bit of money ... I don't know, maybe it's too much for us to pay?"

"Nonsense. We can make it work. How about we set up a meeting with the company in Atlanta, and start the next step, and we'll keep our options open. There's also adoption?"

"I've thought about that too, but I'd like to try for our own baby first. Adoption isn't cheap either," I add. "Any route we decide to go, it's probably going to cost us thousands. If I tried to carry the baby, I bet we'd have to try in vitro ... and you'd have to give me hormone shots."

Raine goes visibly pale at the mention of giving me shots. He doesn't do well with needles, and I can't help but chuckle.

"You're laughing at me having to give you a shot, aren't you?"

"Yep. I'd probably have to get Tracy to do it. You wouldn't last a day."

We're interrupted by the staff delivering our meal. Raine has taken care of everything. And just like the night in his room, we have ribeyes and fresh vegetables, and everything looks and smells amazing. But instead of wine, we toast with water. The pain of recovery lingers for just a moment on Raine's face but passes quickly. After a heavy start to dinner, the night is lighthearted, and it feels like it's our anniversary.

After dinner, we head down to the hotel casino and stop to play a few hands of blackjack. We both enjoy the ease and comfort of being together and not worrying about a thing.

Raine has arranged for the tulips to be brought down to our room, and music is playing as we enter. I whirl around to face him.

"You spoil me so … I just love it. Thank you, hon, it's perfect."

Raine grabs me and pulls me into his strong arms. "No, now is when the real spoiling begins," he says against my lips as one hand goes behind my neck and he places his lips on mine, gently at first, but then with a persistence that leaves me breathless.

As Raine kisses me, I kick off my three-inch heels and my hands reach up, grasping at his tie. He stops to lean back and look deeply into my eyes as he removes his jacket and starts to unbutton his shirt. He shivers when I lay my palms against his chest, and I giggle deep in my throat. "I know … my hands are cold."

"I don't mind warming them up," he teases.

Raine quickly strips off his shirt as I unzip the back of my dress, letting it slide off my shoulders. Raine watches it fall to the floor, staring at my near-naked body with appreciation. I'm in a one-piece bustier, which forms my body with perfection. The light in the room is warm and gives my skin a bronze glow. Raine slips off his shoes, slides his pants down, and then looks at me. I take a step toward him, and he engulfs me in his arms, reaching behind me to undo my snaps until I'm free from my binding clothes. He wraps me up in his arms and steps to the bed. When we reach it, Raine sits down, pulling me down into his arms. I drape myself across his lap as his hands reach up, caressing my face and shoulders. We're soft, gentle, and patient with one another. We have no place to be and are happy to be here, right now.

I lean in and run my lips down to his ear lobe as he sighs. Then he grabs me and places me on the bed, covering me with his body. His eyes glaze with desire as he searches my face. I smile up at him.

Since we've returned from New York and talked about another baby, we've been less careful, and tonight is no exception. We're both caught up in one another and the sweet sensation of being profoundly and hopelessly in love. We forget about anything other than the pleasure of the moment. We make sweet, soft love, long into the night.

Chapter Eighty-Two – Julia

Two days later, I'm sitting in our hotel room with my makeup artist, Jamie, as she fusses with the finishing touches to my hair. Tonight, I've opted for a shorter gold gown that hugs my figure with stiletto pumps to match. My hair is pulled up in a loose updo and it has a disheveled look. I'm glad that I don't look too done up. I want something fun for tonight's appearance. Raine is already dressed in an all-black Armani suit and tie. I smile as I watch him pace the room waiting for me to finish up.

"You're going to wear out the carpet," I say, pointing to the floor with as little movement of my head as possible. I don't want Jamie to goof up.

"I know ... I know, but waiting to find out about Bret's awards will likely kill me. I'm a fucking wreck."

Jamie finishes and I stand, looking directly at Raine.

"I love it. Very hip, and it shows off that ass," he says with a smirk.

"Good," I banter back. "Exactly the look I'm going for," I say as I boldly pick up my small matching handbag. "Let's do this." My bravado must surprise Raine. He smiles and takes my hand, one eyebrow raised in amusement.

We're late to meet Bret, so we scurry down a back elevator to our waiting car. Bret's already inside, and he glances at his watch, frowning at us both.

"You're late."

Raine doesn't say a word but makes a subtle tilt of his head at me. I don't miss it.

"So, it took me a while to get all of this hair up ... what can I say?"

We're still close to leaving at our designated time, and we'll arrive at just the right moment. Not too early and not too late. With the three awards

Bret's up for, Raine thinks we've got a really good shot at Song of the Year, but we figure Album of the Year will go to Catrina Smith, who won last year, or country icon Keenon Castle. We're all praying we have a good night. Bret will sing during the middle of the show.

Our car eases down through the throngs of cars on the strip to the main entrance of the arena. Raine reaches over and grabs my slightly damp hand. I look at him and grimace.

"And I'm not even performing," I whisper to Raine. Jeez. Some things will never change. My anxiety always shows up in sweat or stomach acid.

"You have nothing to worry about, my dear, I'll handle everything," Raine whispers back.

"That's what I'm afraid of," I quip as I roll my eyes.

Raine throws his head back and laughs. We're soon at the entrance and it's time to get out and face my fears, but with Raine gripping my hand, I know everything will be all right.

Chapter Eighty-Three – Julia

We let Bret lead the way and follow, stopping to talk with the media. Raine and Bret are asked to take photos together, but most outlets want shots of me with Raine. They just can't get enough. I smile, pose, and play the part, and it mostly goes well. Many questions are about how we're doing and about our new work, but one nosy interviewer directly asks Raine how he is managing to stay sober. Raine smiles and honestly replies something to the effect that it takes a lot of good food and sex. That shuts that interview down quickly as I walk away laughing. I give him a look and he gives me this huge grin. He's fearless and I love him for it.

When we finally make it to the end and are heading to our seats, I whisper, "Other than the last jerk, that went relatively well."

He replies under his breath with a smile, "As I've said before, darling, no one will ever use any kind of dirt to take us down. Ever." I lean up and kiss his cheek. I've already found out that Trent Austin and I didn't win for our *Next Real Star* performance. Naturally, I'm disappointed, but hopefully there will be other opportunities. Raine's going to be a nervous wreck waiting for Bret's award announcements. He's worked so hard, and I've never wanted anything more for him than to be recognized.

We're seated in the second row from the front. Thank God. I didn't want to be in the front row and under constant TV camera scrutiny. Too much pressure. As we settle in for the start of the show, I take a deep breath. We're scheduled to present the Group of the Year award, which will come up as the first award of the night, so at least we get that out of the way.

The show opens up with a performance by Melinda London, who, with her country-rock song, is fierce as usual. Then she's followed by the show's host, Tristan Adams, and his opening monologue. At the first commercial break, a stagehand gets us from our seats and takes us backstage. I grip Raine's hand hard as we greet fellow artists and industry executives backstage.

Backstage is a beehive. I'd almost forgotten what it's like to be around this kind of energy and action. It reminds me of our *Next Real Star* shows. Part of me misses performing live. With my new album project coming out this summer, I may get my chance to get back to it.

We're led to the side of the stage, and as we wait for the show to start up again, and the cameras go live, my stomach does a dive. This is the first time we'll be in front of a live audience since before Jonah, and suddenly I'm filled with terror.

Tristan walks out center stage to introduce us, "Our first presenters of the night are no strangers to the spotlight. This in-demand producer and his beautiful singer-songwriter wife shocked everyone while on *Next Real Star.* Ladies and gentlemen, Raine Wagner and Julia Tate." Tristan puts his arm up gesturing toward us as we enter the stage from the right. The audience is instantly on their feet, cheering loudly as we walk out to the lone microphone. I raise my head and give the audience a slight wave as Raine grips my hand, smiling for the audience and the camera right in front of us. The audience is welcoming us to the stage and showing their love for all that we've been through, and it touches me deeply. It's overwhelming.

We reach the microphone and both look at the teleprompter. Raine leads us off, but at first, he goes off script, which really shouldn't surprise me.

"Thank you ... thank you so much, everyone," he says, holding up one hand as the crowd starts to die down and everyone takes their seats. "I speak for both of us when I say thank you for your support." He looks down at me slightly before continuing, "It means more to us than you could ever know." And he lifts up my hand still clasped in his and kisses it. Obvious tears start forming on my lashes when the camera cuts to me.

I get us back on script, steadying my voice as I do, "But we're here to do a job and that job is to announce the award for best group, so let's get to it." And from there Raine reads the teleprompter announcing the first two acts up for the award, and then I finish reading the last three.

I'm holding the envelope, and after struggling a tiny bit, I get it open. "And the winner of the Academy of Country Music's Group of the Year is …" We look down at the winner's name and we read it together, "Lucky Seven!" And the crowd erupts as the three members of the famous trio stand up and make their way to the stage to collect their award. I instantly step back, but the group members get on stage and reach for me for a quick hug and to shake Raine's hand.

As Lucky Seven steps up to the mic, I grasp Raine's hand, watching and waiting for them to finish their remarks, and when done, we follow them offstage. Raine never let's go of my hand, which is now wet. I'm actually surprised at how nervous I am, but now that our presentation is over, I let out a huge sigh backstage. Lucky Seven's female lead singer, Hope, gives me one last heartfelt hug, and it feels amazing to have such support from our peers.

During the next commercial break, we make our way back to our seats. We just have to find out if Bret is lucky enough to win any awards. First up will be Song of the Year, which is a song co-written by Raine, followed by Album of the Year a bit later in the night, and then the big final award, Entertainer of the Year.

Tristan comes back out to announce the next performer, country superstar Grayson Nichols, who performs his latest hit, and then there are two more awards, the male and female vocalist awards. It's finally time for the Song of the Year award. I grip Raine's hand hard. He's up against some really strong songs, and I have no idea how this will go. The seconds tick by at a painful pace as we wait to hear the results. And after several breathless moments, we aren't disappointed. Bret and Raine win for one of Bret's latest hits, "I Can't Love You Enough."

Raine stands to accept his award, as I stand and cheer. He takes my face in his hands and leans down to give me a quick kiss, his eyes never leaving mine. Now I'm crying happy tears for him.

Bret, who is sitting front and center, meets Raine at the front of the stage and they clasp hands, walking up together to accept their award. Once on stage, Bret speaks first.

"Man ... oh man," Bret says, looking down at the award in his hands. "Thank you, thank you, thank you!" It's been a couple of years since they've won anything, and you can tell Bret is overcome with emotion. "We can't thank you enough for this. Thank you to our families, the fans, our record label ..." And he continues to thank a few record executives by name. Raine is standing behind him and I wonder if he'll get the chance to speak. At the end of Bret's acceptance, Raine leans into the still hot microphone, "Thank you of course to Bret for helping write an amazing hit, and to Julia ... I love you more than you realize," and that's all he says, but it makes every woman in the room swoon. A camera shoots at me as I blow him a kiss, tears streaming down my face.

The two men give each other a side hug as they walk off the stage. Both are all smiles as the cameras follow them and we go to a commercial break.

When Raine gets back to his seat, he gives me a huge hug, lifting me slightly off the ground and kissing me hard on the neck.

"I knew you'd win," I whisper in his ear.

"Glad you knew ... I didn't think we had a shot."

"I bet you win Album of the Year too. I can feel it," I say smiling.

"Well, we shall see. Bret's performance of our award-winning song is next and one more award before they announce it. I hope you're right."

We sit down as they go back on air and Tristan announces Bret's performance.

"Next, we have the distinct pleasure of hearing an amazing male vocalist and award-winning songwriter. But instead of performing the song that was just the big winner tonight, "I Can't Love You Enough," he's going to sing a song off his soon to be released new album, *Our Time*, called "Born by Song." Ladies and gentlemen ..." And several women scream as Tristan pauses before saying, "Bret Savage."

I'm sitting in shocked silence, realizing that Bret will sing Jonah's song. I look at Raine, and he too looks stunned, not saying a word. We're both wide-eyed and silent as the curtain comes up to Bret, center stage, sitting alone on a stool. The band in the background is visible, but they're muted and it's just

Bret under the lights. The song starts quietly with just an acoustic guitar playing the melody, which is like a lullaby. The entire arena is eerily quiet.

As Bret starts singing, I protectively cross my arms in front of me, and one hand goes up to cover my mouth. Raine drapes one arm across my shoulders and pulls me in tight, almost as if trying to shield me from this. Although I've come to love the song, it's another thing to hear these lyrics live in front of millions of people and know exactly what Bret's singing about. The audience and those watching at home will instantly know the song is about us losing Jonah.

As Bret sings, the crowd pays rapt attention. The first verse and chorus are just Bret with the solo acoustic guitar, and then during the second verse, the band joins in along with a small string section through this verse, and the music builds into the bridge. For the last verse, the dynamics drop to just Bret again, alone with his guitar. Bret sings the lyrics that depict Jonah as older but also the uncertainty of where exactly he is, "You're no longer a child, I can see that now. I promised you once not to lose sight of your love. But where have you been, all this time? I feel like I've left you behind. And I say, ease little one, ease, oh peace, little one, peace." Bret sings this last line acapella, "Don't fear, I'm here. Ease. Ease."

It's at this moment that I can't control the tears. Raine's grips me tighter across my shoulders as he tries to keep his own emotions in check.

The crowd is eerily quiet for several moments, but as Bret stands, the entire room erupts and jumps to their feet. All except for us. Raine and I sit watching the scene unfold as a camera is thrust in our faces, capturing our reaction. After a few seconds, I regain my composure and slowly stand. Raine follows my lead as we join in on the applause. As I expected, the crowd realized what the song was about. We put our arms around each other and hug tightly in front of the TV camera as the audience around us cheers. Then the little red camera light goes black and we're off the air. Finally.

During the break, Bret walks out from backstage, approaching us. I'm still in shock, but I gather myself together and give him a huge hug. Bret's performance was an amazing moment. I realize that he brought Jonah's song to life, which not only helps me and Raine, but may help others who are going through the same kind of pain.

The rest of the night is a blur. Raine and Bret win Album of the Year, and again it's a wonderful moment for us, but Bret wasn't lucky enough to win Entertainer of the Year. That went to Grayson, who had an amazing year with many number-one songs, and he puts on one hell of a show, which is unparalleled.

Several other artists and studio executives stop and congratulate us as we leave, and we promise to hit an after party, but we both agree that we need an early night. I'm emotionally drained, and although Raine is on cloud nine with his wins, he's about done for the night.

We meet up with Bret and climb into our SUV headed to the Bellagio for the after-party with Bret's label. We step inside the room and head to a table in the back as Bret makes the rounds. We're leaving the schmoozing duties up to Bret tonight. Raine's still concerned about me after hearing "Born by Song" live, and he won't leave my side as I sit at the table, relaxing in the crook of his arm.

"What an incredible night, kid, better than I ever could have hoped," he says, leaning down and kissing the side of my head.

"It was a great night," I say, looking up at him. "I know, you didn't know Bret was going to sing Jonah's song, but what do you think? Are you upset?"

"No. Not at all. It's a beautiful song and his performance ... wow. It was amazing. I'll be honest, it surprised the hell out of me, but mainly I was worried about you."

"You saw my face," I say, giving him a slight grin. But I'm glad he sang it and shared it with the world. It brings me peace, and maybe it will help others."

Raine nods, silently looking away. Many people stop by our table to congratulate us, and when we feel like we've done our duty, we quietly make our way to our waiting car, with Raine's arm slung protectively across my shoulders.

Chapter Eighty-Four – Julia

As I think back on the night, a single tear rolls down my face. On this night, the ache in my heart is so strong. The loss will flare up, and tonight is no exception.

I walk into our hotel bedroom and Raine is sitting on the bed, waiting for me. I don't say anything and sit next to him as he gathers me up in his arms, curling me up in his lap. We sit, holding each other for several minutes until Raine gently lifts me up to the pillows, settles me under the covers, and then climbs in next to me. He leans down and kisses me, neither of us speaking as he carefully showers me with love.

We're enjoying a leisurely breakfast while our phones buzz nonstop. I've been ignoring the many phone calls and texts, and Raine has only picked his phone up once. It's clear the media wants to talk to us about Bret's performance, so I reluctantly call Tracy and put it on speaker.

I jump right in, "My phone is going crazy. Tell me what we need to address first."

"The national morning shows, pretty much all of them, want you on tomorrow morning. I can get you both a flight to New York tonight if you want."

We've already discussed our game plan. "Trace, we're heading back to Nashville. You're good friends with a couple of the reporters at the Fox station there. If we speak with anyone, we want to do it locally, and the national stations can pick up the interview."

"Are you sure? This could help Bret's album even more if you guys talk to the national press."

My eyes go to Raine, who answers, "We're positive. We want to go home, and we'll talk to one local station, that's it. Bret's performance speaks for itself."

"You got it. I'll call and set it up. I think you could tape something late tomorrow to air on the evening programs."

We hang up and I look at Raine and smile. I so love this man. Raine takes my hand as we finish our coffee in peace.

At the airport, it's another story. The paparazzi are staking out all flights leaving for Nashville. This is one time I wish we had paid for a private plane. We smile and greet the media. Raine will make a statement if pressed.

A reporter yells at me, "What do you think about Bret's song, Julia?"

Raine replies, a smile on his face. It's not that I can't answer, he's just being protective, and I love him for it. "I wrote the song with Bret, and we both love the song and the beautiful message. We hope it brings others peace as it has brought both of us." And that's all he says as we wave at the paparazzi and head inside the terminal.

Several people in the Vegas airport recognize us and smile. It's a beautiful moment to see strangers give us smiles, but they're polite at the same time. We pose for a few people who ask for photographs, but we arrive at the Delta lounge in relative peace.

"I have to be honest, Jules, this is one moment I really want a drink."

I squeeze his hand for reassurance and lean in, putting my head on his shoulder.

Chapter Eighty-Five – Julia

I've never been so glad to return to normalcy. Vegas was life changing for us in so many ways. Raine's even more in demand than before, and I didn't think that could be possible. And every day I'm feeling stronger and stronger.

The next several weeks pass smoothly. The Fox interview went well, and no one has pushed us about the background of the song. We've been spending weeks choosing new songs for my project and deciding on cover art.

About four weeks after the ACMs, as I lie in bed, I'm giving my body a good stretch when all of a sudden, the room spins. Raine rolls over and watches me run into the bathroom, calling out after me.

"Jules! … Are you okay?"

"I think I have the flu or something."

I run a washcloth under some cool water for my forehead. Great, the fucking flu. Perfect timing. I walk back into our bedroom as he leans up on his forearm, concern clearly etched on his face.

And suddenly I'm quiet as recognition spreads across me like fire. Raine senses something is wrong.

"Julia … what is it?"

"I'm late."

"Late for what?"

And I give him one of those "you really have to ask" looks.

He gets it. "You don't think … how late?"

"A few weeks. But I'm never late."

I slump down on the edge of the bed, looking at him with eyes that are about to pop out. "Could I be?"

Raine jumps up, kneeling before me, and takes my hand in his as he reaches up and brushes a loose piece of hair from my eyes. I look down at his hands, and then meet his eyes with a smile as he lets out the heavy breath he's holding.

I blurt out, "Let's get a test. Right now."

We throw on clothes, run down the stairs, and out to Raine's truck, high tailing it to the local pharmacy. Raine runs inside and comes out with a bag of more than five different pregnancy tests, handing me the bag as I laugh.

"Well, I want us to be sure," he says with a nervous grin.

I try to keep my mood light as we drive back home. I don't want him to see the fear in my eyes as I lightly hold my hand against my stomach. What if we are pregnant, and will I be strong enough this time? I'm filled with excitement, fear, and hope.

Chapter Eighty-Six – Julia

Many months pass as Raine works to promote Bret's album. He's now working with two more new artists. "Born by Song" was Bret's first release on his new album. The song went to the top ten on the Billboard pop chart, and quickly went to number one on the country charts and held that position for eight weeks.

We finished my new project, and I've spent most of the summer promoting my first single to country radio and handling press. I've also written several songs with Candace and a few other new artists, and I'm answering fan mail. Ever since Bret's performance on the ACMs, we've been inundated with mail from others who've also lost a child. I try to answer every letter. Raine thinks this is hard on me, but as I've tried to tell him, it brings me comfort to hear from people who've experienced the same pain.

I glance down at my watch, it's almost two in the afternoon and it's time for me to go as I walk out to my new green Jaguar and pull down the drive. I glance out my rear view and Raine's watching me drive away.

I pull up the long, peaceful drive. The leaves are turning and it's absolutely beautiful. When I stop, I grab the flowers sitting next to me on the passenger side and slide out, heading toward Jonah's tombstone. I walk slowly, more like waddle, to his spot. I come here once a week to talk to him and let him know about his baby sister, who will arrive soon. We've safely made it past week thirty-four and even if I do go into early labor, the chances that the baby will survive are really good. The pregnancy has gone well, and other than terrible morning sickness, her vitals and my ultrasounds are all normal.

We even had a 4-D ultrasound and we got to see her pretty face, although Raine's worried she has his nose. I don't care whose nose she has as long as she has one.

I throw a blanket on the ground and slowly lower my ever-growing body down to sit by him. I've gained a lot more weight with this pregnancy, but I don't care. This time, I refused to tour with my new music and instead I'm posting heavily on social media, and I've had some live events to talk with fans. Even without touring, the first few songs are doing well on the charts. I'm grateful my fans are so loyal.

I lean in and touch Jonah's headstone, setting new flowers down as I remove the flowers from last time. Sometimes, Raine comes with me, but today is a special day. Today is the day we lost him, and I want to visit alone.

"Hey, my sweet boy. Daddy and Mommy miss you," I say quietly, softly rubbing my baby bump. It helps to talk to him. I sit quietly for a few minutes and thank God for giving me the life I have, and the chance to love two children. Even though I won't be able to love Jonah in this world, I know that one day I'll meet him and hold him. A light breeze blows across my face, and I figure it is Jonah, letting me know he's there.

When it's time to go, I roll slightly to my side and slowly stand, and then I lean down and kiss the top of the stone as I do every time I visit. I don't know how often I'll visit after our daughter arrives, but I know that Jonah will understand.

After I climb in my car and start to drive away, "Born by Song" comes on the radio, and I smile, my hand resting on my baby bump. It's a sign. A sign that everything is going to be okay.

END

Blessed by Song

The third book in the Julia Tate Song Series by J. D. Williams

The music continues...

Chapter One – Julia

I'm standing on the side of the stage, anxiously waiting for my sixteen-year-old daughter to perform. I absentmindedly run my hand to my right breast and over the lump just as Raine saunters up, putting his arm around my side. I quickly drop my hand and grab his. I haven't been able to tell him about the spot because I didn't want to worry him. He thinks my doctor's appointment tomorrow is just a regular appointment and he knows nothing about my previous scans, and I've been able to keep the biopsy from him. He looks down into my eyes, giving me a warm smile. The gray around his face and deepening wrinkles around his bright, bold green eyes make him appear distinguished and, to me, amazingly more handsome than ever. I lean into his frame as his strong arm grips me tighter, my head leaning into his chest.

"Was she nervous before she walked out there?" he asks.

I laugh as I look up at him and respond, "Are you kidding? She's my daughter. She about threw up over there on the side of the stage," I say, and we both smile as Raine chuckles. She inherited my stage fright. "I got her calmed down and focused, so I think she's okay now."

"Good. She also inherited my confidence and she'll be fabulous."

"I have no doubt," I say, leaning back to give Raine a sideways glance as he leans down to kiss my cheek.

Just then, we hear the band start up and Aria's guitar starts strumming through the speakers. Here we go! Aria's first real gig here in Nashville. I'm terrified for my baby girl, but she'll be great. My thoughts go to my doctor's appointment, and I say a quiet prayer to myself. *God, they need me. Please make this okay.*

The doctor walks into the room and catches me staring at her certificates and diplomas. Dr. Henley has been my gynecologist, obstetrician, and after all this time, I consider her a good friend. When she looks into my eyes, I instantly know. This isn't good news.

I drive away stunned and my mind travels over the road I've been on for the past seventeen years, from winning the reality music show *Next Real Star;* to my second chance marrying the love of my life, Raine; losing my first baby, Jonah, which almost destroyed me and our marriage; finding the courage to continue on; and then having our daughter, Aria, and all the love, joy, struggles, and triumphs that she brings to our lives. With Raine as stubborn and arrogant as he is, we still have our moments, but our marriage has survived through a tough music industry that continues to challenge us.

After Aria was born, I took a few years off, and then struggled to get anything really going as a performer, so I focused on songwriting. Thank God my writing has been, and still is in demand. I perform now and then, but for the most part, Raine's producing career has sustained us. So I focused on Aria and making sure our baby girl had the best life possible. Now at fifty-seven, I'm likely facing the fight of my life. How in the world am I going to tell Raine it's cancer? *Fuck cancer.*

About J. D. Williams

J.D. Williams grew up in Nebraska, and after graduating from the University of NE – Lincoln, she moved to Minneapolis and toured with a pop cover band. As a recording artist and songwriter, she worked with some of the most talented artists, producers, and managers in the Minneapolis music scene. She has been involved in movie and video production and helped recording artists and bands as a manager and publicist. She is also an award-winning writer for general consumer and business publications and has had work printed in various national and regional publications.

Now living in Franklin, Tennessee, J.D. continues to write music, and her songs are featured in the Julia Tate Song Series of books.

For more information, go to **www.jdwilliamsbooks.com**

Follow on Facebook @jdwilliamsmusic

Follow on Instagram @jdwilliamsbooksofficial

Follow on Instagram @jdwilliamsmusicofficial

Resources for Topics Covered

Grief and Mourning

J. William Worden, PhD ABPP. **Grief Counseling and Grief Therapy, Fifth Edition: A Handbook for the Mental Health Practitioner – Grief Counseling Handbook on Treatment of Grief, Loss Bereavement**. Fifth Edition. Springer Publishing Company. May 28, 2018.

Angela Morrow, RN. **"The Four Phases and Tasks of Grief."** Updated on May 24, 2022. Medically reviewed by Isaac O. Opole, MD, PhD. Fact checked by Elaine Hinzey, RD. verywellhealth
  https://www.verywellhealth.com/the-four-phases-and-tasks-of-grief-1132550

"Coping with Grief When Your Child Dies." Mattel Children's Hospital. UCLA
  https://www.uclahealth.org/sites/default/files/documents/Coping-With-Grief-When-Your-Child-Dies.pdf?f=a608f61f

Litsa Williams. **"Worden's Four Tasks of Mourning."** What's Your Grief
  https://whatsyourgrief.com/wordens-four-tasks-of-mourning/

Dan Bates, PhD, LMHC, LPCC, NCC. **"The 4 Tasks of Grieving. Grieving is a healthy response to loss."** Psychology Today. Posted November 8, 2019.
  https://www.psychologytoday.com/us/blog/mental-health-nerd/201911/the-4-tasks-grieving

Placental abruption

Antonette T. Dulay, MD. **"Placental Abruption (Abruptio Placentae)."** Main Line Health System. Reviewed/Revised Oct 2022.
   https://www.merckmanuals.com/home/women-s-health-issues/compl ications-of-pregnancy/placental-abruption

Pamela Schmidt; Christy L. Skelly; Deborah A. Raines. **"Placental Abruption."**
   National Library of Medicine. National Center for Biotechnology Information.
mation.
   https://www.ncbi.nlm.nih.gov/books/NBK482335/

M. Furuhashi, O. Kurauchi, N. Suganuma. **"Pregnancy following placental abruption."** National Library of Medicine. National Center for Biotechnology Information.
   https://pubmed.ncbi.nlm.nih.gov/12410366/

Medically Reviewed by Traci C. Johnson, MD. Written by WebMD Editorial Contributors. **"Placental Abruption (Abruptio Placentae)."** WebMD. August 09, 2022.
   https://www.webmd.com/baby/what-is-placental-abruption

www.ingramcontent.com/pod-product-compliance
Lightning Source LLC
Chambersburg PA
CBHW050021180626
46810CB00002B/513